VANISHING
ACT

Books by Fern Michaels

Published by Kensington Publishing
Corporation

FERN MICHAELS

VANISHING ACT

ZEBRA BOOKS
KENSINGTON PUBLISHING CORP.
http://www.kensingtonbooks.com

ZEBRA BOOKS are published by

Kensington Publishing Corp.
119 West 40th Street
New York, NY 10018

All Kensington titles, imprints, and distributed lines are available at special quantity discounts for bulk purchases for sales promotion, premiums, fund-raising, educational, or institutional use.

Special book excerpts or customized printings can also be created to fit specific needs. For details, write or phone the office of the Kensington Special Sales Manager: Attn. Special Sales Department. Kensington Publishing Corp., 119 West 40th Street, New York, NY 10018. Phone: 1-800-221-2647.

Zebra and the Z logo Reg. U.S. Pat. & TM Off.

ISBN-13: 978-1-4201-0685-5
ISBN-10: 1-4201-0685-6

First Kensington Books Hardcover Printing: September 2009
First Zebra Books Mass-Market Paperback Printing: January 2010

10 9 8 7 6 5 4 3 2 1

Printed in the United States of America

Prologue

Five Years Earlier

It was a beautiful restaurant, beautifully decorated with well-dressed diners, discreet service, and ambience that had no equal. It was the kind of restaurant where there were no prices on the parchment menus because if you had to ask the price, you didn't belong in The Palm, or so said the owner. Not the Palm Restaurant in New York. This was the Palm Restaurant in Atlanta, Georgia. On Peachtree Road. A hundred-year-old eatery passed down through multiple generations of the same family. When people talked about this particular restaurant, they always managed to mention *Gone With the Wind* in the same breath.

Plain and simple, it was a place to be seen. Not necessarily heard.

Not that the young couple wanted to be seen. Or heard, for that matter. They didn't. They were there because they were celebrating the possibility of a business venture, and what better place than the Palm? Years from now, no one would remember that the couple had been there drinking priceless wine, eating gourmet food served on the finest china, and drinking superb champagne from exquisite crystal flutes.

The woman was striking, the kind of woman men turned to for a second look, the kind of woman other women looked at and sighed, wishing they looked more like her. She was a Wharton graduate. Her professors had given her glowing recommendations, assuring all and sundry that she would go far in the world of finance. She believed them implicitly.

The young man looked athletic, the boy next door, clear complexion, sandy hair. Tall, at six-two, a hundred and eighty pounds. He, too, was a Wharton graduate. He also dressed well—and women stared openly, men took a quick look and turned away, vowing to do something about their receding hairlines and paunches.

They looked like the perfect couple, but they weren't really a couple in the true sense of the word. Partners was more like it, but in time they would drift together, not out of passion but out of need.

The man was fearless.

The woman was a worrier.

They were not compatible.

The only real thing they shared was their mutual greed.

The woman held her champagne flute aloft and smiled. The man clinked his flute against hers and liked the sound. A clear *ping* of crystal.

"So, is it a deal or not?" the woman asked.

"It has flaws."

"Every plan has flaws. Flaws can be corrected," the woman said.

"That's true. I'm inclined to go along with it. But I think I need some reassurance."

The woman set down her glass and reached over for her clutch bag. It was small and glittery and gold in color. She opened it. There was only one thing in the small bag. She withdrew the little packet and slid it across the table.

The man blinked, then blinked again as he looked inside the dark blue covers. At first he thought he was looking at a small stack of passports. What he was really looking at was a pile of old-fashioned bankbooks. Something in his brain clicked as he calculated the last stamped numbers. He pushed the little stack back toward the woman. She, in turn, deposited them in their nest inside the clutch bag.

"Well?"

"There's over one million dollars on those books."

"And I did it all myself. Imagine what we could do together. In five years, we could have a hundred times that amount of money. Offshore, of course. You look nervous," the woman said.

The man sipped his champagne. "Only a fool wouldn't be nervous. I'm not a fool. What you're saying is that you require my organizational skills to continue, is that it?"

She hated to admit it, but she said, "Yes, that's what I'm saying."

The man remained silent long enough that the woman had to prod him. "It's risky," he said.

"Everything in life involves risk," she said, finishing her champagne.

The waiter approached the table and poured more. She nodded her thanks.

The man raised his glass, smiled, and clinked it against hers. "All right . . . partner."

"There is one thing," the woman added. The man's eyebrows lifted. "This is a five-year project, not one day longer. We need to agree on that right now. On December thirty-first, five years from now, our assets are divided equally. You go your way, I go my way. If you don't agree to it, there's no reason for us to stay here to eat the meal we ordered. I'll leave now, and you can pay the check."

"Why five years?"

"Because that's my time line, my deadline."

The man shrugged. "Okay. Should we shake hands or something?"

The woman reached into the pocket of her suit jacket and withdrew a tape recorder that was no bigger than a credit card. She smiled. "It's on record. We don't need to shake hands. Oh, look, here comes our food!"

An hour later, just as they were finishing their

meal, the man asked, "Aren't you forgetting something?"

The woman twirled a strand of her hair as she stared across the table at the man she'd agreed to partner with. Her eyes narrowed slightly. "I don't think so." She let go of the hair between her fingers and started to crunch up her napkin and gather up her purse.

"What about the . . . ?"

The woman froze in position. "Do not go there. I presented the deal to you, and you accepted it. There are no other perks. That's another way of saying what's mine is mine. Not yours."

The man wasn't about to give up. "But—"

"There are no buts. Any other operations I have going on are solely mine. I mentioned them only to show you that the possibilities are endless." She was fast losing patience with her dinner companion. "Well?"

The man still wasn't about to give up. "Can we address this at some later point?"

"No. This is the end of it." She could tell by the man's expression that it was not the end of it. She sighed. Greed was the most powerful motivator in the world. She was on her feet and walking toward the door. *Like I'll really share my little gold mine with someone like him.*

Chapter 1

The Present

The day was hot and sultry, the sun blistering in the bright blue cloudless sky. Even the birds that usually chirped a greeting when the Sisters appeared poolside seemed to have gone for cover in the cool, tall pines on Big Pine Mountain.

"I can't believe this heat! It's only July, and we're on a mountain!" Alexis said as she fanned herself with the book she'd been reading. "It's a good thing we aren't on a mission. We'd disintegrate."

Nikki stood up, a glorious nymph in a simple one-piece pearl-white swimsuit, and headed for the diving board. "Don't even say the word 'mission,' Alexis. We're on hiatus. My brain has gone to sleep," she shouted over her shoulder.

The Sisters watched Nikki as she danced her

way to the end of the diving board. She bounced up, then hit the water, barely making a ripple. A perfect dive that would have been the envy of any Olympic diver who might have seen it.

After Nikki—a glorious bronzed creature—surfaced, she swam to the far side of the pool, climbed out, and walked back to the chair that sat under a monster outdoor umbrella. She immediately started to lather on an SPF 35 sunblock.

Yoko appeared out of nowhere carrying a huge tray, with plastic cups and a frosty pitcher of lemonade.

"What's for dinner?" Kathryn asked.

"Whatever it is, it better be slap-down delicious," Annie warned.

"Then you better get on the stick, my dear, since it is your turn to cook," Myra said with a straight face.

The wind taken out of her sails, Annie got up and headed toward the main building. "Don't you all be talking about my sagging ass while I'm gone," she tossed back.

"Don't worry, dear, when it gets down to your knees it will be time enough to talk about your derriere."

The Sisters giggled as Annie flipped her friend the bird and continued her march to the kitchen.

"Slap-down delicious! I wonder what she'll whip up," Isabelle said.

"Weenies on the grill. Wanna bet? And, she'll talk the whole time about how slap-down delicious they are," Yoko said, laughing. "We had weenies twice last week. I hate it when Annie cooks. A very nice shrimp stir-fry with jasmine rice would be nice."

"With a light, fluffy lemon pie or maybe a pineapple cake for dessert," Kathryn said.

"I'd settle for a corned beef on rye with a ton of mustard," Nikki said.

"Well, none of that is going to happen unless we get up, go to the kitchen, and toss those weenies I know she's going to make down the garbage disposal," Alexis said.

"We could go in and help," Myra said hesitantly.

"We could, couldn't we," Nikki said, making no move to get up.

No one else moved either.

No one said a word.

Because it was suddenly so silent, the Sisters were able to hear the gears of the cable car as it descended the mountain. Suddenly realizing that the cable car was going *down,* the Sisters looked at one another.

They moved then as one, racing to the main building, where the gun cabinet was located. Within seconds, Nikki had it opened and was handing each Sister her weapon. In bathing suits and bare feet, they ran out of the building, across the compound, and stopped only when Annie shouted for them to wait as she flew down the steps, gun in hand and a string of hot dogs dangling around her neck.

"Jack's in court," Nikki said. "I just talked to him at lunchtime."

"Harry's at Quantico," Yoko said.

"Bert is at the White House having lunch with the president," Kathryn said.

Alexis and Isabelle looked at one another and shrugged before Alexis finally said, "Joe Espinosa is on assignment in Baltimore."

"Lizzie?" Annie asked.

"She's in Las Vegas. She checked in early this morning," Myra said.

"Nellie and Elias went to Virginia to see Elias's new grandchild," Isabelle said.

"Then some stranger is on his or her way up the mountain," Annie, the best shot of them all, said. "Wait a minute, what about Maggie?"

"She and Ted went to Nantucket for a long weekend," Nikki volunteered.

"Then it has to be someone who knows us, knows about the cable car, and knows about the switch at the bottom of the mountain," Myra said. "Maybe we should stop the car halfway up until we decide who it is."

"But if someone knows about the car and managed to get it to the bottom, they know about the safety switch inside," Kathryn said. "We should cut the power! As you can see, the dogs aren't real happy. Otherwise, they'd have gobbled those weenies, and Annie would be flat on the ground."

The Sisters looked down at the two dogs belonging to Kathryn and Alexis, then to Annie and her necklace of hot dogs. As the two dogs pranced on and off the platform that housed the cable car when it was inactive, they snarled and pawed the ground.

"C'mon, c'mon, someone make a decision here," Kathryn hissed. "The car is coming up. Now, goddamn it!"

"Wait two minutes and cut the power," Myra said calmly.

Kathryn raced to the platform, her index finger on the master switch. "Tell me when, Myra."

Myra looked down at the oversize watch on her wrist with the glow-in-the-dark numbers. One hundred and seventeen seconds later, she said, *"Now!"*

The dogs went silent, running to their mistresses and panting as though to say, *What now?*

The Sisters looked at one another.

"I suppose we can hold out longer than the person in the cable car. We need to make a decision here," Nikki said.

Annie waved her gun. "Unless there are seven people in that cable car, I'd say we outnumber our visitors."

"Feds? CIA?" Alexis demanded.

Myra shook her head. "Bert would have let us know if anyone at the Bureau was looking at us. I was thinking more like Secret Service, but even that's a bit of a stretch. It is entirely possible some hunter, some stranger, stumbled over the hidden switch and is just exploring for a look-see."

Annie made an unladylike sound. "If you be-

lieve that, Myra, I am going to strangle you with
this string of hot dogs."

"At least then we wouldn't have to eat them,"
Myra quipped.

For the first time, the two dogs seemed to get
the scent of the wieners wrapped around
Annie's neck. As she broke off the weenies and
handed them out, she was suddenly their new
best friend.

"How long are we going to stand here in the
boiling sun?" Yoko asked as she swiped at her
forehead with the inside of her arm. "I say we let
the car come all the way up but stop it before it
hits the pad. Let the passenger swing over the
side of the mountain. We'll still be in control."

Myra thought about that for a moment before she looked at Annie and nodded. Kathryn
flicked the switch that turned the power back
on. They all held their breath as the cable car
started upward, the gears protesting at the sta-
tus change.

Myra looked down at the dogs quivering at
her knees. Their ears were flat against their
heads, the fur on the nape of their necks standing straight up and bristling, their tails between
their legs. A trifecta that could only mean trouble.

· Up high, a fluffy cloud bank sailed past, mo-
mentarily blotting out the orange ball of the
sun. Someone sighed.

Annie looked at her fellow Sisters and liked
what she was seeing. Then she looked at their
hands. Steady as rocks. She took a moment to

wonder how loud the sound would be this high on the mountain if all seven guns went off at the same time. Pretty damn loud, she decided.

Myra licked her lips. "Turn off the power now, Kathryn."

Kathryn turned the switch. The sound of the cable car's grinding gears screeched so loud that the dogs howled. The Sisters rushed to the platform and peered over the side. But all they could see was the top of the cable car and the grille on the side. The identity of the occupant was still in doubt.

"How about if we announce ourselves?" Annie whispered. The others looked at her, their eyes questioning. "You know, a shot over the bow, so to speak. In this case, I think I can shave it pretty close to the grille. If you like, I can shoot off the lock. Of course, if I do that, the person inside *could* fall out. Not that we care, but we should take a vote!"

Knowing what a crack shot Annie was, the Sisters as one decided it was a no-brainer.

"Do it, dear, we don't need to vote," Myra said.

Annie did it. Sparks flew, and the roar of outrage that erupted from inside the cable car made the Sisters step back and blink.

"Charles!" they shouted in unison.

One look at Myra's expression kept the guns in their hands steady as Kathryn turned the power switch back on. They all watched with narrowed eyes as the car slid into its nest, the door swinging wildly back and forth.

Chapter 2

Charles Martin stood rooted to the floor of the cable car. He dropped his duffel bag and raised his hands as he eyed his welcoming committee with a jaundiced eye. Whatever he had been expecting, this definitely wasn't it. He couldn't remember the last time he'd seen so much exposed bronzed oiled skin. Nor had seven women ever gotten the drop on him. One part of him was pleased to see that the guns were steady even though they were aimed at every part of his body. He knew Annie could blow his head off in the blink of an eye. Myra would aim for his knee and hit the pine tree fifty feet away. The others would hit their mark, and he'd wind up dead as a doornail. Then they'd bundle him up and toss him off the mountain. *Cheerfully* toss him off the mountain.

He knew they were all waiting for him to say

something. Anything that would make this little scenario easier. For them. Not for him. He hated the look he was seeing on Myra's face.

Murphy and Grady pawed the ground but stayed near the Sisters. They could not understand these strange goings-on. Charles was the guy who had slipped them bacon, fed them twice a day, and even gave them root beer on special occasions. And he was always good for a belly rub before going to bed. He had a good throwing arm, too, and would throw the sticks for them to retrieve for hours on end. They whimpered in unison, hoping for a kind word. They whimpered even louder when nothing of the kind happened.

Charles had known this little reunion wasn't going to be easy, but he didn't think it was going to be quite so devastating. He cleared his throat. "The way I see it, ladies, is this. I have two choices here—three, actually. One, I can pick up my bag and leave and apologize for this unexpected visit. Two, I can pick up my bag and go to my quarters, and we'll pick up where we left off. Three, you can riddle my body with bullets and toss me over the mountain. Decide, ladies. I'm very tired right now and in no mood to remain in limbo."

Annie risked a glance at Myra, who seemed to be in a trance. "An explanation would go a long way in helping us make our decision."

"As much as I would like to provide one, Annie, I'm afraid that I can't. Do you know you have a string of frankfurters hanging around your neck?"

Annie ignored the question. "Can't or won't?" Annie snapped.

"Both!" Charles snapped in return.

"You think you can just waltz back to this mountain and pick up where you left off with no explanations? You left us flat, to fend for ourselves," Kathryn screeched, her voice carrying over the mountain. "Your conduct is . . . was . . . unacceptable regardless of the circumstances. We deserved more, Charles," she continued to screech. Murphy reared up and pawed at his mistress's leg. "I-don't-think-so!"

"You want us to trust you, but you don't trust us? That's not how it works, Charles," Nikki said, frost dripping from her words. "Kathryn is right, your behavior is unacceptable."

"My situation is different from yours, Nikki. I have to answer to Her Majesty. In the past, you only had to answer to me. If I could, I would answer all your questions. Unfortunately, I am duty-bound to say nothing."

Myra squared her shoulders and leveled the gun in her hand. "NTK, is that it? If there is no trust on both sides, then it doesn't work. I think I'm speaking for the Sisterhood when I say need-to-know doesn't work for us."

Charles looked at his ladylove and noticed that she wasn't wearing her pearls. Chains with circles draped her neck. Annie was wearing the same set of chains. He didn't like this new look. Myra wasn't Myra without her beloved heirloom pearls. He realized at that moment that things had indeed changed here on the mountain since he'd left.

Isabelle stepped forward. "We found out the hard way that we don't *need* you. Back in the day, we may have *wanted* you because you made it easier with your meticulous planning. We managed two missions. And even though we bumbled our way through them, we are standing here in front of you, guns drawn. On you! There is no reason to assume we cannot bumble our way through more missions. Actually, *Charlie*, we're getting rather adept at meticulous planning."

"You used my people. *My people*, ladies," Charles said quietly.

"*Your people* are mercenaries, Charles. Mercenaries go where the money is. We have the money. I rest my case," Alexis replied.

Charles took his time as he looked from one to the other, then down at his bag. Without another word, he picked up his bag and turned around to flick the power switch that would connect the power to the cable car. All he had to do was get in and then hit a second switch that would send the cable car to the bottom of the mountain. "Then I guess there's nothing more to say. Good-bye, ladies."

Yoko stepped forward but not before she clicked the safety on her gun. Her hand dropped to her side. "I haven't spoken yet, Charles. I would like you to stay," she said softly.

Charles turned back to face the women. He

smiled, and his tone matched Yoko's when he said, "I appreciate your vote, but I can't stay unless it's unanimous."

The women watched in horror as Charles pressed the main switch, not realizing he had just turned the power off. Then he sat down inside on the little bench so he could hold the door closed. When he realized his mistake, he stretched out a long arm to hit the power switch. He was going, leaving them again. Murphy and Grady howled. A lone tear rolled down Myra's cheek.

"Mom, don't let him go. If he goes, he will NEVER come back. You have to take Charles on faith. You know that. Pride, Mummie, is a terrible thing. Hurry, Mummie, hurry!"

Myra whirled around as she tried to reconcile what she was hearing from her spirit daughter and at the same time saw Charles reaching for the switch that would activate the cable car and take him to the bottom of the mountain. She literally leaped past the two dogs and pulled Charles's hand away from making contact with the switch. "We want you to stay, Charles."

The collective sigh behind her told Myra all she needed to know. The girls wanted Charles to stay but were willing to send him packing, thinking it was what she wanted. When she stepped back, she felt Annie's arm go around her shoulder. It felt so comforting that she wanted to close her eyes and go to sleep.

"Will you get rid of those weenies already?

Charles will be preparing dinner this evening," was all Myra could think of to say.

Annie laughed as she peeled the string of weenies from around her neck and handed them all out to the dogs, who were waiting politely for the rest of their unorthodox early dinner.

Charles stepped out of the cable car and started to walk toward the main building, the girls following behind. Yoko was the last in line, her head down.

"Honey, I admire your courage," Annie said to her.

"I'm sorry, Yoko. I should have been the one to speak up to tell Charles to stay," Myra said. "It's refreshing to see you for once have the courage of your convictions. I don't know what we all thought we were trying to prove back there," she went on, waving her hand behind her, "other than to make Charles sweat and punish him in some way. It's my fault entirely. The others thought I wanted to send Charles packing, and they went along with it."

"We need Charles," Yoko said softly.

"Yes, we do," Annie said forcefully.

"I agree," Myra said. "But we are going to have a few new rules this time around."

"Do you believe Charles is not allowed to talk about whatever it was that went on over there by orders of Her Majesty, or was he pulling our leg?" Annie asked fretfully.

"Charles never lies. Rather than tell a lie, he simply says nothing. The fact that he even offered up the explanation makes it all ring true. Whatever went on over there, we are never going to know about it, so we had better get used to the idea," Myra said.

"Does that mean you are moving back into the main house, Myra?" Annie asked.

"It means no such thing. I'm more than comfortable right where I am, in the room next to yours. That's not to say I won't be ... uh ... moving back at some point in the future. Then again, I may never move back in. I'm not that same person who followed Charles to England."

"I see that," Annie said, with a twinkle in her eye.

"I see that, too," Yoko added, giggling.

"I wonder what's for dinner," Myra said as she linked one arm with Annie and the other with Yoko.

"Barbara told me to do it," Myra whispered to Annie.

"I know, dear. I actually heard her this time."

"Oh, Annie, did you really?"

"Absolutely," Annie lied with a straight face.

Up ahead, the sound of the door closing behind him sounded exceptionally loud, Charles thought as he walked through the main building that he and Myra had shared for so long. He stopped, dropped his duffel bag, and looked around. He struggled to figure out what was different but couldn't quite hone in on what it was. Everything was neat and tidy. There were fresh flowers in a vase on the coffee table. There was no sign of dust. The windows sparkled.

Charles picked up his duffel bag and walked into the war room. Again, it was neat and tidy, the computers were on, the clocks were working. No sign of disarray anywhere. He flinched at the emptiness. He continued his journey down the hall to the suite he shared with Myra. And that's when he knew what was different. Myra had moved her things out of the suite. He tossed his oversize duffel on the bed and hurried to the closet. All he could see were empty hangers. There were no shoes on the floor. No boxes on the overhead shelf. His eyes burning, he stepped into the huge closet and saw his own clothing at the far end, all enclosed in garment bags. When he'd left, his things had been hanging loosely on hangers. Someone, probably Myra, not knowing when or if he would return, had hung them in zippered garment bags. His shoes were in boxes instead of on the shoe trees. He swiped at his eyes before he looked over at the dresser where Myra kept the jewelry box in which she put her pearls every night. The box was gone, the dresser bare, save his own hairbrush and his own small box for cuff links. His things were now encased in a plastic bag. He bit down on his lower lip as he made his way to the bathroom.

It was a large bathroom, the kind any woman would love, and Myra had loved this bathroom, with the built-in Jacuzzi and the shower, with the seventeen different heads that shot out steaming hot water from all angles. The vanity held only his things on the right side, again encased in plastic bags. The left side, Myra's side, was bare as a bone. He opened the linen closet to see a stack of hunter green towels that were enclosed in a zippered bag. Myra's fluffy yellow towels were gone, as were all her sundries. Only his remained, encased in plastic. Suddenly he had a hate on for plastic.

His eyes still burning, Charles walked back into the bedroom, and this time he noticed that the comforter on the bed was different. When he'd left, there had been a green-and-yellow appliquéd tulip spread with matching pillows. Now a darkish green and brown comforter was on the bed, and there were no matching pillows. It looked depressing. He realized then how alone he was. He hated the feeling. He swiped at his eyes again. Sometimes, life just wasn't fair. He wondered if it would ever be fair again.

Charles stripped down and headed back to the shower, where he stood under the seventeen needle-spray jets and let them pound out the tension in his body.

Forty minutes later, he was dressed, freshly shaved, and on his way to the kitchen, where he was expected to prepare a gourmet meal, the last thing in the world he wanted to do. A smile tugged at the corners of his mouth when he remembered the string of frankfurters hanging around Annie's neck. Obviously, the girls had been eating things that were quick and easy.

A check of the larder and the Deepfreeze gave a lie to that. Someone had ordered and stocked everything just as he'd done. He took a minute to go to the back door that would allow him to see the garden, which—he knew—would be a disaster. He blinked at the neat, tidy rows of plants. The pole beans were tied neatly, as were the tomato plants. Shiny green peppers in need of picking peered up at him. He just knew there were at least a hundred zucchini under the trailing vines. Cucumbers were deep green and plentiful. The broccoli looked wonderful. He knew it would be tender and savory. Thanks to Yoko and her green thumb.

So his girls had managed nicely without him. He had to admit it hurt to know they had not only survived but functioned. Which then brought up a nasty thought. Did he subconsciously want them to have failed without him? The fact that he even thought such a terrible thing bothered him. Knowing and hearing Isabelle say aloud that they didn't *need* him even though they *wanted* him was almost impossible to accept, but it was a sad reality, and he had no choice but to deal with it. He told himself he just needed patience. Well, his time in England had certainly not instilled patience in him.

As Charles checked out the vegetable bin and the freezer, his thoughts raced. If there was some way he could explain to Myra and the others, he'd do it in a heartbeat. But Her Majesty had looked him in the eye and made him swear never to divulge what had gone on during his stay in England. He'd promised, and he would die before he would break that promise.

The best he could hope for now was that time would heal all the wounds he'd created. Women, he knew, were, for the most part, forgiving creatures. He corrected that thought. Most women, with the exception of Myra, possibly Annie, too, were forgiving creatures. The only word that would come to mind was "endurance."

And endure he would.

Shifting his thoughts to the matter at hand, he finally decided on his menu or, rather, his peace offering. He would prepare Shrimp Étoufée. A crisp summer salad from the garden, some of the pole beans in a light, savory garlic-butter sauce, homemade biscuits with soft honey butter. Myra loved his Chinese Almond Rice, so he would prepare that, too, and hope she understood he was making it just for her. For dessert he would make Rice Pudding with Raspberry Sauce and, of course, pots and pots of coffee. He dusted his hands together, satisfied that in the midst of all the turmoil in his mind, he could think of other things.

Charles licked his lips, crossed his fingers for luck, and started to prepare his homecoming dinner.

Chapter 3

The news of Charles's return to Big Pine Mountain flew through cyberspace at the speed of light. In Las Vegas, in a rare afternoon of fun and frivolity, all arranged by Cosmo Cricket for his new bride, Lizzie, the text message arrived just as three cherries appeared on the slot machine she was playing, giving her a win of $44. She whooped and immediately quit playing. Cosmo smiled indulgently as Lizzie steered him to the lounge, where, despite the early hour, she insisted a drink was in order to celebrate her win. While they waited for their drinks, Lizzie called Maggie and Ted on Nantucket.

On Nantucket Island, Maggie sighed with happiness as Ted rubbed her back with sunblock. She looked down at the vibrating cell phone and groaned when she saw that the call was from Lizzie. It had to be business. Maggie tripped right past the greeting, and said, "I just want you to know I'm lying on a glorious beach, the temperature is a wonderful seventy-eight degrees, the sun is shining, and Ted is rubbing my back with some sweet-smelling sunblock. I am drinking one of those frothy drinks with a little umbrella. I am *relaxing.* Are you calling to tell me you're pregnant? If you are, I'll put it on the front page. *When I get back.*"

"No, no, no, I'm not pregnant! I'm sorry to intrude on your short vacation, Maggie, but I thought you would want to know that Charles is back on the mountain. I don't know any details. I'll be back Sunday night. Let's do breakfast Monday morning. By the way I just won $44," Lizzie said happily.

Maggie rolled over as she closed her cell phone. She looked up at Ted and smiled. "Charles is back on the mountain. That was Lizzie on the phone. I wonder what it means, if anything. His being gone changed a lot of things, and I wonder how many of them, if any, will ever change back. I'm getting a feeling, Ted."

Ted groaned as he sat up straighter. He'd learned the hard way never, ever, to ignore Maggie when she said she was *"getting a feeling."* He immediately sent off a text message to Joe Espinosa in Baltimore, apprising him of the news and alerting him to the fact that Maggie was getting one of her feelings. Reporter-speak for *get your ass back to D.C. as soon as you're done in Baltimore.*

Maggie rolled back over, irritated now that she had sand on her oiled back. "Ted, call Nellie and Elias while I call Jack."

In Virginia, just as her cell phone rang, Nellie handed off the two-month-old baby, who'd left a wet spot on her dress the size of a dinner plate, to her jittery husband. Elias handed the squealing infant to his father, who in turn delivered him to his weary mother.

Dismayed at the giant wet spot on her silk dress, Nellie walked to the back of the church, then outside, where she took the call from Ted Robinson. "This better be good, Ted. I'm at Elias's grandson's christening, and the kid just peed all over me."

"Charles is back on the mountain. The girls texted Lizzie, who called Maggie. We're here on Nantucket and headed home tomorrow. Maggie just asked me to call you. When are you going home, Judge?"

"I think that might be a wonderful thing for the girls, especially Myra. At least I hope it will be, but she and Charles may have to start all over again. I know that she felt deserted, even though he told her that he had to stay behind in England. We're leaving as soon as I can drag Elias out to the car. We drove," she said inanely.

"Well, drive safely. We'll catch up on every-one's return," Ted said.

Ted stretched out and rolled close to Maggie. He listened to her conversation, trying to get a bead on what Charles Martin's return to the mountain would mean to all of them.

"That's all I know, Jack. No details. Lizzie called, and she was more excited about winning $44 than Charles returning to the mountain. I wonder how happy Myra is with his return. We're heading home Sunday morning. So, you'll tell Harry, okay? I want to get back to soaking up this warm, delicious sun. It's won-derful here, Jack. I hope you and Nikki get to come to Nantucket someday. Listen, Jack, Lizzie didn't say anything about notifying Pearl Barnes, but I'm thinking she should be kept in the loop. Do it for me, big guy, and I will owe you. See you on Monday."

Ted leaned over and whispered in Maggie's ear the moment she ended her call to Jack. He waited to see what her response would be. When she said, "I've never had sex in the water. Okay, let's go for it," Ted was the first one in the water. The *cold* water. The *really cold* water. He looked at Maggie, who was shivering and watch-ing him expectantly.

Maggie started to laugh when he shook his head. "We could fill the bathtub with *warm* water."

"Yeah, let's do that," Maggie said, scampering out of the water, Ted hot on her heels.

* * *

Back in Washington, Jack jammed the cell phone into his pocket and started to jog his way back to the office. He hated running or jogging in leather shoes, but his sneakers were at Harry's *dojo*. He was dripping wet with sweat when he blasted through the lobby and jogged in place for a moment before he made his way to the elevator.

In his office, he ripped off his jacket and tie and sat down. Slightly winded, he let loose with a mighty sigh as he unpacked his briefcase, his thoughts on Nikki, the mountain, Charles, and wondering where the hell Harry was. He'd been text messaging and calling him every chance he got, all day, with no response. He knew Harry had a midmorning training class at Quantico, and they were to meet up at the Drop Zone for lunch. But Harry hadn't shown for lunch. Jack was getting really concerned because Harry always answered his phone. Always. And the fine hairs on the back of Jack's neck had started to prickle. Somewhere, something was wrong.

Jack sorted, sifted, and collated the papers in his briefcase before he bellowed for his secretary and the two assistant DAs. "Court's dark tomorrow. I'll see you when I see you. Be sure to get those papers to Judge Avalone before five-thirty. Chop-chop, guys. You, too, Melinda." He got snorts of disgust and grimaces that he ignored. "It's all about delegating, guys. That's why they pay me the big bucks." A roll of rubber bands in the shape of a ball hit him squarely in the back of the head.

Jack laughed as he made his way back to the elevator, his jacket slung over his shoulder, his tie trailing out of a side pocket.

In the parking lot, he popped the trunk and tossed in both his jacket and briefcase.

The inside of his car was like a sauna. He turned on the AC to HIGH and then slipped in a favorite Harry Connick, Jr. CD. Sweat dripped down Jack's face. He swiped at it with the sleeve of his shirt. He tooled along, his eyes on the road, hoping to see Harry on his Ducati, but it didn't happen.

Traffic was surprisingly light for a Friday afternoon, when usually a lot of people headed out of the city to cooler pastures, so Jack made decent time to Harry's *dojo* just as the AC kicked in, and he started to shiver.

Jack turned the corner and slowed, his eyes almost bugging out of his head at the sight of the yellow CAUTION tape stretched across the *dojo*'s front door. What made him slam on his brakes was the sight of Harry sitting on the curb in his Armani suit, barefooted. His shoes were next to him there alongside the Ducati. He didn't even look up at the sound of Jack's squealing brakes. Jack slammed out of the car the moment he swerved the curb. He looked around for a sign of smoke that would mean the CAUTION tape was up because of a fire. No smoke. *Christ, maybe Harry finally killed someone. Nah, he'd be in jail if he'd done that, and he sure as hell wouldn't be sitting on the curb in his Armani suit.*

"Harry! What the hell is going on? Harry, look at me! Goddamn it, what the hell is going on? Why are you sitting here all duded up in that fancy suit? Are you going to answer me, or do I have to knock you on your ass?" Jack yelled, his heart beating trip-hammer fast. When there was no smart-ass response, Jack dropped to his haunches and poked at Harry's chest. "At least you're not dead. You had me worried there for a minute. Talk to me, Harry. It's me, Jack. Come on, buddy, let's hear it."

Harry finally looked at Jack, his face a mask of pain, his eyes glazed over.

Jack cupped Harry's face in his two hands. "What, Harry? Are you sick? If you don't tell me what's wrong, I can't help you. Jesus Christ, Harry, will you please tell me what's going on here?"

Harry licked his dry lips and then looked square at Jack. "Someone stole my *dojo*, Jack. The bank foreclosed. They came this morning and kicked me out. Then they stretched the tape, and I'm not allowed to go in. They put new locks on the doors."

"What?" Jack's screech could be heard for blocks.

"I went to the bank this morning about the loan to remodel the *dojo,* and that's when I found out. The bottom line is that my identity was stolen, and the person who did it ran up all kinds of bills, ruined my credit, took out two equity loans they didn't pay on. They cleaned out my bank accounts, savings and checking. I have seventeen bucks in my pocket, Jack. I'm homeless. They don't know about the Ducati. If they did, they'd come and take it. I didn't know what to do or say, so I just left the bank. I've been sitting here for hours. I can't even go inside to get my stuff. That's why I'm still wearing this stupid suit."

Jack lowered himself to the curb and put his arm around his friend's shoulders. "Listen to me, Harry. We're going to make this right. We are. I'm going to call the mountain, and the girls will be on this like white on rice. By the way, Charles is back. That's why I came here. I knew something was wrong when you didn't call and stood me up for lunch. Why the hell didn't you call me, Harry? Give me one reason why. Just one, Harry."

Harry hung his head. "I was ashamed."

"Bullshit! If that happened to me, you would be the first person I'd call."

"It's hard to make phone calls when you're crying and can't talk. Yeah, I bawled my eyes out. My whole life is gone, Jack. *Gone!*"

"Only for the moment. We'll make it right, Harry. I need you to believe that. Now, let's go around back and break into the *dojo* and get your stuff. You're moving in with me till we can get a handle on all of this."

"They told me not to go near the building, or they'd lock me up. I wouldn't do well in jail, Jack."

"Okay, you sit here, and I'll do the breaking and entering. No one told me I couldn't go near the building. My stuff is in there, and I damn well want it. Tell me what you want, what you can't live without."

Harry flapped his hands in the air. "My personal stuff. There isn't that much."

"We need Lizzie!" Jack said as he scooted under the CAUTION tape and raced around to the back door. He eyed the padlock with disdain before he gave the door a kick that sent it flying off the hinges. He walked in and headed straight for Harry's apartment on the second floor. He looked around. The word "spartan" came to mind. He got to work quickly, shoving clothes into a bag he found in the closet. He picked up two pictures of Yoko and added them to the pile. He cleaned out the dresser drawers and collected Harry's bathroom gear. When he was finished he had three bags filled to overflowing. "Not much, my ass," he muttered.

Jack tossed the soft-sided athletic bags down the rickety steps. He followed, then raced outside with the bags and dumped them in the trunk of his Honda. He ran back in and cut off all the circuit breakers. No reason for Harry to be saddled with an electric bill he couldn't pay. He was on his way back to the door when he spotted the huge cardboard carton where Harry tossed his mail. His eyes narrowed. He bent down, hefted the box to his shoulders, and carried it outside. He set it down and propped up the back door. It still looked like it had been kicked in. Oh, well.

The box went into the backseat of his car.

"C'mon, Harry, time to head for your new digs. We're going to hit rush hour, so here's the house key. You'll get there before I will. Just go in and make yourself at home. I'll call Lizzie and Maggie. Harry, look at me, buddy. We're going to make this right. Trust me. Don't kill yourself on the way, you hear me?"

This was where Harry should shoot off some smart-ass response, but all he said was, "Thanks, Jack."

Oh, shit. He liked Harry better when he was snarly and hostile. This new Harry was never going to work. So the girls, and Lizzie, and whoever else, would just have to get done whatever was needed so the old Harry would be back in place in the *dojo* again. Jack didn't know whether to laugh or cry when he thought about what was likely to happen to the identity thief.

Chapter 4

It was almost seven o'clock when Harry, with Jack's help, finished settling into the guest bedroom. It was a pretty room, Jack thought, with the lavender spread that matched the wisteria on the wallpaper in the room. Crispy white curtains fluttered in the early-evening breeze. A woman's room because this was Nikki's house, which she'd deeded to Jack when she and the other vigilantes had to run for their lives. Jack's house now, with the understanding that if things ever worked out for her and the vigilantes, and she was able to return to society, he could deed it back to her.

Harry looked around, his toes wiggling in the pale lavender carpet. His eyes still looked glazed, and his shoulders slumped. The Armani suit had been tossed on the bed, along with the silk shirt and tie. The offending shoes, which he hated, were under the bed. He now wore thong sandals and an outfit that resembled hospital scrubs. "It's a nice room, Jack. Yoko would love it. Lavender is her favorite color. The bed looks comfortable."

Jack knew that most nights when he was alone, Harry slept on a mat on the floor. For the life of him he couldn't remember if he'd brought the mat or not. He asked.

"Yeah, it was in the big duffel. You rolled it up. Thanks."

"You hungry?"

Harry thought about the question. "Yeah, I guess I am. I had an apple at Quantico, but I was nervous about the meeting at the bank, so I thought it would be better if I didn't eat. Good thing, or I would have lost it."

Jack gripped his friend's arm tightly when it looked like Harry was going to go into a trance. "Listen, we're going to make this right. Think of this as a blip on the screen, a bump in the road. Let's go downstairs. I cooked a pot roast the other night, and there's a lot left over. No sprouts, but I have some of that shitty tea you like, and I know how to cook rice. C'mon, let's go."

As an added enticement, he said, "I have a pecan pie one of the girls at the office baked for me yesterday. With ice cream to go on top." But he wasn't kidding himself—it was the shitty green tea that made Harry pick up his feet.

Downstairs in the kitchen, Jack popped a beer and brewed tea for Harry. He bustled about the kitchen, slicing the leftover pot roast, adding it to the gravy. He set the oven timer for fifteen minutes. The rice cooker would offer up perfect rice in less than that. He slid the pecan pie into the oven, next to the meat.

"Jack, the perfect host. When did you *really* learn to cook?" Harry asked. His tone said he didn't care about the answer one way or the other, he was simply making conversation, doing his best to lift the pall that was settling over the kitchen.

Jack chose to answer anyway. "When I took over this house. I used to spend all day Sunday cooking, then parceling it out for weeks. I made a lot of mistakes, but it was a lot cheaper than eating out every night. The money I saved I put into my 401k. Mine's a little down right now, how is yours doing?"

"It's gone, Jack. The son of a bitch who did this to me cleaned that out, too."

"Oh, fuck! How much did you have in there?"

"Almost two hundred grand. That includes my IRAs, too. The bastard took it all. I've been putting in the max and doing without because I wanted to make sure I had enough to take care of Yoko in our golden years—if it should happen that the girls get a pardon. I had another $78,000 in CDs that's also gone. I had a small savings account with $8,300 to draw on for emergencies and $1,600 in my checking account. It wasn't enough to steal all that; the bastard applied for credit cards and put me in hock for over a hundred grand. I used to have an 820 credit score. Now I'm homeless and penniless," Harry said pitifully.

Jack struggled to find comforting words, but none came. All he could do was put his hand on Harry's shoulder and squeeze it.

"What did Lizzie say when you called?" Harry asked.

"Messages were going straight to voice mail, and I didn't want to leave that kind of message. We'll call her after dinner, and Maggie, too. After we hear what they have to say, I think we should call the mountain and ask for the vigilantes' help."

Harry turned around in his chair and looked up at Jack. "I'm not sure I want to do that, Jack. What the hell is Yoko going to think?"

"She's going to think just the way I'm thinking. The same way anyone else who hears this is going to think. Identity theft is a big problem in this country. Just go on the Net, and you'll see it's actually rampant. As soon as institutions get plans in place, those bastards manage to get around them. I promise you one thing, Harry. If the girls get on this, that son of a bitch is toast, and you'll get all your money back. Then if you want to . . . kill that son of a bitch, I don't think anyone will stop you. But the flip side to that is you'll go to jail and won't be able to spend any of that money the girls get back for you. Then Yoko will start to hate you because you made her a widow even before you married her."

"Eat shit, Jack!"

Ah, the Harry he knew and loved had finally

emerged from the sad-sack imposter he had found sitting in front of the *dojo*.

"Soup's on. How come you didn't set the table, Harry?"

Harry clenched his teeth. "Because you didn't tell me to set the damn table, that's why. Furthermore, I'm a guest, and you're supposed to wait on me hand and foot. That's what a good host does."

"Yeah, well, don't go pushing your luck, Harry. We divide everything up here. I cook, you clean up. You do your own laundry. I vacuum, and you dust. We take turns doing the shopping. Yeah, I know you don't have any money, so I'll pay for the groceries, but then if I do that, you should cook. None of that alfalfa shit you eat or those sprouts that grow other sprouts right under your eyes and make you poop green. Deal?"

"I hate you, Jack," Harry said, slamming a plate with purple flowers on it in front of Jack. "Where are the candles?"

"Oh, dear God, mercy me, good heavens, how could I have been so stupid as to forget the candles? You're an asshole, Harry," Jack said as he reached into one of the cabinets for a fat yellow candle, which was supposed to smell like warm summer sunshine, and set it in the middle of the table.

"It doesn't go with the dishes, Jack. It should be lavender."

"Harry! Shut the fuck up and eat!"

*   *   *

Lizzie clicked on her cell phone. There was a smile in her voice when she said, "Talk to me, Jack. I was in the shower when you called. Cosmo is taking me out to dinner. Why didn't you leave a message?"

"I wasn't sure I wanted to leave this particular message. Listen, Lizzie, something terrible has happened to Harry, so that makes this a personal call. That's why I didn't want to leave a message. Someone managed to steal Harry's identity. He's been evicted. All his money, all his accounts . . . gone. He's staying with me right now and has seventeen bucks to his name and his Ducati. And that's it. I'm going to tell you now that I broke into the *dojo* and got his stuff, and, no, I didn't leave fingerprints. There's yellow CAUTION tape all around the *dojo*. One more thing, the person or persons who did this also applied for over a dozen credit cards and ran them up to the max. Harry has over two hundred grand now in credit card debt. He has two cards that he pays off every month. He rarely uses them but will buy something or charge a meal just to keep them active."

"I got it, Jack. I'll be on the first plane out tomorrow. Tell Harry to sit tight, okay? Also tell him he's not the only one this has happened to, and it might make him feel a little better. Forty million Americans get their identity stolen every year."

"Yeah, well, that isn't going to make Harry or me feel any better to know that, Lizzie."

"I know. But it's a fact that we have to recognize and deal with. Call the mountain, and I'll call Maggie. We need to get on this ASAP. Now, relax. I'm going out to dinner with my husband. I'll check in with you the minute I get back to D.C."

"Gotcha. Thanks, Lizzie."

Jack turned to Harry. "You ready for your pie now? Lizzie's on it. She told me that forty million Americans have their identities stolen every year."

"Yeah, I'll take the pie and the ice cream. More tea, too. I don't want to be the forty million and first American who has his identity stolen."

"Look at it this way, Harry. Lizzie has that long flight back to D.C. to map out a strategy. Boy, I can almost feel sympathy for the president of that bank when he goes up against Lizzie. By the way, what's the name of the bank?"

"East Coast Savings."

"Shit! That's where my accounts are," Jack snarled. "Damn it, wouldn't you know this would happen on a Friday, so we have to sweat the weekend? First thing Monday morning, I'm out of that bank, and my money is going into a sock under my mattress." Jack knew he wouldn't do anything that stupid, but he was going to do something. Getting out of the bank was the first thing he had to do. And he wouldn't mince any words when he told them why he was moving his funds.

Harry got up and opened the refrigerator. He popped two beers and handed one to Jack. He clinked his bottle against Jack's, and said, "Here's to the bastard that stole my identity and his imminent death, preceded by total dismemberment and anything else the girls can come up with."

"Now you're clicking, Harry. I think we should just cripple him, make him pee through a straw and poop into a bag. After we break every bone in his body. We could treat ourselves to his misery and go visit him in whatever nuthouse they put him in after we're done with him."

Harry's almond-shaped eyes almost widened. "You'd help me do that, Jack?"

"Hell, yes." Liar, liar, pants on fire.

"You're the best, Jack. Listen, I don't understand any of this. Every January, I pay all my bills ahead for a full year because I don't want to be late on a payment. I even leave a small cushion in case I make a mistake. Like an extra hundred in each account. You know how I hate getting bills. This is just the beginning of July. If I had known, had a clue, I would have done something."

Jack looked over at the cardboard box that held Harry's old mail, the box that he'd dumped by the kitchen door. He pointed to it.

"I bet we find something in that box that's a clue."

Both men dived for the box at the same time. Before they could go through the contents, however, both men's cell phones rang. Jack looked at the ID. Maggie.

Harry looked at his ID. Yoko. His shoulders sagged as he got to his feet and walked out of the kitchen to take his call, leaving Jack to talk with Maggie.

"Jack, Lizzie just called me. I've had my people on this for almost three months, and we've come up dry. Identity theft is a big thing these days. It's the new way for the computer super-literate to fund their retirements. I'm leaving tomorrow, and we'll all meet for dinner with you and Harry. Lizzie said she'd cook dinner for us. I didn't know she knew how to cook, but she volunteered. I think Cosmo must like home cooking. If it was just us, we'd probably get Chinese takeout."

Jack groaned. He wasn't the least bit interested in Lizzie's culinary expertise. "Maggie, tell me there's something we can do. Harry's beside himself, and so am I because I bank at that goddamn place myself."

"It's an identity theft ring, Jack. If you'd read my paper, you'd know we've been doing a series on this for months, but it's been mostly profiles of people and what's happened to their lives since their identities were stolen. It's heartbreaking, and there's no one out there to help them. They don't have the funds to hire lawyers. They try on their own, but in most cases, it's taking *YEARS*, Jack."

"I want you to ratchet this up and go full bore. I haven't called the mountain yet. I've been kind of busy trying to get Harry into a better mind-set. We were just going to go through his box. You know, that box where he throws all his mail that he considers junk mail. Harry definitely has a thing about getting mail. We might find a clue in the box somewhere. So, I guess I'll see you at Lizzie's tomorrow. Did she say what time?"

"Yes, seven o'clock, but she said to come early if we want. Ted wants to leave tonight, so we might do that. I'm not sure yet. You know Ted, he worries about Mickey and Minnie if he's away too long. Espinosa will be back by noon tomorrow. I'm on it, Jack. Call the mountain."

"Harry is on the phone with Yoko right now. I have a feeling he's not going to tell her. He really is an odd duck when it comes to Yoko. He thinks she might think he's stupid or something dumb like that. I'll call Nikki when I hang up. What do you think about Charles coming back to the mountain?"

"I think with all this going on, we can use all the help we can get. I'm going to call Abner Tookus and have him hack into the bank's accounts. You didn't hear me say that, right, Jack?"

"I absolutely did not hear you say you were going to call Abner Tookus to crack into the bank's accounts. Absolutely I did not hear that."

"If Harry doesn't kill you, I will. Night, Jack. See you tomorrow."

"Yeah, tomorrow," Jack said, his eyes on the huge cardboard carton.

Chapter 5

Myra stopped watering the potted plants on the porch to watch Yoko, who was across the compound sitting on a bench under a fragrant pine tree. Something was wrong, she could tell by the set of Yoko's shoulders, the way she was clenching the cell phone to her ear. She looked behind her to see if the others were anywhere near, but she had the porch to herself.

Myra dropped to her knees and started plucking the yellow leaves from a vibrant scarlet geranium, but her eyes never left the little Asian girl sitting on the bench. Myra stood up when she saw Yoko get up and run to the bell. Yoko reached for the round ball, pulled back, and gave it a resounding smack against the side of the huge bell. As the sound reverberated over the mountain, she stepped back and threw her arms wide. Myra had seen Yoko do that on other occasions, and when asked what she was doing, she'd calmly said, "I'm throwing my concerns out to the universe."

The Sisters came from all directions, with Murphy and Grady leading the way.

Breathless from their sprint to the compound, Kathryn bellowed the loudest. "What's wrong?"

The dogs barked, then howled to show they wanted to know what was wrong, too. Their afternoon swim had just been interrupted. Both dogs shook their shaggy bodies to get rid of the excess water dripping from their coats.

The drumming hum of the sound from the bell could still be heard.

"Harry's in trouble!" Yoko shouted.

The Sisters clustered around Yoko.

Myra looked at Annie, and whispered, "It must be serious for Yoko to ring the bell."

Annie nodded as she led the way to the war room. They were all surprised to see Charles at his usual position behind the bank of computers. It looked like old times.

The women all rushed to their respective chairs and waited for Charles to join them. When he did, he simply asked, "What happened?"

Yoko stood up, her slim body quivering. Kathryn reached out and placed a steady hand on her arm.

"I called Harry a little while ago. Jack told him to call me, but Harry didn't want to because of the shame involved. He needs our help. Someone stole his identity. He was evicted from his *dojo*. He is with Jack right now. He is homeless and destitute. We have to help him. Like right now. Immediately. If you all won't help, then I am leaving."

"Darling girl, no one said we won't help," Myra told her. "Relax, tell us everything you know. Give us something to go on, and we will act at the speed of light. Isn't that right, Charles?" she asked briskly.

"Myra is right. Tell us everything you know. Everything, Yoko," Charles said.

Yoko took a deep breath and rattled off everything Harry had grudgingly told her. She ended with, "I'm sure he left out as much as he told me. It is that shame factor, saving-face thing my people cannot let go of. He did tell me he thought Jack probably told Nikki because he thought Jack was talking to her."

All eyes turned to Nikki. "I was talking to Jack, but he didn't get a chance to tell me anything because he had to talk to Lizzie. This is the first I'm hearing about Harry. If we need to vote, you have mine, Yoko."

Yoko nodded. "Lizzie is leaving Vegas first thing in the morning, Maggie and Ted are leaving Nantucket. Joe Espinosa is currently in Baltimore but will be back in the District by noon tomorrow. Judge Easter and Elias are in Virginia and are on the way back. I don't know about Pearl. Harry didn't say anything about her. All of them—well, actually, I'm not sure about Judge Easter and Elias—are going to Lizzie's house for dinner and to talk. What can we do?"

"First, I need to talk to Jack and Harry," Charles said. "Harry's bank is a good place to start, but I'm going to need other information. The person or persons who stole Harry's identity didn't just pop up out of nowhere and ask Harry for it. It's possible that Harry was lax in some way and, Yoko, everyone is careless at one time or another. It's also possible someone hacked into the bank's records and got it that way.

"I'll get on it right now and position my people. In the meantime, go on the Internet and get every tidbit of information you can on identity theft. We'll reconvene after dinner, which, by the way, will be delicious." Without another word, Charles backed up and went to his position at his special computers.

"Business as usual," Isabelle said as she got up.

The Sisters surrounded Yoko and led her back out to the compound, where they started to chatter like magpies, each voice assuring her that they would make it right for Harry. Yoko smiled through her tears and allowed herself to be smothered with affection from her Sisters.

"I think I'm going to like taking on the person who dared to steal Harry's life," Annie said, her eyes sparking dangerously. "The way Harry's life was looted makes me think it's not a person but a ring of people. Maggie did a series of articles in the paper about the subject a few months ago. Actually, she profiled the victims because no one was able to come up with anything that would lead to the capture of the culprits. That has to mean it's an organized group with a leader who has some savvy and a bankroll."

"I think you're right, Annie. Oh, I do relish going after whoever it is," Myra said gleefully.

Yoko giggled as the other Sisters hooted and hollered and stomped their feet.

"And, dear, call Harry now and tell him he's in good hands. Tell him the vigilantes are *on it.*"

Yoko grinned at the vehemence in Myra's tone.

"I know I say this all the time, but, Myra, you absolutely rock," Annie said happily.

That's just what Yoko needed to hear.

"Let's just hope we can deliver on my promise," Myra whispered.

Annie waved her hands in the air. "Myra, if you were a betting woman, who would you bet on? Us or those people who stole Harry's identity?"

"Annie, that is absolutely a no-brainer. Us, of course. I already feel sorry for the people who dared to invade and steal Harry's life and his life savings. They picked the wrong mark this time, and we are going to teach them a serious lesson, one they'll never forget. They might as well kiss their lives good-bye, because they will never recover from what is about to happen to them. Never. I guarantee it."

Annie looked down at her watch, thrilled at the fierceness in Myra's attitude. It had been hard watching the suffering her friend had gone through since she had come back from England without Charles. "It's almost time for dinner. I can't wait to see what Charles has made for us."

"What do you think, Annie? Is it going to work or not?" she whispered.

Annie smiled. "You know, Myra, I think it *is* going to work. Charles wasn't sure what our reaction was going to be. I think he's so relieved, he's positively giddy. Having said that, I think dinner will be spectacular. Women are so forgiving. Maybe we need to harden up or something."

"No, Annie, we are what we are. Forgiveness is a wonderful thing. It really is."

"Then why are you still living in the other building?"

Myra actually giggled. "Because I'm working on that forgiveness thing. I'm not quite there yet. In other words, Charles has to sweat a little more. I earned the right to see him squirm."

Both women laughed as they made their way to the dining hall to set the table for dinner.

Maggie Spritzer rubbed the grit from her eyes. Even though she'd slept the last hundred miles into the District, she was tired and cranky, and she couldn't see any food anywhere in the office. That only made her more irritated. "I need some food," she bellowed to Ted, who was standing in the doorway waiting for his marching orders.

"Maggie, it's four o'clock in the morning. Where do you think I'm going to get food at this hour? No one is in yet, so there are no donuts. Nothing in this area opens till six o'clock. You know no one replaces the fruit and snacks over the weekend. Plus, I have to go home to check on Mickey and Minnie. I can bring you some stuff from home if you can wait. You do know that you are obsessed with food, right?"

Maggie bristled. Ted was right, she did obsess about food, but she also obsessed about sex. She said so, to Ted's chagrin.

Ted hopped from one foot to the other. "So what you're saying is if I don't get you some food, then there won't be any sex."

"Right!" Maggie said, pulling up her e-mails. "It was your idea to drive through the night. We could be in bed right now back on Nantucket, possibly having sex, possibly eating strawberries dipped in chocolate. Strawberries dipped in sweet cream. Instead, I'm sitting here looking at e-mails while I'm starving, and you aren't helping matters."

"Okay, I'm gone. I'll be back. I want to make sure I understand something. If I fetch food back, we can have sex, maybe tonight?"

Maggie looked up from the computer. She loved to devil Ted. "Depends on what you bring back, Teddie."

Ted groaned as he hotfooted it to the elevator.

Maggie mumbled something to herself that sounded like, "Maggie, you are shameless," as she scanned her e-mails, which were hardly earth-shattering. She reached over for her Rolodex and punched in the number for Abner Tookus.

Maggie sighed and nibbled on her thumbnail while she waited for her old friend to pick up the phone. She was *so* hungry. Seven rings, eight rings. "C'mon, Abner, pick up. I know you're there." When the hacker's voice mail came on, Maggie disconnected and dialed the number again.

Finally, the phone was picked up, dropped, then picked up again. "The answer is no. It's four o'clock in the morning. People only call other people at this hour when there is an emergency. No. Take my name out of your Rolodex and forget you know me."

"Abner, sweetie, I'm just as cranky as you are. Otherwise, I wouldn't be calling you. Do you think for one minute that I like waking people up at four o'clock in the morning?" When there was no response, Maggie tried wheedling. "I hate to wake people up at this hour, but I am up, so you need to get up, too. The early bird gets the worm. C'mon, Abner, I need some help."

Maggie heard her old friend sigh. She almost had him.

"I don't do that kind of stuff anymore. I'm on the straight and narrow. I even have a full-time if slightly unusual job working for Big Blue, and I'm getting married. So, hang up and let me go back to sleep."

"What do you mean you're getting married? You said you would wait for me forever. Well, that sucks, Abner. When did you get a job with IBM? If you're lying to me, I'm going to sic the vigilantes on you. Who are you marrying?" Maggie asked, suspicion ringing in her voice.

"Just you never mind who I'm marrying. Big Blue recruited me. I didn't go looking for a job, and they pay a hell of a lot better than you do."

"Yeah, but are they going to give you a smashing wedding present like I'm going to give you? No, they are not. I'm willing to quadruple your usual fee. Furthermore, you and I both know you could retire on what you charge me. All IBM will do is drain your blood, make you work around-the-clock, then what's-her-name will get sick and tired of sitting home alone and divorce you. I rest my case, Abner."

"Jesus, Maggie, it's too early in the morning for this kind of discussion. I have to be in the office at six, and you're eating into my sleep time. Quadruple my fee? What kind of smashing wedding present?"

"How about I pay for your honeymoon to Hawaii, or maybe Paris?"

"Plus quadrupling my fee?"

Maggie sighed, and she was getting hungrier by the moment. She sighed again. "Yeah. That's how special you are to me."

"That's bullshit. You're desperate. I want it in writing, and I want the check in my hands before I do whatever it is you want me to do. And I want to see those airline tickets, too."

"It's four o'clock in the morning, Abner. At nine o'clock I will have it going. That's when the business day starts. Stop by the office later in the morning, and I will have everything ready to put into your hot little hand."

"No can do, Maggie. I'm working, remember. Now, if you want to hand-deliver it to me, that's okay, too. And just for the record, this whole conversation might very well be moot since you haven't told me what the job is."

"Okay, here it is. Listen up. A friend of mine had his identity stolen, and he is now homeless and penniless. I want you to hack into East Coast Savings. Whoever it was that stole his ID took out an equity loan on his property as well as a second mortgage. I want to see the bank records. I also want you to find out if any of the bank's other customers had their identities stolen. In other words, I want it all, Abner. C'mon, you and I both know you're the best in the business. Are you telling me this is above your pay grade? For shame, Abner. I really looked up to you. Don't tell me you're *wussing* out."

"And if I get caught?"

"I'll get you the best lawyer in town: Lizzie Fox. For free. *Free*, Abner!"

"If, and I'm saying *IF*, I agree to this, when do you need it?"

"Like yesterday."

"Ha-ha! Even though it's Saturday, I have to go to work, and when I get there, I actually have to work. W-O-R-K!"

"Call in sick."

"I just started last week; I can't call in sick."

"Sure you can. Say you have the crud. Guys get the crud all the time. You said they recruited you, not the other way around. That means they'll cut you some slack. I need this ASAP, Abby."

"Ten grand bonus on top of the quadruple, and we have a deal."

Maggie pretended to think about it. She was a hundred percent sure Annie would approve this outlandish expenditure. "When can you have it for me?"

Instead of answering the question, Abner asked another one. "How many days in Hawaii? And don't count the two travel days. And an extra day for jet lag. Vouchers for the local airlines to visit the other islands. The only hotel I'll consider is the Fairmont Orchid."

Maggie's antenna went up. "You skunk, that's where you were going all along on your honeymoon, and you just want me to pay for it."

"Hey, you called me, I didn't call you. So, what's it going to be, Miz Spritzer? I'll even bring you back a souvenir."

"Okay, okay! Three full weeks, and that's my last offer. Agree to that, and we have a deal. And you better get me what I need."

"If it's there, I'll get it. See you at nine o'clock. Don't make me wait."

"Screw you, Abner. What's her name?"

Maggie could hear Abner's laughter as he hung up. She looked around to see if anyone had magically appeared with food while she was talking to Abner. She was as alone as before she made the call. She thought about taking a nap but knew she would never be able to sleep if she was hungry. With nothing else to occupy her time, she meandered out of the office, down the hall to the kitchen, where she made the first pot of coffee of the day. While she waited for the coffee to drip into the pot she daydreamed about Eggs Benedict, waffles with cream and blueberries, eggs and bacon, cinnamon apple-sauce on the side, buttery toast, fresh melon, a stack of pancakes with warm butter and syrup. "Oh, God, I'm going to die if I don't get some food." She was so pitiful she couldn't stand herself.

Chapter 6

Lizzie drove her car into the garage and locked it with the remote on her visor. She entered the house through a door that led to the kitchen, where she stopped in the middle of the floor. This was the part that she hated, entering an empty house where there was no sound, no pet running to greet her. It was at times like this that she realized how alone she felt in the world. Oh, yes, her days and the early part of her evenings were filled with people and things to do, but at the bitter end she was still alone.

Lizzie looked around at her neat, tidy kitchen. Cosmo Cricket would not fit into this little house, he just wouldn't. Until they finalized their living arrangements, she would be commuting to Las Vegas on weekends. Not that Cosmo was averse to coming here to Washington; he wasn't. They both recognized that the house either needed to be renovated or they needed to buy a new East Coast home.

Sound was what she needed, so she turned on the under-the-cabinet Bose radio she had ordered last year. Then she turned on the television sitting on top of the counter. A jumble of noise, to be sure, a far cry from the bells and whistles of Las Vegas, but it did make her feel better.

Lizzie's thoughts ran in all directions as she made her way through the house to the stairway that led to the two bedrooms on the second floor. The minute she stepped into the hallway, she started to shed her clothes.

Ten minutes later, her suit was hanging neatly in the closet, her shoes were on the shoe tree, and she was dressed in a pair of sweats and sneakers. She rummaged for combs in the vanity, piling the shimmering silver hair on top of her head. Her two cell phones went into her pockets. As soon as she got dinner under way, she would call Cosmo, and they would talk until her guests arrived. She brightened immediately at the thought of talking to her new husband.

Downstairs in the kitchen, Lizzie hummed to herself as she banged pots and pans, opened jars, and got out her cutting board.

Lizzie was the first to admit that she was no great shakes as a cook, but she did watch the Food Network from time to time. She especially liked the program where the host and cook prepared what she called semihomemade dinners. She'd paid attention, and now was able to pre-

pare spaghetti that tasted like she'd slaved for
hours. Thank goodness, for that was precisely
what she was going to prepare for her guests.

Lizzie dumped a huge jar of store-bought
spaghetti sauce into a pot, squeezed some
tomato paste right from the tube into the mix,
and stirred. A can of fire-roasted tomatoes went
in next. She chopped garlic and onions and
sautéed them in a small frying pan, and the moment the onions were translucent, she spooned
them into the sauce. In the blink of an eye she
chopped basil and parsley and scooped it into
the pot. She frowned as she remembered who
her guests were. Maggie Spritzer could eat the
whole pot of sauce on her own, so she added
two more jars of the bottled sauce, squeezed in
some more tomato paste, then chopped and
sautéed more garlic and onions. Cosmo said his
favorite scent in the whole world was the smell
of frying onions and garlic. She had to admit
she loved the aroma herself.

Continuing with the semihomemade theme,
Lizzie preheated the oven, took a berry pie out
of her freezer, and waited ten minutes before
crimping the edges and making fork marks all
around. What's-her-name on the semihomemade show said guests always looked at the
edges to see if they were cookie-cutter or homemade. Fork marks made it look homemade.
Then Lizzie brushed an egg white over the top,
covered the crimped edges with tinfoil, slid the
pie into the oven, and set the timer.

The kitchen clock told her she had ninety minutes before her guests arrived. Time enough to set the dining room table, cook the pasta, and get a salad ready. Five minutes later she had a bag of four kinds of lettuce washed, drained, and in a wooden bowl. She added some cherry tomatoes, sliced a cucumber and a purple onion, tossed the whole thing lightly with her fancy-dancy salad fork, and the salad was ready. The dressing was a combination of three store-bought bottled dressings that she poured into a gravy boat. Semihomemade was a lifesaver.

She could talk to Cosmo while she prepared the coffeepot, got out the dishes, and carried them into the dining room. The last thing she did was fill a large pot with water, add some extra-virgin olive oil, throw in a pinch of salt, and put it on SIMMER for the pasta. *Finito!*

Lizzie popped a ginger ale and sat down, but not before heaving a huge sigh. Her voice was soft and intimate when she said, "Hi, Cricket, it's me."

Lizzie's guests all arrived within five minutes of each other. All sniffed appreciatively, commenting on the delectable aromas wafting through the house. Lizzie felt smug, it didn't get any better than cinnamon, garlic, and onions. Comfort food, and that was what Lizzie was trying to convey to her guests. From the sounds of their voices earlier, they all needed it.

There was a camaraderie, a genuine fondness for each other as they all hugged and babbled about how good it was to meet in a semisocial situation.

Lizzie served wine and beer as they all gathered around her dining room table. She started off by saying there would be no business conducted until their meal was finished, just the way the Sisters did things on the mountain.

The dinner was family style, everything in the middle of the table so that everyone could help themselves. Conversation was lively and at times boisterous when Ted and Maggie discussed the nude beach they'd visited on their trip north. Lizzie's impressive winnings in Las Vegas were discussed in great detail.

"Then, before we left the casino I decided to play twenty more dollars and guess what? I won a hundred dollars! Twice I got three cherries. Do you believe that? Cosmo said I had the makings of a gambler. I think he was joking, but I was *sooo* excited. Maybe he was serious. Do you suppose I could shut down the law practice and spend my days making the rounds of the casinos?" She giggled.

Her guests were in awe. None of them had ever heard Lizzie Fox giggle. Ever.

"What did you do with your winnings?" Maggie asked as she cut herself a second slice of pie.

"I was going to buy Cosmo a drink, but he said no. He doesn't believe in the woman paying for anything, so I donated all my winnings to the SPCA for a free neutering program they have going on. Cosmo matched my donation, so it was a win-win." She giggled again, to everyone's delight.

Out of the corner of her eye, Lizzie could see that Harry Wong was starting to get fidgety. It was time to get down to business. She was surprised when Ted and Joe Espinosa got up and volunteered to clean up.

When both men were in the kitchen, Lizzie whispered to Maggie, "How hard was it to train Ted to take care of kitchen duties?"

Maggie finished her pie, wiped her mouth, and whispered back. "It was so easy, Lizzie. 'No sex unless you do your share.' Hey, I cook, he has to clean up. That's fair. Wow, I am stuffed. I never thought meatless spaghetti could be so good. How about giving me the recipe?"

Lizzie giggled again. "No can do, old family recipe."

Ted carried in the coffeepot, and Espinosa had the cups and saucers. The table was clear, the signal that pads, pens, and briefcases were ready to be brought out to play.

"Talk to me, Harry, and do not leave anything out. I want you to go back to the beginning of the year and tell me everything you can remember. I don't care if you think it's pertinent or not to this case. I'll decide what's important and what isn't."

Harry talked and talked, from time to time choking up at the injustice of what he was being forced to go through.

When Harry wound down, Jack took the floor and talked about Harry's box of unopened mail. "There were notices of nonpayment on the home equity and second mortgage that Harry had never opened because, like he said, he paid ahead for a year. He had no idea there was an equity loan or second mortgage. There were also credit card bills for all the bogus accounts some person had opened up. When Harry saw the envelopes, he figured they were probably just offers for him to open new accounts. In that sense Harry is not blameless. He should have opened his mail. As you can see by the two legitimate credit cards he carries, he only uses them once in a while, and he pays the outstanding balances in full in the months that he charges something.

"But regardless of whether he opens his mail or not, no one has the right to steal and ruin a person's life."

"You don't have to tell me that, Jack. I'm on your side," Lizzie said.

"Lizzie, how much is this going to cost? All my money is gone. Will you take an IOU?" Harry's voice was fretful.

Lizzie looked Harry in the eye and winced. "Harry, I can't believe you asked me that. I know it wasn't your intention to offend me, but you did. We're family here. Family doesn't charge family. We will not *ever* talk about this again, do we understand each other, Harry?"

Harry turned docile, something Jack never

thought he would live to see. He was further astounded when Harry meekly said, "Yes, ma'am."

Lizzie moved on. "Maggie?"

"I put a hacker friend of mine on it early this morning. He should be getting back to me sometime this evening unless he's hit a snag."

Lizzie looked puzzled for a moment. "Isn't that Charles's job?"

Maggie shrugged. "Possibly. If Charles or the girls don't want my information, assuming I get any, I can use it for the next series I plan on doing. Being in the newspaper business, it's a given that you can never have too much information. Abner Tookus is the best hacker in the world. The FBI and the CIA use him. He even writes software for them and always makes sure there's a back door where he can get in and out without their knowing. It's like being a painter and signing your name on your work. If there is information to be gotten, Abner is the one to get it.

"I had to pay him an exorbitant fee, and I also had to spring for his honeymoon. That's how sure I am he can get us what we need. He knows all bets are off if he can't deliver.

"I spent the day going through the series we ran on identity theft victims. Ted and Joe will be revisiting those same people again to see what if anything will come up. Now that we know Harry's mail habits, we have something more to go on. If he pays all his bills at the beginning of the year, then it falls right into place with the other victims we interviewed, which leads me to think it's a ring of people, as opposed to one person, because that's around the time someone stole all their identities. The major difference is that the other victims were immediately made aware of what was happening when they opened their mail to see their credit card statements and notices from their banks. All the victims were cleaned out like Harry was. Ergo, my reasoning for thinking it's a ring. It's a pattern, and it took a lot of effort on the part of a lot of people to bring it off in a short period of time."

"Definitely makes sense," Lizzie said thoughtfully as she scribbled notes on the pad in front of her. "Did you send copies of the profiles to the mountain?"

"I sent them out midmorning today. I suppose it's possible they might pick up on something, but I doubt it. First thing tomorrow morning, after Ted and Joe visit the other victims again, they'll visit their credit card companies. Depending on what Abner comes up with, I might have to engage his services for phase two. It's a crapshoot, Lizzie."

Jack weighed in. "I find myself wondering if the perp, or perps, is someone all these people know. How were they chosen by the perp? Do they know him or her? Is it someone involved in their daily lives? With Harry it could be anyone. He has private classes. He works with the local police, and he works with the FBI and the CIA. The list is almost endless. A disgruntled class member or parent of one of the kids or some hyped-up kid who thinks he's smarter than the law."

Maggie shrugged. "All of the above. We're blind at the moment, but with Abner, Ted, and Joe on it, not to mention Charles and the girls, we should come up with someone or some group that will pique our interest. We have to start somewhere."

They talked for another hour and a half, with Lizzie making copious notes. When they finally said good night at eleven o'clock, Lizzie knew what she had to do. She gave Harry a quick hug and told him not to worry. Harry just nodded as he followed Jack out to his car.

Maggie stayed on a few moments longer, chatting with Lizzie about her new married life. "It must be hard with you here and Cosmo in Vegas. I know you probably talk throughout the day, but it isn't the same as being together. But"—she winked at Lizzie—"I bet the reunions are spectacular."

Lizzie laughed. "You could say that, Maggie. You could say that."

Ted smirked as he followed Espinosa out to the car. Since Maggie had come by cab, he waited for her, hoping she was in a romantic mood.

Maggie dashed whatever hopes he had of a romantic close to the hectic day when she said, "I'm beat, and I'm sluggish from all that food I ate, so don't go getting any ideas that I'm going to be easy."

Ted huffed and puffed as he got behind the wheel. *Oh, well, Sunday is another day.*

Chapter 7

All the way home in the car, Maggie grumbled about how she couldn't believe Abner Tookus hadn't gotten back to her. She looked over at Ted, whose mind she knew was on sex, and said, "Abby is really an odd duck, works through the night sometimes and sleeps during the day." When there was no comment from Ted, she started to mumble and mutter to herself. "I know Abner will get back to me," she kept saying over and over to herself in the hopes that it would happen. "He promised, Ted, and to date he's never broken a promise." Maggie wondered if her old buddy would really come through for her. Or had he taken her for a ride? She deep-sixed that thought almost immediately. Abner knew she'd either kill him or sic the vigilantes on him. On his honeymoon if he didn't come through, she thought grimly.

Maggie was the first to hop out of the car when Ted pulled to the curb. She looked down the street and waved airily to Jack and Harry. At the last second she ran the half block to Harry and hugged him. "We'll get the SOB, Harry. Count on it. Now go inside with Jack and get a good night's sleep. Dream of Yoko."

Jack stood back, stunned to see that Harry allowed someone to actually touch his person. Not just touched, but *hugged*. He was downright flabbergasted when he saw Harry hug Maggie in return. Harry definitely was not in a good place to allow such shenanigans. There was a lot to be said for touchy-feely where Harry was concerned. Or not said. Jack opted not to comment on his friend's weird behavior. What he did say was, "Lizzie and Maggie are on it, Harry. If anyone can make it work, they can."

Harry mumbled something in one of his eight languages, which Jack took to be not good. He clamped his lips shut as he made his way to the front steps. Then he decided some levity was called for. "You aren't the type that likes to be *tucked in,* are you? I don't mind sharing the house, the shower, and the kitchen, but there is a line I won't cross, Harry."

Harry went off with a string of gibberish, which probably meant that Jack should shut up and open the door. He did, but then he heard the roar of a black HEMI that pulled to the curb in front of Maggie's house. He turned around and walked back down the steps.

Jack made a pretense of fiddling around in

the trunk of his car to see if the black HEMI belonged to Maggie's hacker. When he saw a tall, lanky guy with a ponytail hoofing toward Maggie, he sighed in relief. Maggie had it going on. Still he waited, even though Ted was with Maggie, to be sure the lanky guy was Maggie's hacker.

Jack closed the trunk. He shouted out a second good night before he made his way to his own front door. Maggie and Ted didn't return the greeting, but both waved airily. The minute Jack saw Ted shake the lanky guy's hand, Jack unlocked his door. Harry almost killed him getting inside.

Three doors away, Maggie unlocked her own door, pushed it open partway, and turned to Abner. Maggie hated how jittery her voice sounded when she asked him, "Did you get anything?"

Abner Tookus looked at Maggie in stupefied amazement. He slapped at his forehead in mock indignation. "Did I just hear you ask me if I *got anything*? Do birds fly? Does the sun come up every morning? I should leave right now and let you muck around in the mud puddle you seem to be in. Of course I got it. What I should say is I *got* what there was to *get*. Are we going to stand out here so your neighbors can hear this discussion, or do you want to invite me in?" He waved his hand to indicate two late-night dog walkers who were looking at them as they passed the house.

Maggie opened the door the rest of the way.

Ted followed her in, and, knowing the drill, disappeared. Tookus was Maggie's snitch, and the unwritten rule was there should never be an audience when business was discussed.

Abner tossed a thick envelope onto the coffee table. "You want to look through it first, or do you want the summary now?"

Abner Tookus, like Maggie, had a passion for all things sweet. He looked at the array of candies that Maggie liked to munch on, sitting in little bowls on the table. He scooped up a handful of M&Ms and popped them into his mouth. He reached for a second handful, only to find that the dish was empty. He looked accusingly at Maggie. Guests should be catered to. Maggie opened a drawer in the coffee table and dumped a fresh bag of candies into the silver dish. "Talk!" she ordered.

"The bank's security sucks. Any Tom, Dick, or Harry can access anything if you have a Social Security number. Or if you know how to get in the back door of the program. I know the guy who wrote the bank's software. I printed everything out for you. My guy closed the door, so nothing leads back to me or him. That's high-tech talk, Maggie, so don't worry if you understand it or not. That's just another way of saying your ass, my ass, and his ass are covered.

"Back in January, a block of mortgages the bank held was sold off to another mortgage company. Since Wong paid a year in advance the way you said he did, he probably never opened the mail informing him that his mortgage had been sold off. It wouldn't affect him financially one way or the other, as the interest rate stayed the same. Just a different mailing address to mail the checks to.

"Out of that block of mortgages four people that you profiled were on the transfer list. Wong makes five. Wong is the only one who, at that time, had a sterling credit rating. The other four were iffy at best. The mortgage transfer did not affect the other four in any way either. Like I said, just that change of address.

"I hacked into Wong's credit card company and found out that eight of your profiles have the same credit card company, which is through the originating mortgage bank. Four of your profiles have mortgages that are still at the original bank. So, four stayed, four plus Wong moved. You following me, Maggie?"

"Yeah."

"Seventeen more of your profiles have either mortgages or credit cards with the new company they were transferred to.

"I then hacked into Human Resources, which is a gold mine, bar none, to see who was hired, fired, etc., and came up with a loan officer who was considered hot spit in her department. She got sick around the beginning of January— mono, she claimed—and took a leave of absence. She never returned. She was married but it appears no one knew. She listed herself as single on her employment application. But . . . her husband was a loan officer at another bank in town. How do I know this? From the records at the Watergate Apartments, where they are living now. He left around the same time—two weeks later, I think, it's in the file—and never went back. He told his boss he had to take care of his ailing mother because she was so sick she couldn't get out of bed. From what I could tell, no one followed up. Neither employee filed for unemployment insurance, and the wife didn't file for disability. They moved out of their apartment on Connecticut Avenue and didn't leave a forwarding address. They are paying a boatload of money to live at the Watergate. How am I doing so far?"

"Great," Maggie said grudgingly. She hated sucking up to Abner, especially when she had to pay him for the privilege.

"Neither the husband or the wife is employed. If I were you, the first thing I would do would be to hire a couple of private dicks to monitor them twenty-four/seven and see what shakes out."

"And the bank didn't get suspicious? Didn't the profiles complain?"

"No, why should they get suspicious? When the wife left, she said she was sick. She didn't make waves, just left. Nothing was awry at the bank at that time. The dark stuff didn't hit the fan till around March, at which point the wife had already sent a beautiful letter to HR saying she wouldn't be back and was returning to her parents' home in Texas so they could take care of her. She said how she loved everyone, what a wonderful place the bank was to work, and in the years to come she would remember her working experience with fondness. They probably framed the damn letter, and it could be hanging in the president's office, for all I know.

"If those two are the ringleaders, they had a plan and they stuck to it. They had to have raked in a ton of money to date. Think about it, Maggie. Just take Wong, one guy, and they skinned him out of a quarter of a million bucks. We know of almost thirty others in your profiles. Multiply that by the same number, so they can well afford to live in the Watergate.

"One other thing. What's to say they don't do this in other states? They could do it in New York, Los Angeles, Dallas, anywhere. There is a glitch, though, and I'm working on it. I should know something more tomorrow. I don't know if the husband and wife used their real names when they worked at the banks. They could have been aliases. If they're as smart as I think they are, they probably created new identities for themselves—because I couldn't check back more than five years on either one of them. Whenever I tried to go beyond that date, I simply hit a brick wall. You, Maggie, I could trace back to the day you were born, but not these two, which pretty much confirms what I just said. For all intents and purposes, they were born five years ago. That's when they put the wheels in motion, and this is where we are.

"I have both of their Social Security numbers, and I'm running them. They each have an American Express Black Card, you know, the

Centurion. You flash one of those babies and the world is yours. Since January, they have both traveled quite a bit. She goes east and he goes west. Sometimes to Podunk towns, where they probably rent cars and drive to big cities. They're careful, I'll give them that. Like I said, hire a couple of dicks and sit back and see what shakes out. I gotta go home now. I have to go to work tomorrow."

"No you don't, you skunk. You snookered me. IBM never heard of you. I had my secretary call every office in the land. I'm gonna get you for that, Abner."

"It sounded good, didn't it?" Abner laughed. "Feel free to lose my number. Feel free to forget about me."

In spite of herself, Maggie laughed. "Are you really getting married?"

"Hell, no! Do you think I'm a fool? However, I am taking the lady to Hawaii. To make you happy, we'll pretend we're on a honeymoon."

Abner turned serious. "Maggie, be careful, okay? I'm thinking this is a pretty big ring, and people like that play dirty if they feel threatened."

Tongue in cheek, Maggie said, "Even the vigilantes?"

Still serious, Abner's response sent a chill down Maggie's spine. "Yeah, even the vigilantes. I'll call you when I know more. See ya, Maggie."

Maggie took a step closer. "Listen, Abby, all the bullshit aside, thanks for coming through for me. I won't forget it."

In a rare moment of honesty, Abner cupped
Maggie's face in his two hands. "For you, Maggie,
anything. I'm sorry that you and I . . . never . . .
that we . . . remember that song Whitney Hous-
ton used to sing, 'I Will Always Love You'? I will,
you know. Bye."

Maggie dabbed at her eyes when she closed
and locked the door behind Abner. "I'm really
sorry, Abby. Some things are just not meant to
be," she whispered to herself.

Maggie drifted off for a moment as she
thought of Abner Tookus. Friends for years, he'd
bailed her out many times, just as she'd bailed
him out. Their relationship was always professional. Except for that one time when she'd
dumped Ted and thought that maybe something would happen with Abner. It had, but
then she'd had a meltdown, and Jack Emery res-
cued her in the nick of time.

It was back in the day when the G-String Girls
were in the States to perform, she'd gotten tickets, and Abner was going to be her guest. When
she saw him standing in the hall waiting for her,
dressed in a suit and with a fresh haircut, her
heart had fluttered wildly. This was not the
Abner she knew. The Abner she knew was a free
spirit, who dressed like a bum and thumbed his
nose at the establishment. There was that one
moment in time when she had to decide if she
wanted to step off the path and cheat on Ted.
Not that it was cheating—she and Ted had broken up, and her heart was sore and bruised.
Abner had given her one intense look, knew

what she was thinking, and that it wasn't going to work for them.

He was wrong. It would have worked because she would have made it work. Now she would never even know—all because she'd been gutless. Abner had touched something in her that day. She supposed that she would forever wonder about what might have been had she not had her meltdown.

Ted bounded down the steps just as Maggie came out of her semitrance and whipped around, a tired smile on her face. She looked at Ted. He wasn't much in the looks department, but he was all hers, and she loved him heart and soul.

"You know what I was just thinking, Ted?" she lied. "Let's turn the thermostat down to zero, build a fire, and have wild sex on that bearskin rug in front of the fireplace."

Ted was naked before Maggie could turn on the house alarm and turn out the foyer lights. "I guess we're going to forgo the fire and the zero temperatures, huh?"

"Oh, yeah," Ted said, smoothing out the pearly white bearskin rug.

"You sure you don't want to talk about what my guy brought over here?"

"I'm sure. Boy, am I sure."

"Yeah, me, too." Maggie giggled. And she couldn't help but think about Lizzie's giggling and her comment about reunions with Cosmo. *Well, who needs reunions,* she said to herself.

* * *

Maggie rolled over and looked at the red numerals on the digital clock on the nightstand: 3:00. She rolled back over to her other side. Her leg snaked out, and she pushed Ted out of the bed with one mighty shove. "Wake up, Ted! I just remembered something."

The thump was so loud, Maggie winced.

"What the hell! Is the apartment on fire? You pushed me out of bed! Do you have any idea what time it is? For God's sake, Maggie, what's going on?"

"I remembered something, that's what's going on. Are you awake, Ted? I need you to listen and be alert." Maggie inched her way over to Ted's side of the bed and looked down at her partner. "Do you remember what happened after I ran that first series of articles on all those people whose identities were stolen?"

"Maggie, why can't this wait till morning? I'm freezing."

Heartless, Maggie snapped, "If you'd wear flannel pajamas the way other people do in the winter, you wouldn't be freezing. Just listen and tell me if you remember a conversation we had."

"All right, all right, but why can't I get in bed and listen?"

"Because I want you in listening mode, not lovemaking mode. When you're cold, you always want to have sex. Remember me telling you about that kid who called the paper after the articles ran? I blew him off because he sounded like a kid, his voice changing, you know, from a kid's voice to a more mature voice. He said someone stole his name, and now he doesn't have credit. I thought he read the paper and just wanted to make a crank call. I blew him off, Ted, and that doesn't say much for me. He said he was a mechanic and worked at a garage and he wanted to buy a car, but when he applied for credit he found out he had bad credit and he didn't know how that could be possible. Do you remember me telling you about it?"

"No, I don't! I'm cold, Maggie."

"All right, you can get back in bed, but don't go to sleep. I have to talk this out. We have to find that kid. I remember he said he was in Silver Spring, Maryland. I want you to go there and take Espinosa with you and check out every garage and gas station."

"Are you crazy? Why? That could take days."

Ted punched his pillow with such force that the pillow split and a feather sailed upward, then another. Maggie reached up and caught them. She tickled Ted's ear, and he groaned.

"That kid said he was a foster kid. A foster kid, Ted! He said his friend was in the same boat. The friend wanted to buy a scooter of some kind, and they wouldn't give him credit even though he had a job. God! I can't believe I was so stupid I blew him off. But in my own defense, the calls were coming in so quick and fast, legitimate calls, the switchboard blew out. You remember *that,* don't you?" Maggie snapped.

Ted knew it was worth his life to remember,

so he said, "Yeah. Well, we all screw up at one point or another. So what is your point here?"

"My point is this: Let's just say for the sake of argument the guy or the kid that called is eighteen years old. Let's say he was a foster kid living with some family, and now he's out on his own. He gets a job of some kind, and at eighteen, he's looking for some wheels. He applies for a credit card, and suddenly he finds out he can't get one because someone stole his identity when he was younger and ruined his credit. How many foster kids are in the system, Ted? Thousands, that's how many.

"What I want you to do is go to Child Placement, or whatever department handles foster children, and talk to them. If I'm right, and you know I'm always right, there has to be someone on the inside passing information to those cruds who are stealing those identities. Think about it, Ted! If they start stealing these kids' identities when they're young, they have a four- or five-year head start before the kid finds out. My God! What a perfect scam!

"Why aren't you getting dressed, Ted? You need to get on this right away. Call Espinosa and hit the ground running. Find that kid who called in. Use Dawson if you need extra help. Silver Spring isn't that big."

Ted groaned. He knew there was no point in arguing, but he tried. "What are you going to be doing while I'm doing all that?"

"I'm going back to sleep. Good luck."

By the time Ted was dressed, Maggie was

snoring lightly. He let himself out of the house, his cell in his hand as he called Espinosa and Dawson. His watch told him it was 4:20 as he slammed his way out to the street just in time to see a *Post* truck roll by with the Sunday papers for the citizens' early perusal.

Now that he was wide awake and freezing his balls off as he jogged his way to the paper, he had to admit that everything Maggie had just said made sense. He wished he had half her instincts.

Chapter 8

Charles found himself slipping into what he called a "neutral zone" as he waited for his bank of computers to boot up and the faxes that he expected to spew forth. Outside, he could hear a savage summer rain pound at the windows. When he was in the war room in the underground tunnels at Myra's farmhouse back in McLean, he never knew what the weather was unless he ventured up to the main part of the house. Here, in their mountain fortress, the elements were front and center all day long every day of the year. He wasn't sure if he liked it or not. Not that he had a choice.

His eyes felt like they were full of grit, and they probably were. He'd been in the war room for the past two days, venturing forth only to cook meals and listen to his chicks—that was how he thought of the Sisters, his chicks—berate him, ignore him. They were now making demands on him, impossible demands no human could keep up with. He was trying to placate everyone, especially Myra, but it didn't seem to be working. Yoko was demanding immediate help for Harry Wong and accepting no excuses. Gradually, the Sisters were creeping to her side and voicing questions he didn't have answers for. It was a sad state of affairs.

In a little over an hour they would all meet to discuss, one more time, what they could do to make Harry Wong's life whole again.

Once upon a time, the Sisters had had patience and deferred to him one hundred percent. Since his return to the mountain, they'd treated him like an alien visitor. What Isabelle had said to him, words that wounded him to the core, ricocheted inside his mind. *"We found out the hard way that we don't need you. Back in the day, we may have wanted you . . ."*

It was true that his chicks had bumbled their way through two missions, but when he read the final reports they'd drawn up, he had cringed at how close they had all come to getting caught. What bothered him more than anything was how cocky they had become. He could feel beads of sweat form on his brow when he remembered how they'd gone back to Paula Woodley's house, then been brazen enough to drive the residents of Evergreen Terrace from the White House back to their homes.

As if that weren't bad enough, they'd . . . what they'd done was . . . piss off the Secret Service, the FBI, and local law enforcement. Now they expected him to pull a rabbit out of a hat and get them all back into the nation's capital to help Harry Wong.

Charles shook his head to clear his thoughts when a streak of lightning zipped past the window of the war room. Seconds later, a loud crack shook the building he was standing in. No one needed to tell him the lightning had felled one of the tall pines. From past experience, he knew that more trees would fall before the storm was over. It was inevitable.

The bank of clocks on the wall told him, at a glance, the time all over the world. At the moment, though, he was concerned only with local time and what it meant as far as his culinary duties were concerned. He still had an hour till lunch. At four o'clock in the morning he'd found himself in the kitchen preparing a delectable shrimp and crab casserole and cutting up greens for a salad. He'd also prepared a delicious pink ham and some honeyed yams for dinner. He'd showered and consumed a gallon of coffee that was now having its effect on his nerves. Once, a lifetime ago, he'd been nerveless.

Charles realized suddenly that the war room was quiet. All the faxes he had been waiting for had arrived, his e-mails were all downloaded. He was good to go. He looked down on the right side of his computer terminal to see the thick report that had come in from Maggie Spritzer early yesterday. Whoever her source was, he or

she was good, just as good as his own hacker. He
felt the nerves in his stomach jump. Maybe the
girls were right, with contacts like Maggie had,
did they really need him?

A blue folder with a gold star in the middle
set his teeth on edge. Annie had gone ahead
and purchased the Babylon casino with Lizzie
Fox's help. A done deal, and he'd had no input.
Lizzie had made sure everything was buried
deep. He had to be honest: it was possible Lizzie
had outshone his own people. And now she was
married to Cosmo Cricket, and he hadn't even
been in the country for them.

His eyes started to burn. Would Lizzie take
the job Martine Connor offered as chief White
House counsel? He should know the answer to
that question, but he didn't. He didn't know the
answer because until three days ago he had
been out of the loop, an outsider. There was so
much he didn't know about the Sisters anymore, and there had been no time to be fully
briefed, to read all the reports and notes the
girls had kept in his absence. He needed more
hours in the day, less sleep. What bothered him
the most was where his old pal Avery Snowden
had deviated from the plan and taken Myra and
Annie somewhere at the end of the last mission.
In the report he'd read it simply said, "NTK."
Need to know. It was obvious even the girls didn't
know where Annie and Myra had gone on their
detour. Snowden, when questioned, had simply
refused to answer the question. And that had
been the end of that.

With years of long practice, Charles sifted through the faxes and printed e-mails. Those that were crucial went into one pile, those that needed attention but not immediately went into another pile. Those with tidbits of information went into a third stack.

Fifteen minutes later, Charles thought he had the initial elements of a plan. He made call after call, cryptic messages were left and recorded. He pressed a button, and the plasma screens sprang to life. He wished, as he always did, that Lady Justice would remove her blindfold, but he knew that wasn't going to happen.

Charles reached for a stack of bright yellow folders and proceeded to fill them with stapled reports. Stepping down from his dais, he was meticulous as he placed the folders in front of each chair at the round table. His job for the moment was done.

His eyes were drawn to Maggie Spritzer's blue folder. Annie had been so right when she appointed Maggie editor-in-chief of the *Post*. He allowed a small smile to tug at his lips when he recalled how he'd almost gone ballistic when he found out Annie wanted to buy the newspaper. A smart move. More than smart; brilliant. He'd had misgivings about Spritzer, Ted Robinson, and Joe Espinosa, but those had turned out to be unfounded. All three had performed beyond his expectations. No regrets there. And he had no regrets where Bert Navarro was concerned. He still wasn't sure about the liaisons the girls had formed with the newest members. It seemed everyone had someone to lighten and brighten their lives. Nikki and Jack. Yoko and Harry, Kathryn and Bert, Alexis and Joe Espinosa, Maggie and Ted, Annie and Little Fish. Isabelle was the odd woman out, but he was sure that would change sometime soon. At the moment Isabelle had the company of Myra. Myra, dear Myra. He couldn't think about Myra just then and what the future held for the two of them or—more to the point—whether they even had a future together.

Charles looked at his watch. Five more minutes before the girls would appear to take their seats. Five minutes until they looked up at him expecting a miracle that would turn Harry Wong's life right-side up. For the first time in his life, he wondered if he could make the desired result happen.

Charles's gaze went to the wall of windows to see that it was totally dark outside. The summer storm was kicking up in intensity. Lightning ripped across the sky as thunder rumbled and cracked. It sounded like it was directly overhead. Since there was nothing he could do about the weather, he made his way back to the computers. His nerves were still twanging every which way.

He almost gagged in relief when he heard the door open and the women enter the room. They made a production of taking their seats, murmuring among themselves. The sound of the chairs scraping on the pine floors sounded to Charles's ears as loud as the thunder overhead. He found himself watching them out of the corner of his eye. All expression seemed to be gone from their faces. Two days, he told himself, wasn't all that long to put a plan into action. But to the girls it was an eternity. He could read them like a book.

He didn't know how he knew, but he knew his position was hanging in the balance. All of them, Yoko in particular, wanted a miracle. Could he produce one? Only time would tell. He knew that he was being tested, tested as to whether he still belonged with them, whether they still needed him, whether they still wanted him.

Charles followed protocol and descended the steps that put him next to the round table. He allowed himself the luxury of one last look at the faces staring up at him. Surprisingly, it was Annie's expression that told him he had only one option, and unless he exercised it, his job there was done.

The women were so polite, so blank, it was unnerving. He decided to take the bull by the horns and said in as neutral voice as he could manage, "I have something to tell all of you. When I'm finished, I never want to speak of it again." He had their attention now, especially Annie's. She gave a slight nod of her head.

Charles took a deep breath and said, "My son was a traitor to Her Majesty and to his family. The details are not to be spoken of, it is what it is. I found myself in a position where I had to . . . to make concessions, promises; promises that I've now broken. That means I can never go back across the pond. Never. I will never be able to see my daughter-in-law again. I will never be able to see my grandchildren. My relationship with . . . my childhood friend has come to an end because I refused to stay in England; the reason is that my life is here with all of you. Having said that, I expect you all to make up your minds at this precise moment and decide if we can get past this episode and get back on track."

"Charles, thank you for that disclosure, and I think I speak for all of us when I say thank you and that your . . . your . . . family business is safe with us. Having said that, let's get down to work on Harry's problem," Annie said.

The atmosphere in the room changed as quickly as the weather had outside. Sunlight streamed through the windows, the rain ceased, and Myra smiled up at him. He thought her eyes were full of promises. He'd made the right decision. It was his turn to smile, and smile he did. And then they were all smiling and giggling.

Life was back on track. Charles felt like a peacock ready to strut his stuff, but he stifled the feeling. He risked a quick glance at Myra, who was still smiling. He felt buoyed at the thought she might switch up that ugly comforter on the bed and put her fluffy yellow towels back in the bathroom. He couldn't get emotional at the moment. He had a job to do, and his chicks were waiting.

"First things first. I want to congratulate you on your last two successful missions. I say *successful* because you are back here safe on the mountain. I want to stress to all of you that you broke all the rules. You took ridiculous chances with your well-being. What that means to me and should mean to you is you all got cocky. If it was just one of you, I might be able to understand the attitude, but for all of you to endanger one another is not acceptable. Someday, not today, I want you to tell me what you were trying to prove by going to the White House and driving those people home to Kalorama. What you accomplished is to turn every organization into high gear in regard to capturing you. You acted like teenagers out on a lark. There will be no more of that. Do you understand me?"

The Sisters nodded. Only Myra and Annie managed to look defiant. Charles glared at them.

"And, you two!" he said, pointing his finger at them. "Do not think for one minute that I won't find out where you went in deliberate disregard of the rules that you all stick together. Make no mistake, I will find out.

"I'm going to ask you all one more time. Do you want me to continue in my role as master planner? Are you going to do as I say when I say it? Last but not least, are we all on the same page? And that includes you, Myra and Annie. Just raise your hand."

Seven hands went up at the speed of light.

Charles felt the insane urge to guffaw, but he stamped it down, and said, "Open your folders, girls, and let's see what we're up against."

Papers rustled, feet tapped the pine floors. At

some point Murphy and Grady had come in, but the pair had gone unnoticed until they both barked as if on cue. Charles nodded in their direction. Both dogs dropped to the floor in the middle of the doorway, their large heads on their paws, their eyes alert to what was going on.

"What you're looking at is Maggie Spritzer's report. There is no point in going over it again. I have some additional information such as names. The loan officer at East Coast Savings was a white female named Sara Brickman. According to her employment file she is thirty-two years of age. She worked for East Coast for eighteen months. She claimed to be single when she filled out her employment application. The Social Security number listed is bogus. Sara Brickman was created out of whole cloth five years ago. There is no record of her in any of the databases before that time."

Charles clicked a button, and a picture of Sara Brickman appeared on the plasma screen. "There is nothing outstanding about her or anything that would cause anyone to think she wasn't who she said she was. Blond, blue-eyed. She's five feet four inches tall. She weighed 112 pounds at the time she filled out her employment application. She claims to have been in good health and only availed herself of her health insurance twice in the eighteen months she worked at the bank. Once for a deep cut that required seven sutures when she opened a can and it sliced the palm of her hand. The second time was for multiple bee stings.

"Miss Brickman got sick at the end of her last month of employment and said she was diagnosed with mono. She was away from work for three weeks when she said she'd decided to return to her parents' home in Texas after her recovery was not as speedy as she would have liked. She claimed no benefits from the bank for her illness. She sent a resignation letter to the bank and moved on. The detectives I have on the job said none of her coworkers have heard from her since she left. No one had a bad word to say about Miss Brickman. Her superior at the bank said she was a hard worker, often staying past closing to get caught up on paperwork. An exemplary employee.

"My investigator went to the apartment on Connecticut Avenue where Miss Brickman lived and discovered that she was indeed married and her married name was Carson. Husband's first name was Dennis. Dennis worked for Sovereign Bank as a loan officer. Both husband and wife moved out of the apartment at the end of March, at the same time Mr. Carson resigned his position at Sovereign Bank. It seems Mr. Carson told the manager at the apartment complex's leasing company that his mother was in ill health, and he and his wife had no choice but to break their lease and return to Colorado, where the mother lived. A neighbor said they are a nice couple, had no company that she ever saw, and that the couple kept to themselves. They both drove late-model Honda cars and both of them attended the Lutheran church on Connecticut Avenue. The neighbor said they never missed a Sunday, and she knows because she belongs to the same church."

Charles clicked a button, and Dennis Carson's image appeared next to his wife's on the plasma screen. "These pictures are compliments of both banks' summer picnics.

"The couple look like suburbanites. Cleancut, the kind of people you'd like to number among your friends. The only problem is my people couldn't find any friends, but it's still early in the game for that."

"Do we know where they are now? And how sure are we that they're the ones responsible for the identity theft?" Nikki asked.

"We do know where they are but only as the result of a fluke. The same neighbor who shared her information with my investigator said that in mid-May she went to a dinner party at the Watergate. She said she saw both Miss Brickman and Mr. Carson, as we know them, coming out of Apartment 1206 and getting into the elevator, and, before you can ask, no, they did not see our informant. She, however, took it upon herself to make inquiries about the residents of Apartment 1206. The names under which they had obtained the apartment were Angela and Derek Bookman. Needless to say, the neighbor was most eager to share this information with my investigator.

"Angela and Derek are each driving a brandnew Lexus. My people are checking what they can, and that's pretty much where we stand at the moment. And to answer your other question, Nikki, I think the chances are pretty good that they are the ones responsible for Harry's current problem."

Charles turned his attention to Yoko. "I know you want instant retaliation, but we have to do this right. If we're right about this couple, there is a good chance that we can bring down the whole ring. I think Harry would want that, Yoko. We need hard proof before we can invade their lives."

"When are your people due to check in again?" Kathryn asked.

Charles shrugged. "I have a man and a woman on each of them. I've also taken the liberty of leasing an apartment at the Watergate in the *Post*'s name. We might need it at some point. My best guess would be sometime in the next twenty-four hours."

"So we just twiddle our thumbs until you hear something, is that it?" Annie asked.

"That pretty much sums it up unless you have a better idea. I hesitate to remind all of you that preparation is the name of our game," Charles said quietly.

"How far back were your people able to go in checking Angela and Derek Bookman? Do they only go back five years, too?" Isabelle asked.

"I can't answer that right now. My gut feeling is *yes*. If my feeling turns out to be right, then I think we can safely assume this couple is up to their necks in this scheme. It wouldn't surprise me to find out they're the ringleaders. I say that because they look so normal."

"Are they renters or owners at the Watergate? How did they pass a credit check?" Alexis asked.

"Credit is their business, Alexis. I'm sure they know how to manage anything and everything to safeguard their identities. It goes without saying we could be wrong about this particular pair. We have to be very careful so as not to alert them in any way. Now, if there are no more questions, I have a lunch to prepare."

Charles gave a low, sweeping bow, and winked at Myra, whose hands automatically went to her neck, but her pearls were gone. She felt flustered, her cheeks turning pink. She pretended to sneeze to cover her confusion, not that she fooled anyone.

"So, girls, what do you think?" Nikki asked.

"Could it be that easy?" Alexis asked. "First crack out of the gate, and we have names? Names that will ultimately lead us to the people who ruined Harry's life? I find it a bit of a stretch, but I suppose it might turn out to be right, and we just stumbled into it. Dumb luck at its best. Or red herrings, and everyone is spinning their wheels."

Kathryn weighed in. "Why, if they are the ones responsible, didn't they leave town? Even a lousy crook hits the road after a crime. Why did they stay around? It doesn't make sense to me. So what if they worked at banks? So what if they quit their jobs around the same time? So what if no one knew they were married? Half the people in this town who live together in D.C. aren't married."

"Dear girl, aren't you forgetting that their background checks only go back five years?" Myra asked. "Why would they relocate to the Watergate using different names? That doesn't even come close to passing the sniff test," she said testily.

"I think those two are the leaders of a ring that has been operating in the District, Maryland, and Virginia. It's just my gut feeling, but it's a strong one," Annie said.

All eyes turned to Yoko, who hadn't spoken. "I agree with Annie. It's them."

"We need to call Maggie to see how she's coming along with the interviews she has Ted and Joe working on," Myra said. "If she's ready to go to press with another big story, we don't want to alarm Mr. and Mrs. Carson, or whatever their names are."

"I'll call her, but first we all want to know if you are moving back with Charles, and if you need our help?" Nikki said. "We could have you moved in by the time lunch is over." She grinned.

Myra reached for the pearls that weren't there. "I haven't decided yet," she said primly.

The girls laughed and laughed.

Chapter 9

Lizzie Fox, freshly showered and powdered, stood at the door of her closet. Normally, when she went to sleep she hung her outfit for the next day on a hook outside the closet door so all she had to do was step into it. She hadn't done that last night and didn't know why. Maybe it was because she hadn't decided how to play the game this morning. Did she want to sweep into the bank and bowl over the president? Did she just want to be Harry's lawyer and go with the facts? Did she want to dazzle and bullshit the bank president until he fell at her knees? A different outfit would be required for each of the above.

Lizzie backed away from the closet, her silky robe slithering against her body as she made her way to a little office that was no bigger than an oversize closet, located off her bedroom in a

tiny alcove. She looked around to see where her
coffee cup was and realized she'd finished the
coffee before she'd taken her shower. She ran
back to the kitchen, poured a fresh cup, and
carefully carried it back to her office. She was, as
Annie would put it, at sixes and sevens that
morning. Translation . . . she didn't know which
end was up.

She opened her briefcase and stared at its
pitiful contents. She had so little to go on where
Harry was concerned that she didn't know if
there was anything she could actually do for
him. She'd talked a good game to the nervous
martial arts expert late into the night, doing her
best to reassure him. Damn. That was why she
hadn't picked out an outfit for today. She'd
been so tired when she got off the phone with
Harry that she had just dropped into bed.

She had time, more than enough, to go over
things once more since she didn't actually have
an appointment with Douglas Sooner, the president of East Coast Savings.

She'd Googled him, but she hadn't discovered anything untoward. He was just like all
other bank presidents—boring, well dressed,
perfect banking wife, three children, the requi-
site dog, and a house in Arlington, Virginia,
with a manicured lawn. He belonged to all the
right clubs, his wife was a do-gooder, and the children were above reproach and attended private
schools. Even the dog had a pedigree.

Douglas Sooner was neither handsome nor
ugly. He was just ordinary-looking, someone

you'd pass on the street and label "banker" and
never know why that tag seemed to fit the man.
He had thinning hair, but then most men of
fifty had thinning hair. He was neither tall nor
short; nor was he fat or thin. A box of a man,
she'd decided when she'd stared at the picture
that came with his profile. Just another John Q.
Citizen with a title. She scanned the papers one
more time before sliding them into the shred-
der. No sense carrying around profiles of men
she didn't respect.

A quick glance at the digital clock on her
desk told Lizzie she had plenty of time to make
a plan and get dressed. She even had time, if
she wanted to utilize that time, to stop by the
Post and chat with Maggie, even do lunch if
Maggie was available, before she headed off to
the bank to take care of Harry's business. She ri-
fled through the thin stack of records he had
given her. What she could possibly do to get
Harry back into his *dojo* was still a mystery to
her.

The black leather suit! Definitely. Nothing
cried business better than a severely tailored
black suit. Leather, now . . . leather meant "don't
screw with me because I take no prisoners."
Feeling a little smug, Lizzie wondered if Douglas Sooner would recognize her when she sailed
into the bank's offices, ostrich-skin briefcase in
hand. If he didn't, Lizzie was sure his secretary
would Google her just the way she'd Googled
Sooner.

Maybe she should have another cup of coffee
and call Cosmo just to chat. An early bird, he
was probably up and getting ready to start his
day. She hated the three-hour time difference,
but there was nothing she could do about it.
Cosmo told her not to worry about time, to call
him any time of the day or night. She loved talking to her new husband, loved the deep timbre
of his voice, which he considered a whisper even
though it could be heard a mile away. She
melted inside whenever he called her Elizabeth.
She hit the number 1 on her speed dial and
waited.

"Elizabeth! How wonderful to hear your
voice. What are you doing?"

Feeling like a teenager in the throes of first
love, she told him. "I'm not sure how to play it,
Cricket."

The booming, intimate laugh that greeted
her ears made her smile. "Sure you do, honey,
you just want to hear me say, *go for it.*"

"How'd you get so smart, Cricket?"

"Hanging around you, Elizabeth. I miss you.
We never decided if I should come east or you
should come west this weekend. I think it
should be me who does the traveling this time.
It sounds to me like you have your hands full. Is
there anything I can do for you from out here?"

"I wish there were, Cricket. I have to play this
out on my own. Unless you know some people
in the credit card industry you can squeeze."

The silence on the other end of the phone
told Lizzie there was a ray of hope somewhere.

Her fist shot in the air was when Cosmo asked, "Which credit card companies?"

"Chase and Barclays were Harry's legitimate cards, the ones he paid off at the end of the month. The fraudulent ones are Citi Platinum Select, American Express, Capital One Platinum Prestige, Wells Fargo Prime Rate Visa, Wells Fargo Platinum, and there's one for Hooters and one for Walmart."

"Do you have the credit card numbers, honey?"

"I do." Lizzie rattled them off. "Are you saying you can help, Cricket?"

"I'm going to try. Five will get you ten that some of those wheeler-dealers have a history here in Vegas. I'll just have to find that history. Are you smiling, honey?"

"Cricket, I am grinning from ear to ear. How long will it take you before you know something?"

Cosmo countered with a question. "What time is your meeting at the bank?"

"I don't have an appointment, Cricket. I was going to wing it. The surprise element, you know."

"In that case, give me forty-five minutes to get to the office and another ninety minutes to see what I come up with. Will that work for you?"

"Yes, Cricket, that will absolutely work for me. I was planning on stopping at the *Post* to talk to Maggie first, anyway."

"Elizabeth, how much money are we talking about in regard to Harry Wong?"

"At first we thought it was around $200,000,

but when I did my final tally, it's a few dollars shy of half a million. This is some really serious money, Cricket. Multiply that number by whatever number you pull out of your hat, and the amount is staggering. The *Post,* Maggie in particular, is working on it. She's still totaling up the numbers other consumers have lost, then she's going to go full bore, a big, black WAR headline to gain the readers' attention. The timing is something we have to work on because we don't want to alert the credit card ring before the girls can go after them. Did all that make sense, Cricket?"

"Perfect sense, Elizabeth. I'll call you when I have something worth reporting."

Lizzie didn't feel silly at all when she made little kissing noises into the phone; nor did Cricket when he returned them.

The smile stayed with Lizzie as she made her way to the bathroom to apply makeup she didn't need. Brush in hand, she did a few artful swirls with it, and the silvery fall of hair completed Lizzie's *look* for the day.

The black leather suit was so soft, so buttery, so thin, it felt like a second skin. Lizzie whirled and twirled in front of the mirror a few times to make sure there were no flaws anywhere. There weren't. Shoes. Shoes were always a problem. She had tons of shoes, loved, just loved, shoes. She wished she had a conveyor belt like Aaron Spelling had had in his house so she could press a button and all her shoes would circle around her until she found the pair that she wanted. She looked

down at the shoe trees on the floor and the shoe
bags hanging on the closet door until she finally
decided on a pair of stilettos with pointy toes
that made her legs look like those of a Vegas
dancer.

Maggie Spritzer knew something was going
on outside her office. Something other than the
clacking computer keys and the muted sound of
twenty different voices all talking at the same
time. And then she smelled Lizzie Fox's per-
fume, which, for some reason, always seemed to
arrive before the lawyer appeared in person. It
was a heady scent, unlike anything she'd ever
smelled. When she'd asked Lizzie, the lawyer
had replied that it was a mixture she'd had
made up in Paris just for her. Lizzie had gone
on to say she had powder, lotion, shampoo, and
bath salts all with the same fragrance. "I call it
'Me.'" Then she'd giggled and told Maggie that
Cosmo Cricket claimed to get drunk on the intoxicating scent.

Maggie couldn't help but wonder if Ted
Robinson would ever say anything like that to
her. As long as she smelled like anything fla-
vored with vanilla, it worked for him. She sighed
mightily as she got up to hug Lizzie.

"Good God, lady, where are you going? You
look . . . I don't know a word to describe you,
and I'm a damn journalist. Like ten million
bucks!"

"To East Coast Savings Bank to see Douglas

Sooner. Listen, Maggie," Lizzie said as she closed the door behind her, "I was on the phone with Cosmo a little while ago, and he seems to think some of the credit card officials might have a history of some kind in Vegas. What we do with that information is something I'm not sure about yet. Want to go to lunch?"

"Yes, yes, yes! A few weeks ago, a new restaurant opened up a block from here. I've been dying to try it out. I heard they deliver, too."

Lizzie smiled. Maggie always had food on the brain. "Do they have a specialty?"

Maggie already had her handbag over her shoulder and was putting on her shoes. "Uh-huh. Goulash. My people tell me it's like Mom's home cooking. It's called Sallie's. Crusty homemade bread and every cobbler under the sun for dessert. Is there a reason you want to go out to lunch, Lizzie?" Maggie whispered as they stood by the elevator.

"More or less," Lizzie said, unaware of the stir she was creating just by being herself.

Marveling at the way Lizzie tripped along in her spikes, Maggie cursed herself for wearing her high heels instead of her sneakers.

Sallie's proved to be a small, quaint food emporium that didn't serve alcohol, but the delectable aromas more than made up for the absence of a liquor license. It was still early into the lunch hour, so the two women were shown to a table immediately.

Once seated, Maggie looked around, and said, "I like it. It's not too big, and it's like eating in your mom's kitchen. I really like it, and I sure hope the food lives up to the reviews I've heard. Guys for some reason know good food when they eat it. Small menu, that's a plus, makes choosing something so much easier. What looks good to you, Lizzie?"

"Caesar salad, I guess, ice tea, and I might try the blackberry cobbler. What looks good to you, Maggie?" Lizzie twinkled.

"Everything." Maggie sighed as she finally made her decision to go with a double order of goulash and gave her order to a pink-cheeked woman with curly white hair.

"Now, Lizzie," Maggie said as she leaned across the table, "tell me why we're here and what I can do to help whatever you have in mind."

Lizzie leaned forward until the two women were almost nose to nose. "First things first, you have to call the mountain to okay this. Text me as soon as you get an okay. Now, tell me what you think of this . . ."

Chapter 10

Lizzie Fox sashayed across the lobby of East Coast Savings to a small area that proclaimed it to be the bank's information center. She held out her business card and handed it to the preppy-looking guy seated behind a desk whose nameplate said he was Gerald La Blanc. In the blink of an eye, Lizzie's assessment was that he was a fussy little twit. She offered up a dazzling smile and remained standing even though the twit stood and motioned for her to take a seat. She remained standing, waiting to see what La Blanc would do. She knew the man's dilemma immediately. Remain standing, and customers in the bank would see she towered over him. Man versus woman, and woman wins. If he sat down, she would still tower over him. First adversarial rule was to have the upper hand. Standing gave one an advantage, seated you were at the standee's mercy.

La Blanc twittered a moment, his gaze sweeping the austere bank lobby. "How can I help you, Miss Fox?"

Lizzie felt her BlackBerry vibrate. She knew it was Maggie, she didn't have to look. "I'd like to see Mr. Sooner and, no, unfortunately, I do not have an appointment. I represent Harry Wong."

La Blanc suddenly had a limited-edition Visconti pen in his hand and was twirling it between his fingers. He's either terribly overpaid or has a rich girlfriend, Lizzie thought.

"And Harry Wong would be . . . ?"

Lizzie wagged her finger back and forth. "That's all I'm comfortable saying at the moment, Mr. La Blanc. I really don't have much time, so if you'll show me to Mr. Sooner's office, we can perhaps . . . take care of Mr. Wong's business."

La Blanc looked around again, and saw that six new customers had entered the bank since Lizzie Fox had walked to his desk. Everyone was looking at them. "Let me check with Mr. Sooner's secretary. He was in a meeting a short while ago. I'll just be a moment."

Lizzie nodded but remained standing. The moment the young man's back was turned, she whipped out her BlackBerry and read Maggie's text message, which said simply, "Annie says okay." A series of numbers followed the message. Lizzie smiled as she meandered around the small alcove. She was admiring a Jackson

Pollock on the wall when La Blanc returned and motioned for her to follow him.

La Blanc opened a mahogany door and stepped aside. A pleasant-looking middle-aged woman rose and extended her hand. "Miss Fox, I'm Annette Bloom, Mr. Sooner's secretary. I understand you're here about Mr. Wong. That was such a terrible thing that happened to him."

"Yes, it was a terrible thing. That's why I'm here. I appreciate Mr. Sooner's agreeing to see me without an appointment."

"Just follow me," Sooner's secretary said.

The door closed discreetly behind Annette Bloom. Douglas Sooner rose and walked around his desk to shake Lizzie's hand. He motioned for her to take a seat. This time she did. She knew what would follow. Sooner would walk back to his desk, grab the crease in his trousers, sit, then he'd shoot his cuffs, lean forward, and clasp his hands. He'd make eye contact, and say, *"Mr. La Blanc said you wanted to talk about one of the bank's clients. How can I be of service to you today, Miss Fox?"*

The Google profile of Douglas Sooner was on the money, Lizzie decided as she held the banker's gaze. "I represent Harry Wong. This bank holds the mortgage on a building he owns. Unfortunately for Mr. Wong, his identity was stolen while he banked with you. His original mortgage is paid ahead by five months. Several days ago you foreclosed on Mr. Wong's residence and evicted him from the premises. The way I see it, Mr. Wong is not responsible for your bank's approving a fraudulent equity loan and second mortgage on said property. As far as Mr. Wong and I are concerned, Mr. Wong is current in his payments. I would like the keys to the property and all the paperwork completed to reinstate ownership."

"I'm sorry, Miss Fox, but that is not how this bank works. We have rules and regulations we have to adhere to. I'm really sorry, but I can't help you."

Lizzie leaned back and crossed her legs. Then she smiled. She thought she saw a flicker of alarm in the banker's eyes just as a discreet knock sounded. The door opened, and Annette Bloom walked over to Sooner's desk and handed him a sheaf of papers. Lizzie knew what the papers were; her own Google profile with a short summary on a sticky note affixed to the first page for Sooner's immediate reading pleasure.

"Oh, I think you can help me, Mr. Sooner. In fact, I know you can. Before I came here, I stopped at the *Post* and had a rather lengthy conference with the editor-in-chief, Maggie Spritzer. They're planning an all-out exposé of identity thefts that have arisen out of the banks in the area, and your sixteen branches are at the top of the list. Now, I am prepared to work with you, as is Miss Spritzer, so that you and your sixteen branches will come off as saviors instead of a bunch of uncaring, hard-nosed bankers. Front-page coverage, top of the fold, Mr. Sooner.

Personally speaking, Mr. Sooner, as a bank customer, nothing would give me more confidence than to know my bankers care about me and my deposits, as opposed to a . . . say, a run on your sixteen branches."

Lizzie looked down at the diamond watch on her wrist and smiled. "Time is money, Mr. Sooner. My offer is on the table for exactly five minutes. After that . . ." She threw her hands in the air and shrugged.

"I need more than five minutes, Miss Fox. I have people I need to call."

"Please, Mr. Sooner, don't insult my intelligence. Read through those papers your secretary just gave you. I never say anything I don't mean. You have full authority to do what I asked, and we both know it. It would be a wise man who comes in before the time expires. If you need an incentive, let me be the first to tell you that I heard from a very reliable source that the *Post* is going to be receiving some unorthodox help in the way of the vigilantes."

Sooner flopped back into the depths of his burgundy Naugahyde chair, raised his eyes to the ceiling, and said, "Sweet Jesus! All right, Miss Fox, you win. I'll bring our legal counsel in, and the two of you can work out the details." He pressed a button and asked Ms. Bloom to come into the office. She poked her head in the door and waited for instructions. "Tell John Tyson to come to my office, then get the keys to Mr. Wong's property out of the vault and bring them to me."

"See," Lizzie said brightly, "that wasn't so hard, now, was it? And you're doing the right thing, Mr. Sooner." She offered up a wicked smile. "Let's not kid each other, Mr. Sooner, you don't want to go a few rounds with the notorious vigilantes. I can't say that I blame you."

Sooner was saved from a reply when a knock sounded and the door opened at the same time. A tall, handsome man walked into the room, and asked, "You wanted to see me, Douglas? Lizzie!"

"Hello, John," Lizzie said as she gracefully rose out of her chair. She allowed herself to be air kissed, then extended her hand. "It's been a long time," she said, her voice breathless and intimate-sounding.

"Four years at least. So, tell me what's going on."

Douglas Sooner told him while Lizzie sat back down and crossed her legs. She waited while Tyson made a tepid argument that Sooner waved away.

"Just do it, John. The bank does not need any bad publicity or a run on any of our branches."

Lizzie licked at her glistening lips and did her best not to smile when Tyson winked at her behind Sooner's back.

"Let's get to it, then. Come with me, Lizzie. I think we can wrap this up lickety-split."

"To my satisfaction?"

"Always." Tyson laughed.

Lizzie turned just as the secretary entered the office. In her hand she held a key ring. She looked at her boss, then at Tyson, and last at Lizzie. With a nod from both men, she handed the key ring to Lizzie.

Sooner walked around his desk, shot his cuffs, and extended his hand. "You'll be in touch?"

"Absolutely."

An hour later, Lizzie walked out of the bank into bright sunshine. In her briefcase were the papers that restored Harry Wong's life. In addition, there was a check and a creative contract approving a loan for renovations to Harry's *dojo*. And a special account had been set up with Tyson's help so that Harry could bank online. As long as Harry didn't get too curious, his life was now back on track, with Tyson promising to monitor the account and report to Lizzie on a monthly basis.

Chapter 11

The Sisters looked like a row of bronzed water nymphs as they sat poolside, their feet dangling in the water. A few feet away, Myra and Annie sat under a bright orange and green sun umbrella, sipping from frosty glasses of lemonade, compliments of Charles on his last break from the command center. They were close enough to the others that they could participate in the conversation without shouting.

"It's been five days since Charles put the investigators on Bonnie and Clyde," Kathryn said, referring to the couple under investigation. "So far all we know is they change their names the way we change our underwear. I even think Charles is having a hard time keeping their names straight."

"The only bright spot this past week is that

Lizzie managed to get Harry back in his *dojo*. He is so happy. I am so happy," Yoko gurgled.

"Charles said he would have solid information by the end of the day and we would have something to work on. You know how meticulous he is when it comes to planning a mission. I have to admit I'm getting a little antsy myself," Annie said as she adjusted the massive sun umbrella over her and Myra.

"I went online early this morning to check out what kind of tenant security they have at the Watergate. Nothing we can't handle," Isabelle said happily. A moment later, she was in the water and daring the others to follow her, which they did.

"Do you miss being young, Myra?"

"I can't believe you asked me that, Annie. I wish I was young again and know what I know today. And if you think for one minute getting those tattoos is going to make us younger, you're wrong." Myra sniffed.

"That's why you haven't moved back in with Charles, isn't it? Oh, for shame, Myra. I look at mine all the time and just wish there was someone to see it. You need to come alive, Myra. We're old, we should be having fun or doing something we can pretend is fun."

Myra's face turned pink. "You're being silly, Annie. I'm simply not ready to go back. I may never go back. That ink on my backside has nothing to do with anything."

"Oh, yeah, well then, prove it to me," Annie snapped. "Right now, right this minute, march into the command center, pull down your draw-ers, and *show* Charles your artwork." At Myra's horrified expression, Annie leaned back, crossed her legs, and looked smug. "I thought so. You're afraid."

"I am not afraid," Myra said indignantly.

"Then prove it!" Annie challenged.

In the pool, Alexis nudged Yoko. "Look, something's going on between those two."

The others stopped splashing and turned to see what Yoko and Alexis were looking at.

"Something's going down," Isabelle said as she swam to the ladder, the others following. "Act like we didn't notice anything," she hissed.

Chattering among themselves and drying off, the other Sisters watched their mentors argue in harsh whispers. When Myra stomped off, they clustered around the table, wanting to know what was going on.

A devilish gleam in her eye, Annie said, "I just dared Myra to do something. She accepted the challenge, albeit regretfully."

"What? What?"

"Can you keep a secret, girls?"

The response was a unanimous *yes.*

Annie got up, turned around, and mooned the girls. Her shorts went back up at record speed. As one, the girls gasped.

"Myra has one, too, but it's a little more . . . artful. That means it took a lot of ink. Her art-work is the reason she hasn't moved back to the main building. She wants to be back with Charles so bad she can taste it, but she's afraid of what he'll think or say when he sees it. I told her to get over herself and show Charles now. She could be moved in by dusk if she doesn't change her mind. Do you think I was wrong to do that, girls?"

When there was no response to her question, Annie sat back down.

"Myra had Charles's name tattooed on her ass!" Kathryn guessed, her eyes as round as saucers.

The others started to laugh.

"It took a lot of ink, too. Colored ink. She went all out. We were there a very long time. She made the decision either in memorial to Charles, or else she was hoping Charles would come back, which he did. As you saw, I just went with a rose."

"Way to go, Annie," Nikki said, hugging the older woman. "That took a lot of guts. Are you sorry you did it?"

"Not at all. I look at it all the time. You know what I mean. It was . . . it was like an act of independence. Nellie wants to get one. Believe it or not, Pearl Barnes has two of them. Pearl said it goes with this new life she's leading. It's just . . . exhilarating!"

"So, what do we think Charles will do or say?" Yoko asked.

"I think he'll be speechless," Nikki said.

"Myra isn't wearing her pearls these days, so I don't know how he's going to equate the two. Speechless is good," Isabelle said.

"Well, I think he's going to be so flabbergasted that she cared enough to put his name on her ass that he's going to swoop her back to the bedroom," Kathryn said, then laughed until she almost collapsed.

"I think I agree with Kathryn," Yoko said.

Alexis agreed, too.

"Maybe we should go up to the command center and see what's going on," Nikki said.

Annie looked flustered. "Maybe we shouldn't. I wasn't supposed to tell you all what we did. It has to be a secret."

"Get off it, Annie. Everyone knows you can't keep a secret, especially Myra. So we just sit here and wait—is that what you're saying?"

"Pretty much. She should have come back by now," Annie said, nibbling on her thumb. "The ice has melted in the lemonade. Maybe it's time to replenish it, and I saw some peanut butter cookies on the kitchen counter." A second later Annie was on her feet, leading the parade up to the building that housed the dining room and kitchen.

Annie made a huge production out of replenishing the lemonade, jabbering nonstop as she told the girls to get fresh glasses and put the cookies on a platter, all of which was carried to the front porch next to the building where the command center was located. Not a sound carried through the open door.

Inside, Myra paced the huge living room of the main building. How in the world was she going to do this? She alternated between feeling like a giddy teenager and an old lady doing stupid things . . . to I-don't-give-a-shit . . . to I-do-give-a-shit. Finally, she squared her shoulders, gave the gold bangles on her neck a hitch, and marched down the hall to the command room. She announced herself, and said, "I need to talk to you, Charles."

Charles poked his head around the corner and responded, "Can it wait, Myra? I'm knee-deep in some things, and I can't get sidetracked right now."

"No, Charles, it can't wait. We don't have to talk. In fact, you can stay right where you are. I just want to show you something."

Myra strutted up the three steps to the dais next to where Charles was standing at the computer. She took a huge gulping breath before she turned around and yanked at her capri pants. Charles's intake of breath sounded so loud Myra thought her eardrums had ruptured.

"Take a good look, Charles! Now, I'm leaving. You think about this all afternoon now, you hear me?"

Myra bounded out of the building like the Hounds of Hell were on her heels. She pulled up short when she saw the girls sitting on the porch eating cookies and drinking lemonade.

"All right, I did it! Are you all satisfied? And don't pretend you don't know what I just did. Annie can't keep a secret to save her life. I'm not showing it to you all, so don't bother asking."

"Lemonade?" Nikki asked with a straight face.

"Cookies?" Alexis asked solemnly.

Myra accepted both. "Maybe I'll show it to you later." And then she giggled.

"What did he say?" they asked as one.

"Not a word. I think he choked, but I didn't stick around long enough to be sure. He could be dying in there for all I know. I don't think we should worry about it, girls."

"Myra, I like your chutzpah." Annie laughed.

Charles was indeed gasping for breath one door away. Did he just see what he thought he saw, or did he fall asleep for a few seconds and merely dream about an apparition that had just presented itself?

Was it possible that the love of his life, the very breath of his life, actually had a tattoo on her derriere? And not just any common tattoo but a tattoo that bore his name? He was suddenly so light-headed he had to go down the steps to sit at the round table, and drop his head between his knees.

How in the name of all that was holy was he supposed to work now after having seen what he'd just seen? Was Myra punishing him? Was Myra the shill the Sisters sent to bedevil him with some kind of insidious mind game? He needed advice. Absolutely he needed advice, but where to go for it and whom to ask? Avery Snowden immediately came to mind. Then a second thought came to mind, and that was Snowden spiriting Myra and Annie away at the end of the last mission. Ha! Well, he wouldn't be asking

Avery Snowden anything anytime soon. He made a mental note to take care of Snowden at some point in the future. Rules were rules, and to be obeyed.

Jack Emery? Harry Wong? Bert? Elias Cummings, Nellie's new husband? But did he want to air his linen to any of these men? Surely he was old enough, mature enough, to deal with his lady's tattoo on her derriere. Maybe he was looking at this all wrong. He should be flattered.

Charles raised his head. The realization hit him that he was outmanned, outmaneuvered, and under fire. The Sisters were going to be watching him like a bunch of hungry hawks to see what he would do, so they could pounce on him. While they'd all said they forgave him, they still held some resentment toward him. Only a fool would believe otherwise. One way or another they were going to make him pay, vigilante style.

Charles shook his head to clear his thoughts when two different phones shrilled to life, the fax machine went off, and he heard the *pinging* from the computer announcing new e-mails coming through.

On legs that had gone rubbery, Charles got up and made his way to the platform, where he worked literally nonstop. He closed his eyes for a moment, but all he could see was his name on Myra's buttock. Maybe if it was just blue ink, it would have been different, but the confetti colors that made up his name were so eyeball-popping obvious he was still thunderstruck. He finally admitted to himself that he couldn't wait to see the rainbow of colors again.

Charles gave his head another shake and got down to business, but the wicked smile stayed on his face as he tried to make sense of all the reports coming through faster than he could staple them together.

Dinner that evening on Big Pine Mountain was a festive affair. The dinner plates were a fiesta of colors, the enameled handles of the silverware matched, a veritable rainbow. The food was superb, with vegetables picked that day from the garden that Yoko had tended so lovingly. A luscious Pecan-Crusted Salmon, fresh garden peas, baby carrots, and new potatoes the size of a quarter, drenched in butter and savory herbs. The salad was new Bibb lettuce with fresh chives, the first tiny red garden tomatoes, and thin slivers of cucumbers. But it was the white layer cake with confetti frosting that sent the women off into gales of laughter.

Myra found herself laughing along with the girls, then winked at Charles as she dipped her fork into the cake on her plate.

Tonight, she thought, might be interesting.

Chapter 12

With twilight settling over Big Pine Mountain, Charles Martin set aside his personal desires and turned inward to the matter at hand. At first he thought the Sisters would be smirking and itching to make snide comments, but they proved him wrong. If any of them, Myra included, were thinking even remotely about Myra's tattoo, you couldn't prove it by him. The women were in work mode, chomping at the bit to get this new mission under way, especially Yoko, who was taking the whole affair personally.

The Sisters looked upward to where Charles was standing on the platform, their gazes expectant. Charles waved a stack of printed e-mails and began. "Reports from my operatives. I'll give you the short version, ladies. In the four days my men and women have been tailing the suspects they've garnered a wealth of information. I have here eight different aliases that the subjects go by. I want to thank Kathryn for naming them Bonnie and Clyde because it makes it so much easier when we refer to them that way.

"I also want to point out that we have not been able to find any records of a marriage taking place under any of the names we have discovered. Even though Bonnie and Clyde live together and *say* they're married, there is absolutely no evidence that they are. And at this time we have not been successful in determining Bonnie's or Clyde's real identity.

"Surveillance began four days ago, when my people first staked out the Watergate. Bonnie and Clyde have been under the microscope. Bonnie left the Watergate, drove her Lexus to Reagan National Airport, and took a 7:00 A.M. flight to Newark, New Jersey. In the long-term lot, she picked up a black Honda that had obviously been left there for her. She then drove to Menlo Park and went straight to the Hilton. She didn't register, but she had previously rented one of their conference rooms. She ordered fruit, coffee, and Danish. Within an hour, ten people entered the room. All ten people appeared to be business types, and all of them carried briefcases. My operative managed to get pictures of all ten plus Bonnie. He also videotaped the parking lot, making sure to get the license plate numbers of all the parked cars. We're in the process of running the plate numbers now, but so far nothing has come back. There were hundreds of cars in the lot.

"Our current thinking is that the business types would have been using their own cars, not rentals or stolen vehicles. Also, for your information, Bonnie's Lexus is registered under the name Angela Bookman, the name she's using at the Watergate.

"Bonnie reserved the conference room under the name of Carol Stewart. She used a credit card under the same name to pay for the room and food. The meeting lasted a full ninety minutes. My man stayed with Bonnie and followed her back to the airport, where she next boarded a flight to Pittsburgh. We had just enough time with her layover to get another operative onboard. He flew with her to Pittsburgh, where she did exactly the same thing she had in Newark. She picked up a car, another black Honda in the long-term lot, and drove to another Hilton. This time she used the name Tammy Jessup. My man followed through just the way the operative had in New Jersey. Ten people, all business types. Same food ordered, and the meeting lasted ninety minutes.

"This time, though, we had an extra operative, one who followed one of the business types. We are now profiling her, and I'm waiting for that report. My man followed Bonnie back to the airport and waited to be sure she boarded the flight back to Reagan National, at which point another one of my people picked up the trail and followed her back to the Watergate.

"Dennis Bookman, Clyde, if you prefer, did exactly the same thing, but he went in another direction. The MO was exactly the same as Bonnie's. He flew south to Florida, then to Georgia on his second leg. He arrived back at the Watergate an hour after Bonnie arrived. On the third day, they did exactly the same thing, only with different destinations. With each name change, there was also a change in appearance. Different hair, a change of jacket, high heels to low heels, different purse for Bonnie, that kind of thing. Clyde was more casual, baseball cap, jeans, jacket, all either reversible or he carried a spare in his backpack. The alias he used on the first leg was James Ferris; the second was Timothy Black.

"So, girls, what do you think?"

"What I think," Nikki said, "is we stepped into a giant hornet's nest, and what we thought was some couple scamming a few dozen people is now a giant fraud ring. The big question is, are Bonnie and Clyde the ringleaders, or is there someone over them?"

"My gut is saying Bonnie and Clyde are the ringleaders," Myra put in.

The other Sisters all agreed.

"So where do we go from here?" Kathryn asked Charles.

"We need to formulate an airtight plan. We're now open for input. Bear in mind, we just purchased an apartment in the Watergate complex that is in move-in condition. This," Charles said, waving a sheaf of papers in the air, "is a schematic of the entire complex, along with their current security system. At best, it's mediocre. My people also learned that there is no maid, live-in or otherwise, in Bonnie and Clyde's apartment. When the couple leaves, the place is empty. A little B&E might be called for. Their security system can be dismantled in under sixty seconds if you know what you're doing."

"Are we sure Bonnie and Clyde had no idea they were being followed?" Alexis asked.

Charles looked out over the top of his glasses and squelched Alexis with a stern look. "Puh-leze! I do not operate a Mickey Mouse operation. The couple are clueless at the moment. As far as they are concerned, it's business as usual. Which is good for us. I would like surveillance on both of them for at least another week. I think they're big, but not *that* big. If it's as my operative suspects—that they take a trip every two to three days—it's just the Eastern Seaboard. Who knows where they were operating before they descended on the nation's capital. Documentation, as we all know, is everything."

"Are we going to wait it out here on the mountain, or are we going to go to the Watergate?" Annie asked.

Charles looked around at the expectant faces staring at him. "I'm going to leave that up to all of you. If you think you can be more effective on the scene, then I will arrange transportation for you to the Watergate. If you prefer to stay here on the mountain until all our information is confirmed, that's all right, too. It's your call."

Isabelle frowned. "Seven people . . . seven new faces in a condo might raise eyebrows."

"I could stay at my old house if I have enough cover," Nikki said.

"I can stay at Harry's *dojo*," Yoko volunteered.

"I would be happy to stay with Joseph," Alexis said. "That leaves only four to move in. Myra, Annie, and their two daughters, Kathryn and Isabelle. My personal opinion is it would be too dicey for Kathryn to hang out at Bert's pad." The others nodded, even Kathryn. "If you want to count it down to three, Kathryn or Isabelle could stay with Maggie. Then we could *visit* as the need arises."

Charles pondered the suggestions presented to him. He nodded. "Work it out among yourselves, and get back to me first thing in the morning. I have a mountain of work ahead of me, so we're adjourned for now."

The Sisters walked out into the dark summer evening, each busy with her own thoughts, until Myra said, "I think I just got the brush-off."

"I think you did, too, dear," Annie said. "What are you going to do about it?"

Six very ripe and unorthodox suggestions followed Annie's question, all of which sent Myra off into gales of laughter. The one Myra liked best was where they had Avery Snowden bring Gaston, the tattoo artist, to the mountain under cover of darkness after they drugged Charles with enough of something to fell an ox so Gaston could do some artwork on Charles's nether regions. "Let's do it, but not until we finish our mission."

"Myra, I love the way you think. Can we watch?" Annie asked, clapping her hands together in excitement.

"Annie, my dear, I wouldn't have it any other way," Myra said.

"When we corner Bonnie and Clyde, what are we going to do with them?" Nikki asked, bringing matters back to hand. "What kind of punishment are we going to mete out?"

"Let's get a snack and meet up in our common room and kick it around. I have a few ideas," Annie said. "Good ones!"

While the Sisters were kicking around suitable punishments, Jack Emery was banging on the door of Harry Wong's *dojo*. At his feet were Harry's belongings, along with the paperwork and check Lizzie had left for him to give to Harry.

Harry appeared in the dim light and peered out at Jack. "What? Don't you ever sleep, Jack? What's with this nocturnal visit?"

"You're so damn ungrateful, Harry. I'm returning your belongings because I care about you and didn't want you sleeping directly on the floor. And to return your cell phone, which you left at the house. I also come bearing messages from the mountain and one in particular from Yoko, who said she was going to kick your ass all the way to Kentucky. I didn't even know Yoko knew where Kentucky was, but that's where you're going when she gets hold of you."

Harry's arm snaked through the door, and a second later, Jack was sliding across the slick floor. "What the hell . . . Now I'm going to have blisters on my ass. What the hell is wrong with you, Harry?"

"That was for breaking my damn door."

"How'd you expect me to get your stuff, you dumb shit! You were sitting barefoot on the curb in your Armani suit when I got here. You didn't even have your toothbrush. I got you your toothbrush. And, you asshole, you even thanked me for getting you all your stuff. I want an apology," Jack blustered.

"Climb in the window like any other burglar. Thanks for bringing my stuff back," Harry said grudgingly. "Are you telling me the truth about Yoko?" His tone was so worried, Jack enjoyed the moment.

"Would I lie about something that stick of dynamite would say? In case you don't know it, I'm almost as scared of her as you are. You got some major sucking up to do, buddy, and I can't wait to see it. Serves you right, you ungrateful . . . *terrorist.*"

Harry's concession to making peace was to play the host. "You want some tea?"

"No, I don't want any of your shitty tea. Don't you have any beer?"

"I do. Do you want one?"

"Well, yeah," Jack said, getting to his feet.

Tea in hand, Harry led the way into the

practice room. Jack with his beer followed. Together, they sat down cross-legged on a deep-
blue practice mat. "So, talk to me, Jack."

"The girls are coming soon, probably within
the next couple of days. Yoko will be staying
with you, at least temporarily." Jack quickly out-
lined all that Nikki had told him. Tongue in
cheek, he said, "You better start sprucing up the
place, Harry." Harry favored him with the evil
eye, which then made Jack hurry to explain all
that Lizzie had told him. "Here's the check for
the renovations. A letter of apology will be coming from the bank. Lizzie wasn't sure how long
that would take, but it *is* coming. If I were you,
I'd frame it when it gets here. From now on you
will be banking online, and Lizzie and some guy
at the bank will be monitoring your account
since you have such a phobia about mail.
They're still working on the credit card stuff, so
just be patient. You can still use the two cards
you have, it's been cleared, and new card numbers have been issued. You following me here,
Harry?"

"Yeah, but I don't like that online part."

"Harry, you are such a Neanderthal. That's
another way of saying you don't have a choice in
the matter. It was part of the deal Lizzie made,
so suck it up and shut up. How about another
beer?"

"What, now you want me to wait on you, too?
Gratitude goes just so far, Jack."

"Listen, your ass could be sailing over Kentucky as we speak if it wasn't for me, so, yes, I ex-

pect you to wait on me. Hand and foot. Then I'm going to help you spruce up your place for when Yoko arrives. That means we have to wash the sheets, preferably new ones, in some sweet-smelling stuff, get some fresh flowers, dust with lemon something or other, clean the dust off the paddle fan, and *really* clean up that scuzzy bathroom of yours. I'm thinking you need new pink bathroom rugs. Women love pink. New towels, too, big and soft. Soap that smells good, new toothbrushes, all that junk you saw in my house. I'm sleeping here since today is Friday, and we can hit the stores first thing in the morning."

Harry's eyes were as round as he could make them. "Tell me you're jerking my string, Jack."

Jack laughed. "It's either that or you're going to Kentucky. Your choice."

"I hate your guts, Jack. If I find out you're lying to me, you're the one who will be going to Kentucky!"

Chapter 13

The Sisters were clustered together on the platform where the cable car rested as they waited for Charles to join them with whatever last-second information was coming in by the minute. It was four in the afternoon, and their trip into the nation's capital would get them there soon after dark. It was the perfect time for the six-hour trip.

"I can't believe it's taken six days to get all this information," Kathryn grumbled. "My head feels like it's going to explode with all the information Charles drummed in to me . . . us. Finally." She sighed as she pointed to Charles crossing the lawn, the two dogs at his side. "Damn, will you look at that stack of folders he's carrying. They must weigh a ton," she continued to grouse.

Charles handed a folder to each of the women, then stepped back. "Ladies. There's been a change of plan. Annie, Myra, instead of waiting until tomorrow to go into Bonnie and Clyde's apartment at the Watergate, you'll be doing it right after you arrive. Word came in from the men and women who have been tailing them that both Bonnie and Clyde have checked in for the night at the Hiltons where they had their business meetings. No one knows why the change in routine, but it works out well for us.

"So, good luck! Call in every three hours, and I don't mean every four hours. Three means three, and it also means no one acts independently under any circumstance. Should that happen, you will be extracted. I have already alerted Jack, Harry, Bert, Ted, and Joseph to these new rules. Do any of you have any questions?"

They all shook their heads no. It was Annie who opened the gate to the cable car. She stepped in, Myra behind her.

As the dogs barked, Charles waved nonchalantly and slowly made his way back to the command center.

Alexis shoved her Red Bag, which looked like it weighed a ton, into the cable car before she followed Annie and Myra.

"You look more like Tyra Banks than Tyra does," Nikki shouted at Alexis. "See you tomorrow."

Alexis laughed at what she'd accomplished

with her Red Bag. She did look like Tyra Banks. She could hardly wait to see Joe Espinosa's expression when she let herself into his apartment. Would he think that somehow the wrong woman had come calling? What a hoot that would be.

"Do you think we look like two spinster sisters?" Annie asked Alexis.

"You do. Trust me, no one will give either one of you a second glance. I don't mean that the way it sounds. What I mean is no one who sees you will think of either Annie de Silva or Myra Rutledge. And if, when you're around people, you can remember to speak that awful German language Charles forced us to learn, you'll ace your new identities."

Dressed in prim suits, walking shoes with stout heels on their feet, and look-alike wigs fitted perfectly to their heads, the two women did resemble sisters of a certain age. Both wore glasses with wire rims and had no jewelry other than plain gold wedding bands. Widows, both of them. Each carried a small leather duffel bag that was worn and battered. Two suitcases waited for them at the bottom of the mountain. They were in the trunk of a two-year-old Ford Taurus, complete with an onboard navigator, set to show them the way to the Watergate and its underground parking garage.

Alexis, on the other hand, looked just like the model and movie star she was supposed to be. She wore skintight jeans, spike heels, and a crisp white shirt tied in a knot at her waist. A rakish jeweled cap pulled low over her forehead at an angle matched the gleaming bracelets and rings she wore. Huge gold-hoop earrings dangled from her ears. A car waited for her, too—in her case a Ford Mustang convertible, which also had a navigation system. It would take her straight to Joe Espinosa's apartment, where she would park in an underground parking spot, at which point she would take the elevator to the floor where the photographer hung his hat. She was so excited at the prospect that she had trouble breathing. This would be the first time she was actually going to be *alone* with Joe. Giggling, she said, "I am ecstatic!"

Myra and Annie smiled indulgently.

The cable car came to a stop and slid into its nest. The women exited quickly, and Myra pressed the button that would send the car back to the top of the mountain. Within minutes, all three women were in the waiting cars and out on the highway. Their destination: Washington, D.C.

Back on the mountain, Yoko, Kathryn, Isabelle, and Nikki stepped into the cable car. Sadly, there was no one to wave good-bye.

Charles had issued new identities and driver's licenses, the procurement of which had also contributed to the weeklong wait on the mountain.

Nikki, sporting a dark auburn wig with feathery bangs, was dressed as her old cleaning lady,

Cleo Kilpatrick, whom Jack had sent on a two-week vacation. Isabelle, wearing a navy business suit, heels, glasses, and a short blond wig, looked just like Kelly Ripa. She could have been anyone—a lawyer, a banker, an executive of some sort. Women dressed like her paraded the streets of Washington every day. Kathryn, her hair bunched up under a ball cap and dressed in jeans, work boots, and a skinny mini tee that showed off her bronzed, muscled arms—seemingly attesting that she worked at something in a man's world. A tool belt that looked to weigh at least forty pounds was around her waist. She carried the weight well.

Yoko was dressed casually, carried a backpack, and had the credentials of an exchange student from Taiwan. A motor scooter waited for her, and it had a navigator programmed to take her to Harry Wong's *dojo*.

At the foot of the mountain, the Sisters hugged, gave each other a thumbs-up, and climbed into their respective vehicles. Yoko slid onto a powerful Honda motor scooter and was off before the others could even turn the key in their ignition. Then Nikki drove off in an ancient dark green Toyota Corolla, Isabelle in a sleek black Audi, and Kathryn in a white van that said it belonged to the Carpathian Plumbing Company.

Once all the Sisters were in their nests, the plan called for telephone contact only, until told otherwise.

The mission was on.

* * *

The German sisters, aka Myra and Annie, pulled their well-traveled suitcases behind them as they made their way down the hall that would lead them to their newly acquired apartment on the eighth floor of the Watergate. Annie opened the door and gasped at the nicely decorated, comfortable apartment Charles had managed on such short notice. "For however long we're going to be here, Myra, I think we'll be quite comfortable. I like that the eighth floor isn't that high up."

Myra nodded as she walked around, looking at things. While she wouldn't want to live in a place like this, she could and would adjust for the short-term.

Within minutes, they were unpacked and checking to be sure the computer, the printer, and the fax machine were up and running. Suddenly beeps and whistles could be heard throughout the three-bedroom, three-bath apartment.

Annie smiled. "Avery's people playing with the electric breakers. They were obviously keeping track of our arrival and gave us some time to get ready. That was number one. Four more, and we hit the hall and do our thing. I think we should be waiting by the door for the fourth surge. That's when we hit the stairs and walk up to the twelfth floor, so we can do our power walk. The cameras in the stairwells will pick us up, but Avery's people will erase or adjust the film. When the power goes off completely, we scoot right into Bonnie and Clyde's empty apartment. Charles said we'll have ten seconds before the power comes back on for five minutes, time for us to do what we need to do inside and get back out to resume our power walk. That's the way you see it, right, Myra?"

Myra nodded. "That was three, Annie." She opened the door and stepped out into the hall just as the fourth power surge caused the hall lights to flicker.

Both women went directly to the stairwell, where they huffed and puffed their way to the twelfth floor and immediately went into their power walk, arms pumping.

"There it is, 1206, and Charles was right, the door is slightly ajar. Slow down, Annie, we don't want to get too far down the hall." She looked down at her watch. "Two seconds, turn around," she hissed. "Now!"

Annie and Myra barreled back down the hall and were inside Bonnie and Clyde's apartment the moment the windowless hallway went black. Myra counted to ten. The power came back on, and the apartment came to life. Whoever had entered first and left the door open for them must have been the one to turn the lamps on. Undoubtedly they would return and put things back the way they were after Myra and Annie left. The overhead light in the foyer gave off enough light to illuminate the dining area, the kitchen, and the living room.

The apartment was sparsely furnished.

"I don't know for sure what rental furniture

looks like, but I think we're looking at it," Annie
said, indicating the dark, bland furniture that
looked neither comfortable nor fashionable.
The women separated, Annie taking the bathroom and bedroom, Myra the kitchen, living
room, and dining area. It took only four minutes before the women met up in a short hallway that separated the living area from the
bedroom.

"No one lives here, Myra. There's no *stuff*.
Everyone has stuff. Everyone brings something
with them from the old place to the new place,
even if it's only a dying plant. There's always a
bit of the past you want to bring with you to the
present to remind you where you've been. This is
just a shell, a cover of some sort. Everything is new,
the sheets on the bed still have the creases on
them from being packaged, and they smell new.
Everything is minimal, drugstore cosmetics, all
new. Clyde's shaving kit and his sundries are new
and unused. They forgot to take the tag off the
towels. The chest of drawers holds brand-new
clothing from JCPenney. Seven of everything. It
still smells new. The closet has shoes, they're new,
too. No DNA anywhere in this place, and that's
a guarantee."

"It's the same thing in the kitchen," Myra
said. "There are four of everything. Nothing
extra. Two pots, two fry pans. The refrigerator
has a bottle of wine, three bottles of beer, and a
six-pack of bottled water. There are two dried-
up oranges in the fruit bin. In the freezer there
are two frozen TV dinners, a can of frozen juice,

no pitcher to mix it in. That's it. The coffeepot has never been used, and the can of coffee hasn't been opened."

"This place is carpeted, but there's no vacuum cleaner. No cleaning supplies. I don't think Charles was expecting this. What do you think, Myra?"

"I think you're right. This place is just a cover. I think like you do, there must be another apartment inside this complex where they *really* live."

Myra looked at her watch. They both ran to the door and waited for the power to go back out. Just as Myra turned the knob on the door, the apartment went dark. Like the conspirators they were, they raced to the end of the hall. The only light to be seen was the red EXIT sign over the stairwell door. Inside the dark stairwell, they waited for the power to come back on before they made their wild scramble back to the eighth floor and their apartment.

Inside, both women collapsed onto a soft, nubby off-white sofa.

Her voice sounding jittery, Annie said, "That was fun, wasn't it, Myra?"

"About as much fun as a root canal. Do you realize you could live in a place like this for years and never see or know your neighbors?"

The two women waited through three more power surges, darkness, then light before Annie called Charles to report in. "There has to be another apartment here. All your people saw was

Bonnie and Clyde exiting and entering the building. They didn't see which apartment they came out of. Myra and I are tired, so we're going to bed. That means we will not be checking in during the next eight hours." Annie rolled her eyes at Myra, and so it was obvious Charles was berating her for something.

In a voice loud enough for Charles to hear, Myra said, "Tell him to sit on it!"

Annie immediately broke the connection.

"I think the correct expression according to Kathryn would be, 'sit on a pointy stick and twirl around,' or, in other words, 'perch, pivot, and rotate.'"

"Whatever," Myra drawled as she got up and made her way toward the bedroom. "Tomorrow is another day, Annie. Do you have a good feeling about any of this?"

"Actually, I was just thinking about Lizzie and wondering if she's going to take the job as chief White House counsel. But to answer your question, I'm thinking positive thoughts. It's going to depend on all of us working together. Think positive, dear."

"I don't think she's going to take the job. She has a new husband, and with all the work we've been sending her way, I just don't see her leaving the work she loves behind, however prestigious the new position is. Lizzie has her own reputation and prestige. She doesn't need the White House," Myra called over her shoulder as she yawned elaborately.

Ten minutes later, Myra came out of the bathroom. She was wearing silky pajamas with butterflies all over them, a long-ago birthday gift from Nikki. She sat down on the edge of her bed and looked across at Annie, who was taking off her shoes. "I like it that there are two beds in this room. I hate sleeping in a strange place by myself."

"Me, too." Annie yawned. "Myra, wouldn't it be wonderful if our Lizzie found herself pregnant and had a little girl? A boy would be nice, too, but a little girl is kind of special. I wonder if she'd let us both be the baby's godmothers?"

Myra started to cry. Annie swiped at her own eyes. "It never goes away, does it, Myra?"

Myra shook her head no. She swiped at her eyes. "We shouldn't talk about sad things before we go to sleep. Has anyone heard from Maggie?"

Annie reached for a tissue from the box on the nightstand that sat between the two beds. "Not that I know of. I wonder if we should call her and ask her to have her . . . you know, that person who . . . uh . . . *helps* her out from time to time, and ask him if he could somehow find out if we're right and there's another residence here at the Watergate that belongs to Bonnie and Clyde. It might take Charles a while to find out. If her person can do it quicker, he doesn't have to know we asked her. I know, I know, we're undermining him, but we're wasting valuable time that could be put to better use if Maggie's guy can come up with something."

Myra whirled around. "And you want to do this *now?* I thought you said you were sleepy."

Annie marched into the bathroom, where she took out her cell phone and called Kathryn, who was staying at Maggie's place, told her about what they had discovered, and asked her about trying to get Maggie to have her guy find out where Bonnie and Clyde were really burrowing. When she returned, she was wearing a granny nightgown that covered her from head to toe. "I was tired when I said it, but now my brain is whirling and twirling. I just called Kathryn at Maggie's to bring her up to speed. She said she'd talk to Maggie when she got home.

"I wonder how much money I made at my casino today. Myra, are you listening to me?"

"I am," Myra said as she massaged a thick, gooey night cream all over her face.

"You should rub some of that on your ass, old girl."

"Annie!"

"I just said that to wake you up. You look like you're half in a trance. It couldn't hurt, you know. That is a rather large encryption you have back there. Block letters, no less." Annie sniffed to make her point. "I thought we were going for, you know, tiny, delicate—and what do you do? You order up psychedelic colors and block letters."

"I don't care to discuss my rear end, thank you very much. I got carried away in the moment. Do I wish I hadn't done it? Yes. But I'm stuck with it. I have no intention of talking about this ever again."

Annie wadded up her pillow and threw it at Myra, who in turn threw her pillow at Annie. "Night, friend."

"Night, Annie."

Chapter 14

Jack stood back to look at his and Harry's decorating handiwork. "Done in the nick of time," he said, shaking his hands in the air. "What do you think, Harry?"

"What I think is I hate you, Jack. When you said pink, I thought you meant pink like a peony. That's a flower, Jack. My people love peonies. The color is delicate, almost white. This," he said, shaking his fist, "is fucking *PINK!* Men do not have pink bathrooms. And men do not have pink bedspreads with flowers all over them."

Jack backed up a step. "And your point is?"

"When you aren't looking, I'm going to kill you. How can I live with this?"

"We did it for Yoko. Don't lose sight of that, Harry. Stop being so selfish. At best Yoko is only going to be visiting short-term. *Very* short-term. We did it to make her happy. We did it so she could see your creative, sensitive side. She's absolutely going to melt when she sees all the trouble you went to. I guarantee it!" Jack said, his voice sounding a little more brave.

"And if she laughs and mocks me?"

Jack danced away. "You are so damn negative, Harry. How do you live with yourself? Just look at everything. It's *pretty*. Women love pretty. Those rose-scented candles are the topping on the cake. I hope you remember to light them. You need to be suave, Harry."

"Eat shit, Jack."

Jack danced even farther away. He dusted his hands together dramatically. "Well, my work here is done. Yoko should be arriving any minute now. That means Nikki is probably already at my house. I really have to go now. I hope you appreciate all the help I've been to you. You know, I could have just left you to your own devices. What that means is Yoko would have said she wanted to go to the Hay-Adams. I saved you money. A thank-you would be nice."

Harry turned, tilted his head. A look of pure panic covered his face. "She's here!"

"I don't hear anything."

"She's a block away."

"You expect me to believe you can hear something a block away?"

"No, you're too stupid to believe that. See, she's turning into the driveway. She's here. You need to get out of here."

"That's well and good, but your front door is

still padlocked, so that means the only exit is over there," Jack said, pointing to the back door. "Wow, look who's here! Hi, Yoko! I was just leaving. Did you have a good ride . . . trip . . . journey?"

"I did, thank you for asking." She looked over at Harry and bowed slightly. Harry bowed in return.

"Well, like I said, I was just leaving. By the way, Yoko, before I go, do you want to see Harry's new . . . uh . . . renovations? Come on, let me show you!" Jack was more than careful to keep a good distance between Harry and himself. "Of course when the actual renovations start, I'm sure Harry will ask you for your input. This is just, you know, temporary."

Jack grinned from ear to ear as Yoko walked around, squealing with pleasure. "Oooh, Harry, how did you know I love pink? Oh, my goodness, mercy me, this is just so beautiful. Harry, this was so sweet of you. To think you did all this for me!" Yoko started to make kissing kootchie-koo noises that Jack thought were none of his business. "Harry, honey, say something. How did you know? Do you love it, too? It makes such a difference. Pink is so peaceful, so serene. And you did it all for me!"

Harry looked over at Jack, his eyes defying him to say something. He did.

"Harry did his best to convince me that pink was the way to go, but I argued the point. He was adamant, though, and this," Jack said, waving his arms around, "is the perfect result. I'm sorry, Harry, you were right, and I was wrong. I'll see you two later . . . at some point . . . maybe tomorrow . . . if not, oh, well."

To Harry he hissed, "Man you owe me big-time, and I'm going to take it out of your hide at some point. You got that, you *schmuck*?"

Harry nodded.

"For sure my work is done," Jack mumbled to himself as he made his way back to the *dojo* and let himself out.

It was his turn now. Time for some quality time with Nikki. He crossed his fingers that she would be sitting in the kitchen or the bedroom waiting for him. *Oh, yeah! Life is good right now.*

As always, when Maggie arrived home and exited her chauffeur-driven car—a perk of her job at the *Post*—she looked up and down the street. She saw Jack's car parked two doors down and a green car of some sort that belonged to his two-day-a-week housekeeper. She couldn't help but notice a white plumbing van parked directly in front of her house. Her driver walked her to the door and waited until she was inside.

"Guess you left your lights on this morning, Miss Spritzer."

"I finally got around to setting the timers over the weekend. Thanks for bringing me home, Will. See you in the morning."

The driver wagged his finger but waited till she was inside and the door closed. The moment he heard the lock snick into place he turned on his heel and walked to the Lincoln Town Car.

Inside, Maggie stood stock-still as she waited to see which of the Sisters was in her house. Kathryn emerged from the kitchen, a chicken leg in hand. Kathryn's appetite was as notorious as Maggie's.

"I didn't know I had any chicken in the fridge," Maggie said inanely.

"You didn't. I stopped at a deli and bought two bags of food. I was starving. I didn't know you worked this late, Maggie. It's almost midnight."

"I try not to, but with the profiles pouring in, I have to stay on top of it. Ted and Espinosa are working overtime. I want to start our new series midweek if possible.

"We're going to run with something else, too. It's a long story, but, fast-forward, I remembered something that has been niggling at me. There was this kid who called in to the paper right before the switchboard blew out. It was right after we started running the series. I hate to admit this, but I sloughed him off at the time. You know what they say, everything happens for a reason, so maybe even if I had paid attention, I wouldn't have attached any importance to what he said. I just don't know. What I do know is we are definitely onto something now.

"I sent Ted and Espinosa to Silver Spring, Maryland, to look for a garage where I think this young man might be working. The kids aren't just in Silver Spring, they're all over the map—Arlington, Alexandria, Bethesda, etc. They finally found him, and his name is Antonio Vargas. He had a story to tell, and Ted got it all. Espinosa has the pictures to back it up. The young man gave us a few other names, and those people gave us more names, kind of like a domino effect. In total, Ted and Espinosa, along with Dawson and his partner, managed to profile sixty-seven kids. I call them kids because the lot of them just turned eighteen. Male and female. Those profiles just broke my heart, Lizzie. Here are these kids living in foster care and not having the love and affection of a set of parents. Don't get me wrong, I'm not saying the foster parents didn't care about them, but nothing can take the place of a set of birth parents.

"Each and every one had a refrain: 'I can't wait till I'm eighteen, so I can get out of here.' And when they did get out, look what happened to them. One girl, Melanie Blackman, is so musically inclined and gifted she was accepted to Julliard, but when she tried to apply for grants and open a bank account, apply for a part-time job, she was told she had such a poor credit history it wasn't possible. Not one of them understood about credit reports, FICA scores. Each one of those kids has a story. We're going with six of them in the paper. Ted did a superior job on the profiles. While we're only doing six profiles, we are listing the names of all the others.

"I called Annie right away, and she's working with some of her people to, as she put it, 'arrange something for those youngsters.' She'll

make it happen, too. One way or another, she'll
see to it that those kids get their lives back.
Count on it."

"That's great, Maggie. I can't wait till we get
ahold of the people responsible for all of this.
When we're finished with them, Bonnie and
Clyde are going to wish they had never been
born. Just imagine each of them having their fifteen minutes of fame going up against Harry or
Yoko!"

Maggie laughed. "It won't be pretty when it
happens." Maggie kicked off her shoes and sent
them sailing across the room. Her backpack
landed on the sofa, then her suit jacket settled
on a chair next to it. She followed Kathryn to
the kitchen. "Talk," she said as she peered into
the fridge.

Kathryn brought her up-to-date. "So, to account for my leaving the van in front of your
house, what you're looking at is major plumbing problems. I'm going to need another vehicle. Do you think either Ted or Espinosa can
come up with one for me?"

Maggie carried a load of food to the counter,
where she prepared to make a Dagwood sandwich. "Yeah, they probably can come up with
one; if not, we'll get you a rental. So what's the
deal?"

"Everything is pretty much in place, but we
hit a snag. A big one. Annie and Myra discovered that Bonnie and Clyde's apartment at the
Watergate, 1206, is a shill. That means they
must have another apartment in the complex.

At least that's what we think. Until we know exactly where they're living, we can't do anything. Annie wants to know if you can have your guy check that out. Charles has his people on it, but we need speed right now. Her thinking is two . . . uh . . . hackers working on it will bring quicker results. She said pay whatever you have to pay to get the information."

Maggie bit down on her sandwich. She chewed thoughtfully before she responded. "Okay, I'll make the call, but he's going to fight me on this."

Kathryn grinned. "Maggie, Maggie, just tell him the vigilantes will hunt him down and kill him if he doesn't do it."

"Hmmm. That might work. Common sense tells me we should be hiring private detectives by the dozen to man the doors and elevators, so when Bonnie and Clyde do go in and out, we can take them. When I spoke to Nikki earlier, when you guys were still on the mountain, she said that Charles's people have pictures, good ones, of Bonnie and Clyde. If the detectives have pictures, we should be able to get a bead on them."

"Paper trail, Maggie. We need hard information that they either own or rent the space where they're actually living when we turn it over to the proper authorities. You're going to want that, too, for your articles."

"Okay, you're right." Maggie's cell was in her hand before Kathryn could blink.

A voice barked into the phone. "No!"

"I have a message for you," Maggie barked in return. "Just to prove I'm serious, look around and tell me what you see."

The voice on the other end of the phone sounded wary. "Why?"

"Tell me what you see," Maggie said, her voice ringing with frost.

"Lots of people. The ocean, waiters. White sand. What do you want me to see?" The voice was still wary and jittery-sounding.

"Among those people are two members of the vigilantes. There is also one local FBI agent. Right now they don't know who they're looking for, but if you don't do what I want you to do, they're going to zero in on you in the next five minutes. You told me you weren't going to go to Hawaii until next week. You lied to me, Abbie. How much?"

"You're lying, Maggie Spritzer!"

"You want to bring it to a test?"

"All right! All right! Tell me what you want."

Maggie winked at Kathryn, who was trying not to laugh.

"I want . . . no, I *need* a list of all the tenants, owners, and renters who live in the Watergate. It seems our . . . birds . . . have a shell there but actually live in a different apartment. How hard can that be? You hack in and get the list. You're done and I pay you, and you can stay in Hawaii for another two weeks."

"I don't want to stay here another two weeks. I might want to come back in January, when it's cold back in D.C. What you're asking me for is

stupid. That information is not going to tell you
what you want. The Watergate and Crystal City
are havens for young couples and singles as
well. It would take me weeks, maybe longer,
even if I worked round-the-clock to sift through
it all. The bottom line is: as much as I hate to
admit it, I can't do it. But, if you have time and
don't need the information in the next twelve
hours, I'll take a shot at it. My fee will depend
on what you want me to do. I'm serious, Maggie,
you're grasping at straws. Want some advice?"

"Do I have a choice? What?"

"I can't believe I'm saying this to you. Use the
money you'd be paying me and hire a batch of
private eyes. Position them as needed and wait
for whatever shakes out. People have to go outside from time to time. You said you have pictures, so hand them out to the detectives and sit
back and wait. I'm sorry, Maggie, I hate turning
down business, but this time it's a no-brainer.
Were you lying to me about the vigilantes and
the FBI?"

"I absolutely was not lying to you," Maggie
lied, fighting to keep a straight face but crossing
her fingers. "You rained on my parade, Abbie. I
hate it when people rain on my parade." She
broke the connection as Abner Tookus started
to sputter.

Maggie stared across the table at Kathryn.
"No dice. He could do it eventually, but it will
take weeks. We have to hire detectives."

"Annie said she was going to mention that to
Charles. I'm thinking it's already in the plan-

ning stage unless his hackers are better than your guy."

"Trust me, no one is better than my guy. So, do we hire some dicks or let Charles handle it? I wonder how many entrances and exits there are."

Kathryn rolled her eyes. "I don't have a clue. Parking garages have all kinds of exits. Didn't you say Charles's people know the makes and models of their cars?"

Maggie shrugged. "I'm pretty sure, so that's another avenue his people can pursue. I think it would be better if you call Charles, Kathryn. Ask him to stake some dicks in the garage area. He views me as stepping on his turf when I think outside the box."

Kathryn yawned elaborately. "The morning will be time enough. You look as tired as I feel. C'mon, I'll help you clean up."

"What's up with Lizzie?" Maggie asked, finishing the last of her glass of milk.

"Other than making Cosmo a happy camper, not much. Just wait five minutes, and that will change. Do you think she'll take the job as chief White House counsel? And what effect do you think that would have on Connor's giving the Sisters the pardons she owes us?"

"Nothing at this point in time. Having said that, I think Martine has a plan down the road. The last time we had a personal chat, she said something about putting the wheels in motion in regard to those pardons."

Kathryn nodded. "What time do you get up?"

"Five o'clock. You can sleep in. I'll make arrangements to get a car for you. I'll call and tell you where it's parked, okay? Night, Kathryn."

"Night, Maggie."

Chapter 15

Lizzie Fox was opening her front door to head for her office when her BlackBerry came to life. She stopped, and walked back to the kitchen as she said hello to her husband. "You're running late this morning, Cricket?"

There was a smile in her voice that Cricket couldn't help but hear. He responded in kind. "I am, but I can't start my day without talking to you before I go out the door. I have news, no smoking guns, but you might find it useful."

"Fire away," Lizzie said as she fixed herself the last of the coffee. "You never know, Cricket, I might be able to turn whatever your news is *into* a smoking gun. Let's hear it."

"I spoke with Damon Finn, he's on the third or fourth tier of the Chase credit card division. I hate to admit this, but I had to bribe him to get the information he was willing to part with, and, like I said, it isn't much. Two years ago they, meaning Chase, had a promotion for their people for signing up new accounts, then they brought them all here to Vegas as a thank-you. We met, nothing out of the ordinary, just a meeting. Nice guy. His people were nice, no drunkenness, no rude behavior. That's all I had to go on when I spoke to him. I laid it out, told the truth, and promised him and his wife a week at the Babylon, fully comped, plane fare, food, chips for $100 a day. I'm not sure his information is worth what it cost us, but I'll let you be the judge.

"In October of last year, a young woman by the name of Bethany Nolan was hired. The reason her name came to his attention was because of the strange hiring requirements she insisted on."

Lizzie frowned. "Which were?"

"She said she was a law student and was just a hair away from taking the bar, and could only work two full weekends a month. But she was willing to work double shifts and once in a while maybe a Friday or a Monday if she could arrange it, so in essence it was the equivalent of a four-day or five-day workweek. She didn't care that she wasn't eligible for health benefits, said she was covered under her husband's policy where he worked, so she was hired with Finn's approval.

"She was everything you could want in an employee, according to Finn. She came in, worked sixteen hours a day, then they had to hire someone else to process all the new accounts she brought in. She stayed until the end of February, when she said she had to quit. She said she was run-down and needed to fall back and regroup so she could study for the bar. She sent a lovely letter thanking them for giving her the chance to work for such a wonderful company. On her last day she bought her fellow workers, six of them, pizza and gave them all a little token gift and promised to stay in touch. She even offered free legal advice in the future. No one ever heard from her again."

"And this means what, Cricket?"

"Check Bonnie's employment records when she worked at East Coast Savings. Fax Finn a picture of Sara Brickman. Isn't that the name you told me she used when this all came to light? I told him to expect one."

"But, Cricket, that isn't going to tell us anything. So what if she worked weekends? She didn't work weekends at the bank here, so there won't be a record of her taking off."

"Finn did say on occasion she would work a third day, depending if she needed extra money. Sometimes she would work a Friday or a Monday. That you can check. But it will be the clincher if the picture of your person matches up with Finn's employee.

"Finn just thought you might be interested in this because you comped a trip to Vegas?" Lizzie's fingers tapped on the kitchen table. She'd been hoping for so much more.

Cricket laughed, the sound booming over the

wire. "Not exactly. The *Post* started to run articles on identity theft along with human-interest stories, and, lo and behold, most of those cases were Chase card holders. Finn said at first he thought it was just something they had to deal with, and the next time it would be American Express or Citi. This time they had to take the hit. They brought in a forensic CPA to do an audit, and that's when they found out that all the new accounts that Bethany Nolan set up were fraudulent. Moreover, remember telling me something about minor foster children being targeted? Well, twenty percent of those accounts were for minor children in the foster care system.

"They tried to find her, even hired private detectives. Nolan was not a law student, they found out to their dismay. She didn't live where she said she lived. She had no past beyond five years, just like your Sara Brickman. He said he would help but don't count on it. Chase doesn't want the exposure a full-court press will bring. He said as much. Finn is afraid people would stop using their Chase credit cards, turn them in, go to other cards because Chase doesn't protect their interests, that kind of thing."

Lizzie chewed on her bottom lip as she digested her husband's information. "What's your gut feeling, Cricket?"

"My gut says Bethany Nolan is your Sara Brickman and all the other names you said she used. My advice would be to fax Finn the woman's picture and wait to see what he does. I did mention that I heard through the grapevine that the vigilantes were hot on her trail."

Lizzie found herself smiling at what Cosmo Cricket probably thought was a hushed whisper. "What did Mr. Finn say?"

Cosmo chuckled. "I can give it to you verbatim. 'Good Christ, don't tell me that!'"

This time Lizzie laughed out loud. "What did you say to that?"

"I just wished him luck, then he hung up."

"Thanks, sweetie. Talk to you later."

Lizzie sat for a few minutes longer as she ran the conversation with Cricket over and over in her mind. When she was satisfied she had it clear, she called Maggie, reported in. She rattled off the information Cosmo had given her. "Just fax the picture to Finn, and call me as soon as you hear something. The fact that the *Post* is on it might make Finn a little more cooperative. I think I just gave you your next headline, Maggie. And kudos on your following up on the foster child angle. Imagine, twenty percent of those accounts for kids in foster care. Talk about lowlife scum."

Lizzie broke the connection and called Myra and Annie and relayed the same information, with instructions to call Charles immediately.

Charles Martin looked at the blizzard of papers spewing out of his fax machine. His e-mail *pinged* and *zinged* as if vying for attention over the faxes coming through. Two phones started buzzing as they, too, wanted their fifteen minutes of fame. Charles knew in his gut that something was wrong even before he answered the phone or checked his faxes and e-mails. He shrugged; that was what he was there for, to deal with each crisis and resolve it.

He listened to one of Avery Snowden's operatives, a seasoned professional, as a frown built between his brows. "But you aren't sure is what you're telling me, is that correct?" He listened again. "You know what to do, Leigh. Call me when your replacement is in place. Check in with Avery and stay out of sight."

Charles pressed a button and took the second call. He listened, the frown growing deeper. "If she's in the garage and about to take her car out, she's going somewhere. Stay with her. What do you mean she changed her mind? She's going back to the elevator? Can you see what floor she punched in? Six? Did she act like she forgot something, or is she spooked? Leigh just called in, and she thinks Bonnie is spooked. Said Bonnie looked around, then right at her. A new face, and Bonnie can't decide if she recognizes it or not. Anything is possible. Where's Clyde? Usually he's right on her heels. Okay, stake out the sixth floor, the stairwell, and make sure that the GPS you attached to the vehicle is on good and tight. Can you dismantle the locking system and dust the steering wheel for fingerprints?" He listened a moment longer, then said, "Get someone there to do it ASAP."

Charles's next call was to Myra, and it was

short and sweet. "Get down to the fifth floor and walk up to six. Keep your cell phone on and do your power walk. The second you get to the sixth floor, call me, and we'll keep the line open." He cursed loudly and ripely as he attacked the stack of papers still coming through the fax machine. The e-mail was *pinging* so loudly he wished he had earplugs.

Murphy let loose with a loud bark, which triggered one from Grady. Both dogs were on their feet before Charles could turn around.

"It's okay. I know I don't usually use language like that, but there's a first time for everything."

Charles took a moment to wonder if he'd put too many operatives on this particular case. Never one to voice self-doubt, he shook his head to clear it. He needed every single operative and probably should have assigned a dozen more to Bonnie and Clyde. He closed his eyes for a moment as he tried to figure out what the couple's next move would be.

First and foremost, Charles now realized, the couple was suddenly seeing too many new faces in a short span of time. No operative was perfect, sometimes no matter how they disguised themselves, no matter how nonchalant they appeared, a subject would pick up on it. Maybe they were too close, the clothing didn't sit right with the subject, or the operative made eye contact. Whatever it was, Charles knew that Bonnie and Clyde were now on the alert.

He also knew that if either Bonnie or Clyde left the Watergate, there was a good chance they could successfully elude his people. It happened all the time, and it didn't matter how good the operative was. Bonnie and Clyde were pros, and there was too much money at stake for them to suddenly get sloppy. In addition, most criminals had Plan B, C, D, and, if necessary, the rest of the alphabet in place. Right now, he knew, they were kicking Plan B into place. All it took was one little thing to warn the subject that things weren't quite right. People like Bonnie and Clyde had built-in antennae that were always on alert for possible trouble.

Charles's cell phone was at his ear the instant it rang. It was Myra announcing she and Annie were on the sixth floor and starting their power walk. "Remember, Myra, only German when you and Annie are walking. Don't talk loud, keep your voice normal. I'll be able to hear everything with my earbud. Be careful."

He was already calling Jack and Harry as he spread out the stack of faxes on the table: reports on all the people who had attended Bonnie and Clyde's seminars at various hotels over the past two weeks. As he scanned the reports, viewed the attendees' credit histories, their mundane jobs, and unimpressive work performances, he understood how easy it would be for Bonnie and Clyde to recruit them to the identity theft ring. The number of cash advances was staggering.

Charles suddenly knew how it all worked: Bonnie and Clyde stole the victim's identity, farmed out the identities to the people who attended the seminars. Probably each person was assigned, at the most, a dozen victims. They'd charge up a storm, buying merchandise that was sent to various drop zones, then sold on the black market. Before they moved on to the next victim, they would take a cash advance in whatever amount the card would allow. He knew now that the couple wasn't running a *big* operation, they were running a *huge* operation. They had to have a quality forger in place, along with people whom they trusted to monitor the drop zones and peddle the merchandise. Even with a seventy/thirty split, they were racking up huge profits, stealing money from unsuspecting people at the speed of light.

The big money, he knew, came from the second mortgages and home equity loans they perpetrated. Timing was everything, Charles knew, which meant from the moment Bonnie or Clyde applied for either a mortgage or home equity loan they had to have dozens of people and various bank accounts in place so they could cash the checks and move on. Just the banking alone was a mind boggler. Having only two people working the financial end of it bothered him. Would they trust a financial man, or did they do it all themselves? His gut told him it was a two-person operation. Where were the records? Was there a set of books? Unlikely. Was it all done on the computer and transferred to a memory stick? Probably.

If their real apartment was on the sixth floor,

was that where the computer was? Or did they have yet another place where they actually conducted business? An office of some kind with electronic equipment? The Watergate had thousands of office units for rent. Another needle in the haystack for him to find. He sighed mightily as he listened to Myra and Annie jabbering on the open cell phone line.

Annie stopped by the elevator, and Myra bumped into her. "Listen, Myra, as long as there is no one in the hallway, we don't have to do that long-legged stride with our arms windmilling. If we hear the elevator, we go into action; otherwise, I say we just walk up and down this hall. We could listen at doorways to see how many people are actually home. You know, the sound of televisions, radios. We might even get a whiff of food cooking. There aren't any cameras on these floors, which I find very strange. What good are cameras in the stairwells if you get mugged in the hallway?"

That was all Myra had to hear. She pointed to the cell in her hand, then put her finger to her lips, the signal to Annie that she should whisper so Charles couldn't hear what they were saying. Annie nodded as she trotted to the nearest door, Myra on the other side of the hallway.

Uptown, downtown, and in midtown, on orders from Charles, the Sisters moved as one even though they were separated by blocks, if not miles.

In Georgetown, Nikki donned her cleaning-lady attire and waved good-bye to Jack, who stood in the doorway of the bathroom dripping wet, a towel around his waist. "I'll call you."

Outside, Nikki headed to the green car she'd arrived in and slid behind the wheel. Out of the corner of her eye she noticed Kathryn, dressed in jogging clothes, climb into a champagne-colored Honda Civic.

In the *dojo* at the other end of town, Yoko's cell phone pealed at the same time Harry's rang. Yoko was up, dressed, with a backpack on her shoulders and almost out the door before Harry knew what was happening. He pretended to catch the kiss Yoko blew at him before she raced out of the bedroom, answering her call on the way. Harry waited a few seconds.

"What the hell is going on, Jack? Yoko just blew out of here like a hurricane."

"What's in it for me if I tell you?"

"Your life!"

"Yeah, well, Mr. Martial Arts Expert who has pink towels in his bathroom and who sleeps under a pink comforter and I have the pictures to prove it, what makes you think I know what's going on?"

Jack had a vision of Harry clenching his teeth and banging something with his fist and wishing it was Jack's head he was banging. "Well, yeah, but like I said, what's in it for me if I tell you what I know, assuming I know anything?"

Harry sighed. "Name it."

"I know that cost you, Harry, and in your heart you didn't mean it, but since I love you like a brother, I'm going to tell you. I-do-not-know. All I know is Nikki got a call, and she barreled out of here and didn't look back. She didn't say anything other than that she would call me. However . . . before you punch a hole in the wall, Charles did call right before I headed for the shower. He said they think, *think,* Harry, that Bonnie and Clyde are in an apartment on the sixth floor of the Watergate. One of his operatives was on her trail and something spooked Bonnie and she went back inside. That's it. Don't even think about acting independently, Harry. Your time will come with those two. The girls will make sure that happens.

"Look, I have court this morning, but I can leave around noon. I'll come by the *dojo* and pick you up. In the meantime, Myra and Annie are power walking the sixth floor. Dive back under that pink comforter and catch some more sleep."

Jack blanched at what he heard next before the connection was broken. Harry's speech could be so colorful sometimes. Ten minutes later, Jack was out the door and on his way to court to file a motion to suppress something or other on a case he couldn't even remember.

* * *

Alexis Thorne walked down the street after she exited Joseph Espinosa's apartment. She was smiling as she walked along, remembering the stunned look on Joseph's face when she hopped out of bed, donned her Tyra Banks outfit, and winked at him. "I have to tell you, Joseph, that was some really good sex. Time permitting, I'll be back for an encore."

Alexis stepped to the curb and hailed a cab, gave the address of the Watergate, and leaned back to enjoy the ride. Her BlackBerry vibrated. She looked down at the text message from Isabelle, announcing she was safely inside Myra and Annie's apartment awaiting her arrival.

Thirty minutes later, on the mountain Charles's closed fist shot into the air. All his chicks were accounted for and were safely in their nest. As far as he was concerned, the Watergate was as good as in lockdown mode. Snowden had assured him every single exit was manned, the garages covered, and, unless Bonnie and Clyde had wings, they weren't going anywhere.

Charles realized then that he was talking to Murphy and Grady, who surprisingly looked interested in what he was saying. "I think we deserve a break and a treat, gentlemen. Let's take a walk; I have some bacon strips."

Both dogs barked their approval as they trotted to the door, where they knew Charles would not only walk them but would throw a ball for Murphy and a stick for Grady.

The warm summer day wrapped its arms around Charles when the old-fashioned screen door closed behind him. The golden sun immediately warmed him all over as he walked to the bench under a giant hemlock tree, where he liked to sit late at night to contemplate life. Today, though, he wasn't contemplating his life; he was trying to figure out how Bonnie and Clyde would evade his people. He was certain they would get out one way or the other.

Chapter 16

Huffing and puffing, Myra looked at Annie, and said, "I can't keep walking these halls any longer. There has been absolutely no activity. It's like no one lives on this floor, and I can't believe this building is so acoustically wonderful that all noise is blocked. These people work. In my opinion, Bonnie gave Charles's operatives the slip, and she's not anywhere near this floor."

Equally winded, Annie leaned up against a wall and took deep breaths. "I couldn't agree more. I say we head back to our apartment, all the girls should be there by now. *We* need to make a plan since this one doesn't seem to be working." Annie heaved herself away from the wall and was about to follow Myra when the door to the stairwell banged open. Both women almost jumped out of their skins.

"Ladies!" a man dressed in blue coveralls said

by way of a greeting. "I'm here at Mr. Snowden's request."

"Oh!" Myra and Annie said as one. "We were just leaving."

"Not yet, I need your help." He handed each of them a clipboard and pens. "This," he said, holding up a square box, "is a heat sensor. It will detect the presence of humans, even animals, in these apartments. We'll know soon enough if our subject is inside hiding. The only exits to these apartments are the doors to the hall.

"This is what I'm going to do. I'll flash this, get a reading, and if it registers heat, we'll knock on the door, and I'll say I'm going to be spraying for bugs tomorrow, and we want to be sure the tenants don't have any allergies. You two will be making fake notes on your clipboards. Are you ready?"

Annie shrugged. "It sounds like a plan. Actually, a pretty good one," she said grudgingly. Myra nodded.

An hour later, Avery's man called a halt. "Okay, we have human occupancy in five apartments. "I don't want either of you doing any talking, let me do it all."

"What's your name?" Annie asked as the man pressed the first doorbell. It chimed inside, a five-note melody.

"That's NTK, ma'am."

"Need to know, my ass," Annie hissed into Myra's ear. "Who does he think we're going to tell?"

The door to the apartment opened and a nurse

in a white uniform looked at them inquiringly. She was middle-aged and had a no-nonsense look to her. "Yes?"

The NTK man went into his spiel.

"It's not a problem," the nurse said. "Mr. Donahue has no known allergies, and I don't either. Spray away."

Annie and Myra made check marks on their clipboards. They moved on.

An hour later they all knew the birds had flown the coop, if they had even been there to begin with.

"Now what?" Annie asked.

"Now we separate. You never met me. I never met you. This floor is secure. Good-bye, ladies."

"He's watched too many spy movies," Annie said as she and Myra headed for the elevator.

The other Sisters clustered around Annie and Myra the minute the door closed behind the two women. "Talk to us," they all babbled at once.

"James Bond II is on his way to wherever he goes after a mission. Whatever-her-name-is got away," Myra said. "We aren't sure she was even headed for the sixth floor to begin with. All Charles's operative saw with his binoculars was her pressing the number 6 on the elevator. She could have gotten out and walked to any floor. This was a big to-do over nothing."

"So what do we do now?" Alexis asked.

"I say we eat something," Kathryn said.

"That sounds like a plan," Nikki said. "Breakfast will be right up. Someone call Maggie and see what's going on at her end. Isabelle, check in with Lizzie, and, Myra, call the mountain to see what Charles wants us to do."

Maggie looked at her star reporter and photographer. "I can tell by looking at both of you that neither one of you has anything that's going to make my blood sing. Why is that, gentlemen?"

"Not so fast, Miss EIC, we do have something. We just don't know what it is we have," Ted said.

"No riddles. Either you have something, or you don't. Do not tease me, I am not in the mood to be teased. Talk to me."

"You told me to go to the Watergate, so I went. Espinosa got there five minutes after me. We saw Harry Wong roar up on his Ducati, then off he went like a bat out of hell, and he didn't even see us. That has to mean he saw something we didn't see and took off. The only thing is, there was nothing going on. Espinosa took some pictures, but it's going to turn out to be traffic, pedestrians, and not much else."

"Did either one of you think—mind you, I said *think*—to call Harry to ask him what was going on and what *he* might have seen?"

"Well, yeah, Maggie, I did, but Wong didn't answer his phone. I think the guy is acting independently, which is not good. Everyone knows Harry Wong is like a one-man army."

"Jack always seems to know what Harry's up to. Did you try calling him?"

"I did, but the call went straight to voice mail. He's probably in court, so I left a message for him to call either you or me."

"So we have nothing more on the original fraud victims other than that two of them have died of natural causes since we ran our last series. It's a damn good thing that, despite all your whining, I had you two go out and follow up on that foster care angle. Here's something else on that you might be interested in, gentlemen."

Maggie proceeded to tell them what Lizzie had learned from Cosmo about Chase's discovery when it hired a forensic CPA to conduct an audit of the fraudulent credit cards opened by their "law student" employee.

When she had finished, Ted grinned sheepishly. "Okay, we are properly humbled, Madam EIC. What do you want us to do now?"

"Espinosa, let me see those pictures you took. Ted, keep trying to reach Jack and Harry."

Espinosa handed over his camera.

"Load them onto my computer so I can print them out. I want you both to go back to the Watergate and stay there until I tell you otherwise. Check in with the girls. They might have some info for you. They're in Apartment 809. Go!"

Maggie sat in front of her computer, staring at the pictures Espinosa had taken earlier. Nothing. Life in Washington early in the morning. People. Cars. Traffic. A dog walker, a woman pushing a stroller, an elderly lady shuffling along with a pull-along grocery cart. An ambulance going by. Four young girls, their arms linked, laughing. A group of pigeons clustered at the curb. What? What had Harry Wong seen? Frustrated, Maggie threw her hands in the air but not before she sent the pictures off to Charles. Then she hit the SEND button again, and they were off to Nikki and Lizzie. Maybe one or the other of them would see something she wasn't seeing.

Jack Emery pulled into the skinny driveway that led to the back of Harry's *dojo*. He blinked when he saw that the Ducati was gone. He looked down at his watch. He was right on time. Where the hell was his friend? He let himself in through the broken door and started yelling for Harry. He whipped out his phone and hit the speed dial. "C'mon, c'mon, Harry, answer the damn phone." He was about to hang up when he heard what he thought was Harry's voice. "Harry, izzat you? Where the hell are you? I'm here at the *dojo*. You were supposed to be here, Harry. You are not here, Harry!"

"I know I'm not there, Jack. I'm here. You on foot, or do you have your car?"

"I drove. Judge Dumas has a medical appointment this afternoon, so I'm off. Where the hell are you, Harry?"

"Get in the car and come here, 1454 Monarch Street. I followed the chick from the Watergate, and this is where she came. I'm waiting to see if her partner shows up. It's in Mt. Pleasant, Jack. Just get here. I called some of my guys; we need surveillance here."

Jack was already backing his car out of the skinny driveway. He debated all of one second before he reached down for the strobe and slammed it on the roof of his car. He cranked the siren, the sound splitting the air as the red-and-blue strobe warned drivers to pull to the side. One eye on the road, the other on the navigation system, Jack roared down the road, marveling at how the drivers of other vehicles moved out of the way. He loved every minute of it.

Three blocks from Harry's stakeout point, Jack cut the siren, yanked the strobe off the roof of the car, and tossed it under his seat. He pulled to a curb a block from where Harry said he would be. It was obvious that Harry wasn't budging from his parking spot, which meant Jack had to get out of the car and walk back to where Harry sat straddling the Ducati.

"You want to tell me what the hell you're doing here, Harry? Why didn't you call me?"

"Because you were in court, and I did leave a voice mail. Didn't you get it?"

"I guess I should have asked what the hell you were doing at the Watergate. I told you to stay away from there. You cannot act independently on this. I told you that, too."

"Listen up, Jack. It's a damn good thing I didn't follow your orders. And I just *went* there. I wasn't going to do anything. It made me fucking nuts

to know those skunks were hiding out in there
after what they did to me and thousands of other
people. Screw Charles and that Chinese fire drill
he has going on. They got away. Somehow or
other, one of those professionals spooked them,
and they bugged out. I followed the woman, and
here I am. I have two of my guys in the back.
There's an alley behind the houses and a row of
garages. The guy hasn't showed up yet, but he
will. I think we need a few more guys. What do
you think? Actually, it doesn't matter what you
think since they're on the way."

Jack didn't know what he thought. "How do
you know you followed the right person?"

"Read my lips, Jack. I-do-not-make-mistakes.
I-have-the-eyes-of-an-eagle."

"*Okayyyyy*. But who did you recognize?"

"I really studied those pictures Maggie sent
us. I memorized every detail. I studied them for
hours because those people ruined my life."

"Okay, I'll give you that one. But how did you
nail the woman?"

"She was pushing a baby stroller. She herself
looked a little different, bulked up in sweats,
but because I have the eyes of an eagle, I could
see that it wasn't a real baby in the damn
stroller. Then she dumped it in an alley and
took off running. After that, she swooped to the
curb and grabbed a cab. She had a diaper bag
over her shoulder. It had little yellow ducks all
over it."

"I'm impressed, Harry."

"And well you should be."

"How come you didn't call Charles to ask for some of Snowden's people to help out?"

"Because . . . Jack . . . Snowden's people are the ones who blew it."

"Okay, that's a good point. So who's coming?"

"My guys. These people are not going to get away again."

Jack shuddered. He'd seen Harry's guys in action. Skinny little guys with fifth-degree black belts. There was never enough left for identification after a melee.

"You wanna do lunch, Harry? Then we should go to the Watergate and tell the girls we have the situation in hand. Yoko is going to be so proud of you."

"What's that *we* stuff?"

"Don't worry, I'll make sure you get all the credit. Harry, I really hate to ask you this, but how sure are you that the woman's partner is going to show up?"

Harry tilted his head to the side and stared at Jack. He didn't say a word.

"Yeah, yeah, I take that to mean you're damn sure. Okay, so we're waiting for your guys, who, I assume, know what to do when they get here. Do you think by any chance you and I might both be blowing this gig by standing here talking? Well, actually, I'm standing, and you're sitting. Do you not think this is just a little suspicious?"

"Take a look around you, Jack. This is a mind-your-own-business neighborhood. I could be slitting your throat, and no one would come to your aid. People in this neighborhood *lurk*. We're lurking. I'm not leaving here till the guy shows up."

"Which guy, Harry?"

"The dog walker."

"You're that sure, huh?"

"Do birds fly, Jack?" Suddenly he looked down at the wide mirror on the right side of the Ducati. "Here he comes, and he's still got the dog. Light a cigarette or something, but don't look. Pretend you're new to the hood, and try to look slick."

Try to look slick. "Kiss my ass, Harry." Jack fumbled in the pocket of his sweatpants for the cigarettes he always carried but smoked only when under acute stress.

Across the street, a fight broke out with loud yelling and cursing. The dog walker was the only one who didn't pay attention. The fight carried out to the middle of the road just as the dog walker approached the six steps that led up to a decrepit front porch.

"Okay, Jack, let's do lunch now."

"Huh?"

"Squire's Pub, and you're buying," Harry said as he roared down the road without a backward glance.

Jack turned around to see how the fight was progressing, then it dawned on him. "Fight, my ass. Harry's guys on the job."

He felt like a fool as he trotted to his car and climbed in. Just for spite Jack put the strobe on the roof but didn't turn on the siren until he caught up with Harry. He laughed himself silly when Harry pulled to the side. He laughed harder when he saw Harry offer up a single-digit salute.

Apartment 809 was crowded to capacity when Harry and Jack arrived two hours later. The Sisters listened in awe, their jaws dropping as Jack praised Harry to the hilt.

Annie ushered everyone to the dining room, where she served coffee and pastries that no one wanted.

The moment everyone was updated, Myra looked around the table and voiced the question they had avoided until then. "Does Charles know?"

"We can't blame Charles or Snowden's operatives," Nikki said. "Something spooked the woman. It's that simple. Besides, we're not here to bash Charles, so let's move beyond that. Harry was in the right place at the right time, which works for us. We all know that what can go wrong will go wrong. What we have to decide is what we do next. I can't believe those two are going to stay in that house for any length of time. They're going to move soon. That's a given."

"Maggie's first headline about identity theft hits the street tomorrow. If they see it, they might spook quicker," Ted said.

Espinosa mumbled something about pictures he'd uploaded onto Maggie's computer. His eyes were on Alexis, who was smiling and winking at him.

"They're good for three days," Harry said.

No one questioned the authority in Harry's voice.

"Then that means we have three days to reel them in. Why wait? Why don't we just do it now?" Kathryn asked. "Too many things can go wrong the longer we wait. Harry said they're good to hold out for three days. That doesn't mean they'll wait the whole three days. For all we know, they could be planning their escape as we sit here hashing this out. I think we should take a vote whether to wait or not to wait."

"Maggie's not ready. Her special edition doesn't hit until tomorrow," Ted said as he looked over at Harry.

Suddenly, cell phones rang, one after the other.

"It's Maggie."

"It's Lizzie."

"It's Charles."

Harry looked down at his cell phone, and said, "Oh, shit!"

Chapter 17

The inside of the house on Monarch Avenue was empty of furniture, with the exception of two kitchen stools buttressed up against a counter whose ceramic top was cracked and pitted. There were no appliances, and the water and electricity had been turned off months ago.

The lease on the property testified to the fact that Edgar and Anna Penn had paid for a whole year's lease with the intention of refurbishing the property if the owner would cut them a deal on a possible sale—something the owner had readily agreed to.

The Monarch property was little more than a way station for the two occupants who were staring out the window at the fight going on across the street. While the man watched the fight move onto the road, the woman watched the thin man on the motorcycle and his companion, who was puffing on a cigarette.

His eyes still on the ongoing fight, the man said, "I know the guy on the cycle. Do you remember when I did the pay-per-view of the martial arts exhibition in Las Vegas a while back?" The woman nodded. "He's the number-two expert in the world. Do you think it's strange that he's right outside this house?"

The woman nodded again. The little dog he'd brought with him barked, then lay down on the filthy floor and went to sleep.

"The men scrapping with each other are of Asian descent, like the man on the cycle."

The woman looked up at him. He was so detached about everything. With what was going on outside, he sounded like he was discussing preparations for an evening at home with his friends. Nothing fazed him. Nothing. She, on the other hand, was a worrier; she even had a set of worry beads. "We need to leave *now*. What about the dog? We can't leave the animal here."

"I'm going to call a messenger service to pick him up and take him back to his owner. I'm not heartless."

Yes you are, she wanted to say but didn't. "They're too close. We've always had ample warning before. What are you waiting for? Do you want them to come up and knock on the door?"

"You worry too much, honey. When you rush, you make mistakes, and that's when things go wrong. I do not make mistakes. Aren't you the one who drilled into my head at the beginning that we had to have foolproof contingency plans in place due to your paranoia? At the risk of repeating myself, this was all your idea."

Honey. The days when that term of endearment thrilled her were long gone. So was the passion, the adrenaline thrill. These days she hated the man standing next to her, but she feared him even more. She wished for a fairy godmother who would come and whisk her away to someplace safe. The urge to reach up and snatch the skin off his face was so strong, she had to clench her fists at her sides. She'd spoken, so now there was nothing she could do but wait.

She watched out of the corner of her eye as her partner whipped out his cell phone and made a call. She strained to hear his soft voice.

"Yes, it's a small live animal. The dog weighs about twelve pounds, his name is Stewart. He's to be taken to the Watergate Apartments, Apartment 1406. The owner's name is John Mulberry. I'll be paying cash. Please pick up a dog carrier, and I will pay your messenger when he gets here. I need the animal picked up immediately. Thirty-five minutes will be just fine. Thank you."

"We'll be on our way in precisely thirty-seven minutes. That's assuming the messenger is on time. Do you have our things?"

The woman pointed to the diaper bag with the yellow ducks on it. Within seconds, she had the contents out on the floor and the bag turned inside out. Now the diaper bag was a rich tartan

plaid. She adjusted the straps, added an exten-
der, and, voilà, the bag became a backpack. She
knew she could change her appearance in less
than five minutes. Her partner could do it in
three.

She paced as her partner continued to stare
out the filthy window.

"Here comes the messenger. Twenty-nine
minutes. I do like punctuality."

The man scooped up the little dog and
walked to the door. He had two hundred-dollar
bills in his hand when he handed over the dog
and waited until he was secure in the canvas carrier. "Take good care of him. His owner loves
him very much."

The messenger scribbled off a receipt and
handed it over. The man waited until the messenger was in his Jeep and halfway down the
street before closing and locking the door.

The woman peeled off her sweats to reveal
shorts and a tank top. Her blond hair was now
red and in a pixie cut. She wore wire-rim glasses
and dangling earrings. The man was now wearing running shorts and a sleeveless ragged T-shirt.
A bandanna was tied around his forehead. The
woman tossed him the tartan backpack. She
watched as he settled it comfortably on his shoulders. She herself had a small purse looped cross-
ways across her chest.

The man led the way to the kitchen and the
door that led to the cellar. It was cool and damp,
and strange scurrying noises came from all directions. With the aid of a small penlight, the

man led the way to a small window and pried it open. He helped the woman go through. Then, by standing on an empty wooden box, he followed her and settled the window back into place.

In the narrow space between their house and the one adjacent, which was no more than a foot and a half and smelled of dankness and moldy leaves, he pried open the cellar window next door and helped his partner through it. He knew for a fact the building housed a bunch of crackheads who would never venture into the cellar. Part of his contingency plan months ago had been this very drill. In the darkness, with the aid of the tiny light, he waited for his eyes to adjust to the contents of the cellar before they exited through yet another window.

They repeated the same process four more times. Finally, they came out of the back alley five houses away from their starting point. They moved off, apparently just a couple out for a midafternoon stroll. No one looked at them, no one called out. Totally ignored they walked a good mile before they found a cab.

Avery Snowden felt quite smug when he looked through his rearview mirror at the cluster of Asians slouched against a scraggly tree as he steered the Yellow Cab away from the curb. Silly amateurs!

Maggie Spritzer looked down at her littered desk and winced. If she didn't clean it off soon,

she'd have to relocate. She looked away just in
time to see Ted and Espinosa loping down the
hallway on their way to her office. The moment
both men skidded to a stop, she grinned from
ear to ear. "Tell me my headline isn't the work
of a genius."

Both men laughed.

"It is," Ted agreed.

"Things are working out just perfectly. I know
that a few hours ago, all of you were bumming
because Harry's guys lost those two snots. In a
way the reprieve was good for me because we
get the paper out, and, bam, even though they
think they got away, they aren't going anywhere."

"They're toast," Espinosa said. "Once the
paper hits the street, the whole world will be
watching for those two, and a disguise won't
make a difference. There's always someone who
will see through it."

"I like that you led off with the retired couple
from Alexandria who lost everything," Ted said,
"even their retirement because of those two.
The public is not going to like it that a seventy-
eight-year-old couple who were living comfortably, certainly not lavishly, are now being forced
to live in a one-bedroom furnished apartment
and count their pennies.

"Bringing in the foster kids whose credit had
been ruined years ago, when they were minors
and couldn't have possibly prevented it, also
worked. I'm glad that the interviews Joe and I
did with Antonio Vargas and Henry Workman

gave you so much to work with. You used their stories brilliantly.

"Which brings me to something I just heard on the news on the way over here."

"Whatever it is, tell me it isn't going to interfere in my series."

Ted bit down on his lower lip. "It could, Maggie, but not by tomorrow morning."

Maggie poked around on her desk to see if there was possibly a cookie or something under the piles of papers—anything edible she might have missed. "You going to make me pull it out of you or what? Why do you guys always have to rain on my parade?"

"Trust me, it's not intentional. What we heard is three brothers right here in our very own nation's capital bilked thousands and thousands of people, as well as some very large corporations and charitable foundations, out of huge amounts of money. Apparently, these brothers have been running a Ponzi scheme to the tune of tens of billions of dollars. That's billions with a *b*. All three brothers are considered A-list. What you have going on with the identity theft is small-time compared to that trio. Politicians, movie stars, union pension funds, university endowments—they showed no mercy. Small investors, big investors, they duped them all."

"Oh, God, I feel a headache coming on. You two want to run with this, is that it?"

"Yeah, we do. There's nothing more we can do with the others for now, we've pretty much come to a dead end on finding out who helped the dynamic duo with the foster-kid scams, but if something comes up, just squeal and we're there. You might want to . . . alert . . . the others. This is something they could really sink their teeth into if they have a mind to go into action."

"Who is it? Give me names." Maggie's mind started to race. She could do a dual headline, split the top page. This just might be the time to go with *color.* Red, like in a bloodbath.

Ted laughed. "The brothers Grimm. Adolpho, Vincenzi, and Eduardo. The Big Three of the financial world. The news is calling them The Munchkins. Last name originally Grimaldi but changed to Grimm twenty-five years ago so they wouldn't be confused with the Mafia Grimaldis. Can you chew on that one for a while?"

"Chew? Did you say *chew*? If this turns out to be what I think it might, then forget the chewing part. Let's just gobble those bastards up whole. Go!"

Maggie felt so gleeful, she forgot how hungry she was. How often did the gods of journalism smile twice in the same day? Where was she going to put all her Pulitzers? She needed to give serious thought to having some extra shelves built into her office. But she really didn't want to get ahead of herself.

A moment later she had her phone in hand as she called the Sisters to report in.

*   *   *

The temporary tenants in Apartment 809 at the Watergate were sitting around the dining room table grumbling among themselves. Harry looked so glum that Yoko was patting him on the shoulder and whispering soothing words of comfort.

"Stop being such a *nebbish,* Harry. Your people are warriors, not spies. You told them to watch and report in. You didn't tell them to break in or start World War III. I really don't see blame here. I say we should be thankful Snowden was on the scene and knows how this crap goes down. It's what he does for a living. We're just fringe players."

"Jack's right," Annie said. "As soon as Mr. Snowden reports in, we move. Are we all agreed?"

Every hand in the room shot upward.

Myra twirled her chair around, and said, "That was Maggie. She really had some interesting information. I'll get to that in a minute. She wants us to turn on the computer. She sent us a mock-up of the morning paper. She said—and this is a direct quote—'I hope you all pee in your pants when you see it.' End of quote."

The group got up as one and ran to the bedroom, where Nikki booted up the computer.

"Would you look at that!" Kathryn marveled.

Nine pairs of eyes stared at the bold black headline that read:

DO YOU KNOW WHERE SARA
BRICKMAN AND DENNIS CARSON ARE?

Underneath the headline it read:

If the answer is no, do you know people
with the following names? Those are among
the aliases Brickman and Carson used in
their identity theft of thousands of people,
possibly people only you, *Post* readers, can
identify.

"Check that out!" Nikki said. "Six columns
straight across the page and above the fold. The
Post's switchboard is going to blow up when
the paper hits the street. You know there are
people out there who knew those two under
one of the aliases they used. Good God, there must
be close to four hundred names there! The AP
will pick it up, and the whole East Coast will be
on red alert. Maggie kept her word and thanked
Damon Finn of Chase for his invaluable help
when the *Post* called upon him. This is beyond
clever!"

Jack poked Harry in the arm. "See! I told you
that you weren't the only one whose identity was
stolen. None of them were as lucky as you either."

"Wow! A double headline," Isabelle said as
she pointed a finger at the dark lettering under
the fold that said simply:

THE BOTTOM LINE
$100,000,000

Under the second headline there were pictures of some of the identity theft victims, in-

cluding two whose identities had been stolen when they were minors in foster care, and alongside those pictures were pictures Espinosa had taken of Brickman and Carson, as well as pictures Ted had gotten of them from various bank's archives. Pages two and three carried more pictures of the victims and the various stories of how their lives had changed since their identities were stolen.

"I'm so glad I bought that newspaper and hired Maggie. She's been doing a masterful job," Annie chortled.

When the little group trooped back to the dining room, Yoko held Jack back and whispered in his ear, "Jack, how could you do that to Harry? The pink bathroom, bedspread, rugs, towels? I *hate* pink. So much for what you know about women."

"I wish Charles would call so we know what the next step is," Kathryn said.

"Patience is its own reward," Myra said. "Now, do you want to hear what else Maggie told me? I'm thinking we might want to get involved, but of course we would have to take a vote on it." When she had their undivided attention she said, "You've all heard of the Brothers Grimm, the financial gurus of Wall Street, right? Well, here's the poop on that . . ."

Chapter 18

Bert Navarro took the call personally, something he didn't normally do as director of the FBI.

"This particular call," his secretary said, "sounds ominous. The man says he's seen the vigilantes. Before you can ask, Mr. Director, the phone is a throwaway. The trace is saying it's the Crystal City area. I've kept him on the phone for a few minutes until we could complete it. If he knew what I was doing, he didn't give any indication. He is refusing to talk to anyone but you. I'll put him through now, sir."

"Navarro," Bert said briskly. "What can I do for you today, sir?"

"It's not what you can do for me, Mr. Director, it's what I can do for you." The voice lowered in tone to a soft whisper Bert had to strain to hear.

One of Harry Wong's *people.* Or, possibly one of Charles Martin's operatives. It had to be one or the other, he was sure of it. He leaned back into the soft leather of his chair and waited and listened to the voice coming over the wire.

"I saw two of the vigilantes in Crystal City! I don't want to tell the FBI how to do their business, but if I were you, I'd send a contingent of agents to check it out. I hate the way those damn women make fools of the fine institution of the FBI. So are you going to do something about it, Mr. Director?"

"I'll have my agents look into it, sir. Now, would you care to give me your name?"

"I prefer to remain anonymous at this time for purely personal reasons. You'll look into it, when? Later in the day, tomorrow, next week? Those women are like greased lightning. If they're here, something is going on. You snooze, you lose. Aren't you people at the Bureau tired of always being made fools of? You're as bad as the pathetic Secret Service agents those damn women hog-tied in a Dumpster out there in Kalorama. And then they went to the White House, brazen as hell, and nobody did anything. Where the hell are my tax dollars going these days? You people are pissing them away, that's where they're going, and I damn well don't like it."

"In other words, is it safe to say you're going against the females in your family—at this time?" Bert had to fight not to laugh out loud when he heard the man's response.

"Yeah, it would be safe to say that. I can see where I'm not making any headway with you, but you really need to take care of business, Mr. Director. I'm going to hang up and make some other calls now."

Bert did laugh then.

The game was on. He felt a small thrill of excitement when he buzzed his secretary and told her to put all calls through directly to him from any and all media.

Next he called in the two agents sitting outside his office, and simply said, "We have another vigilante sighting in the Crystal City Underground. Check it out and report back to me. I think it was just some ticked-off citizen mad at his wife for something, and he's acting out, but you never know. Those women are wily."

Joyce Hart, Fox 5's evening news anchor, picked up her extension a mere five minutes after Bert Navarro's anonymous caller hung up. She listened to the rapid-fire explanation of the call, her jaw dropping.

"How sure are you? Which vigilantes? Can you describe them? How do I know you aren't some dumb schmuck who wants his fifteen minutes of fame? You do have a point, they're world-famous, and they do have unforgettable faces. What's your name? Yeah, right. Before I take my crew and go chasing over to the Crystal

City Underground, I'm going to need a little more information. Just so you know, I don't pay for information. Who else did you call? If you say no one, then it becomes an exclusive and maybe we can talk about some kind of monetary remuneration. What do you mean you called the FBI first? What am I, chopped liver? I don't much care if you like my attitude or not, and I don't care if you *think* you're doing your civic duty or not. I think you're calling because the females in your personal life have stood up to you, and the vigilantes somehow, some way, have made your life miserable. Good-bye, whoever you are."

Hart broke the connection, snapped off her recorder, then dialed the offices of the FBI, where she identified herself and asked to speak to the director. She was surprised that she was put through immediately. She got right to the point, and then asked, "Can you give me a comment, Mr. Director?"

Bert clucked his tongue, but he was smiling from ear to ear. "Miss Hart, you know we don't make comments to the media. I will say, however, that we field thousands of calls a day, most of them anonymous. Have a nice day, Miss Hart."

On Big Pine Mountain, Charles Martin did his best to wade through the tsunami of intel that was coming in via e-mails, faxes, and cell phone calls. This was what he loved, the second-by-second coordination of all the minutiae, pickups, drop-offs, drop zones, and transportation by either air, land, or sea, and sometimes even by bicycle or horseback. He allowed himself a visual of Harry Wong on horseback, which made him laugh out loud.

His fingers were like magic, his eyes sharper than an eagle's as he scanned the faxes that kept shooting out in all directions. He'd always excelled at multitasking, and that trait was working overtime. His words were bullet-fast when he spoke to Avery Snowden. "Everything is in place. Do it! Good work, Avery."

Charles pressed a number, and Annie picked up. "Go!"

The activity or lack thereof in Apartment 809 in the Watergate accelerated to beehive speed.

Jack and Harry were the first to leave. "We can get there faster on the Ducati, Jack. It's up to you if you want to take your car. Those people must really be stupid. They split, and now they're going running at the Tidal Basin. How dumb is that?"

"No, they're smart, they have to be somewhere until it gets dark. What better place to blend in until nightfall?"

Five minutes later, Harry sprinted over to his motorcycle, and asked, "What exactly is our role in this?"

Jack climbed on the back of the Ducati, plopped his helmet on his head, and asked, "What the hell are you waiting for, Harry? Charles said to *go*. We're just sitting here. Oh, you want to know what our role is. We pick up two hypodermic syringes from the guy at the Sno-Cone machine and pass them on to the girls when we spot them. Now, go!"

The Ducati shot forward and hit a speed bump. Jack cursed. "You did that on purpose, you terrorist. Now I have whiplash."

Harry ignored him as he gunned the powerful machine. Jack hung on for dear life.

"I have a gun, Harry. I just want you to know that."

"Black belt warriors have no need of guns. Obviously you aren't as good as you think you are."

"Yeah, well I'm an officer of the court and as such am authorized to carry."

"Where is it?"

"What do you care?" Jack shot back. "In my pants, if you must know."

"Front or back?"

"If it's that important for you to know, the front. My shirt covers it. Why?"

"Because when I hit the next speed bump, I don't want you shooting your dick off."

"The only thing you have to worry about is me shooting you in the ass if you hit a speed bump, so I hope that explains why the gun is in front."

Harry's response was to bend low over the handlebars. Jack did the same. He didn't think it was possible for Harry to drive any faster than he already was, but they now seemed to be *flying*. Jack held on, the July heat searing his face. He was so light-headed when Harry finally came to a stop that he had to hold on to the Ducati until his equilibrium returned to normal.

"Wuss."

"Eat it, Harry, and remember I have a gun."

"I'd be worried if you could hit the broadside of a barn, but you can't."

"And your point is?" Not bothering to wait for a response, he added, "That's why you have to be worried. Eventually, I'll hit something. Look around, what do you see?"

"People," Harry snapped. "Lots of people. Some are jogging, some are running. Some are sitting under the trees eating. I see the vendor's cart. I don't see the girls. I also don't see our quarry. Do you see any of Snowden's people?"

Jack shifted his sunglasses. "I don't see anyone I know. Jesus, you don't think this was a dry run, do you? It would be just like Snowden to pull something like that."

"Why?" Harry asked, his gaze sweeping the crowds of people.

"Because you attempted to usurp his authority by having your people out there on Monarch. In case you haven't figured it out, Harry, Snowden is very territorial. And he's afraid of you, you terrorist, you."

Harry took his gaze away from the crowds to look at Jack in disbelief. "Do you really believe that?"

"Nah. But you have to admit, it sounded good. C'mon, we need to pick up those syringes. The girls should be arriving shortly. You know Charles, everything is synchronized down to the last second. Move it, Harry!"

"Shit, Jack! Look at that line!"

"I have the magic bullet, Harry." Jack held up a crisp hundred-dollar bill and waved it in front of Harry's face.

"And when those sweaty people standing in line attack you for trying to cut ahead of them, what are you going to do?"

"I'm going to let you take care of them. Strawberry or blueberry? We have to make it look good. The third one will have the syringes in it. Oh, I'm supposed to say I'm picking up the senator's Sno-Cones. That's my ID."

"How stupid is that? Snowden, right?"

Jack laughed. "Yeah. I think he saw the same episode of *Law & Order* that I did.

"If he acts up, I can always shoot him in the ass instead of you. Now do you feel better?"

Harry looked at Jack and smiled. "You know what, Jack, that does make me feel better. I'm seeing the silly side to you, and I actually like it."

Jack moved away. Harry never complimented anyone. "Oh, goodie, we're here!" Walking up to the front of the line, Jack asked the vendor, "Hey, buddy, you got the strawberry, blueberry, and the surprise-him-with-the-third-one the senator wants? He said he called ahead."

Disgruntled sweaty runners started to mumble among themselves.

"Hey, cool it, dudes. The senator said your cones are on him." Jack whipped out a fifty-dollar bill and handed it to the first guy in line. "Be honest," he warned.

Harry reached for the cones. Jack steered him away. "The strawberry is mine. Hey, look, there's Nikki." He moved forward and handed over the cardboard carton. "It's in the one that looks like banana." He moved off.

"Where's mine, Jack?"

"They didn't have tofu or that shitty green-tea flavor. You want a lick of mine?" A second later the Sno-Cone was in Jack's eyes, up his nose, and trickling down his cheeks."

"Now I really am going to shoot your ass off, Harry Wong."

"You're going to have to postpone that. I see one of Snowden's people. See that guy in the purple shorts, the one with the high-and-tight haircut? He's at three o'clock. I can't be sure of this, but I think our quarry is at eleven o'clock, and they appear to be eating a packaged lunch. Hot dogs would be my guess."

"Then we go counterclockwise, so we're behind the quarry. Are they looking around or are they eating or pretending to eat?"

"They're having an intense conversation, and, no, they aren't paying attention to the runners or joggers or the food. This is just a guess, but from what I can see, it looks like they're fighting."

"Let's get into position and wait to see how this plays out."

Across the Basin, Nikki Quinn and Kathryn Lucas did a few stretches and limbering-up exercises before they jogged off.

"First lap will tell us what's going on. We can always stop and wait to see if they get up or if they just keep sitting there," Kathryn said. "If they stick with the picnic scene, we're going to have a problem. I wish the others were here."

"There was nothing for Annie and Myra to do. Besides, it's too hot out here for them. And they have to be available to take the deliveries Charles has arranged. Yoko and Isabelle are here somewhere, but not as a duo, just as single runners. Alexis is replenishing her Red Bag, and I think at the last minute Charles wanted her to go to the *Post*. I don't know why."

Kathryn chewed on her bottom lip. "Did anyone say what's in the hypodermics?"

Nikki laughed. "Just something to make them slow down. They'll suddenly feel lethargic. It will be hard for them to put one foot in front of the other. It should last about four hours. We'll be right there to help them out. Too much sun, not enough water. We don't have refills, if that means anything."

Kathryn shrugged. "It means nothing. A good left hook will take care of that situation.

What are they doing now? Where are the guys? Damn, I wish I could see better."

"Everyone is behind them. We're at two o'clock now. Uh-oh!"

"What? What!"

"Looks to me like a small band of hoodlums coming up fast. The backpack is just sitting there on the ground. The woman still has the purse around her neck, it's just a little one, no weight to it. The backpack looks like it's loaded and heavy. Jack and Harry see it, too. They're moving faster. Some runners are in between them. Faster, Kathryn!"

"Where's Snowden's guy?" Kathryn huffed.

"I don't know, can't see him."

And then it all went wrong.

Sweat dripping into her eyes, Nikki brushed at her forehead with the inside of her arm as the group of slovenly youths closed in on the couple. A second later they had the woman's purse and the backpack and were running like race-horses.

"What the hell? They're just sitting there? Now what?" Kathryn exploded.

"Of course they're just sitting there. If you were them, you'd be doing the same thing. Do you really think they're going to call the cops? I-don't-think-so!" Nikki said.

"Then why aren't they chasing those kids to get back their belongings? The guy looked pretty buff and in condition in the pictures we saw. Maybe there was nothing important in the bags. There were six of them against two. Mostly women runners ahead and behind. Maybe they thought no one would help them."

"Or, was it all a setup? Those hoodlums moved in, took the bag, and will return it at some point in time. Maybe they made us," Nikki said.

"What now?" Kathryn asked, skidding to a stop close to where Jack and Harry were standing mopping their faces with the tails of their shirts but close enough that she could converse with them. "Where's Snowden's guy?"

"Up ahead, the guy with the high-and-tight haircut. Says it was a setup."

Nikki felt like shouting that she'd called it, but she kept quiet. "Did any of his people take off after those hoods?"

"I think so, but you know Snowden's guys. Everything is NTK."

"Yeah, well, that's getting real old, real quick. We need to know what's going on," Nikki said.

No sooner were the words out of Nikki's mouth than her cell buzzed in her pocket. She mouthed the words, "It's Yoko and Isabelle." She listened, her jaw dropping, and then ended the call. "You guys are not going to believe this but those two ran after the hoods. Yoko took them all out. Isabelle said it only took her three intense minutes. They have the bags, and Isabelle called 911. They're on their way back to the Watergate."

"Holy shit!" Jack said.

Harry grinned from ear to ear.

Nikki looked at Kathryn.

Kathryn looked at Nikki.

Jack and Harry shrugged and moved off.

"Which one do you want, Kathryn?"

"I'll take the woman."

"Guess I have Mr. Charisma. Let's do it!"

Chapter 19

Nikki settled the billed cap a little lower on her forehead. Kathryn did the same thing. With their shorts and sneakers, their bodies dripping with sweat, they looked just like all the other runners and joggers. They slowed as they approached Bonnie and Clyde. Then, on the whispered count of three they were behind the couple, their hands pressed hard into the duo's shoulders.

"Well, hi there, Clyde!" Nikki said cheerfully. "Don't be foolish and make a move. Breathe shallowly, or I'll snap your neck. My partner will do the same to that lovely lady sitting next to you. I want you to sit really still so I can give you something."

When Bonnie moved her head, Kathryn gave her a swat and jabbed the syringe deep into her well-muscled arm.

The man ignored Nikki and looked up.

Nikki clamped her hands tightly over the man's ears. "I told you not to move." The syringe found its mark. "Anyone paying attention to us?"

"Doesn't look like it," Kathryn said, her gaze raking the runners and joggers.

She sat down and wrapped her arms around her knees. Nikki did the same thing.

"How you doing there, Clyde?" Nikki asked. "Remember that Gumbi doll you had when you were a kid? Well, that's how you're going to feel for a good long while."

"Who . . . what . . . ?"

"Need to know, big guy," Kathryn said as she kept scanning the runners and joggers.

"Vigi . . . vig . . ." Bonnie bleated.

Nikki laughed as she said, "Viti, vigi, vegi," referring to an old *I Love Lucy* segment, her very favorite. "Well, you got it half-right. Isn't it great, Kathryn, that these *skanks* recognize us as the infamous vigilantes?"

"Yeah, just great," Kathryn said. Her gaze never left the Basin. "No one is paying attention."

"We still need to wait a little while. Some of those runners are going to do a second lap. We want to appear the same as when they did the first lap, just four friends enjoying a picnic on a hot July afternoon." Nikki scooted around until she was facing the dopey-looking pair. "Thought you were smart with that little heist a while ago, huh? Just so you know, it didn't work."

Clyde tried to hold his head up, but he was fighting a losing battle.

"Look alive, you two! Well, *try* to look alive. Over there, past the Sno-Cone guy and through that stand of cherry trees. I see cops! I see six kids being handcuffed. I can't see that plaid bag or that itty-bitty purse that was hanging around your neck. You know why I can't see them?" Kathryn singsonged. "Our partners have them. And now we have you, and the police have those kids. My questions would be: Where did these two make contact? And are those kids going to point us out? Oh, yeah, they're all looking at us as I speak. Think, Nikki! Quick! Those cops are going to split up and be here before you know it. Where the hell are Snowden's people?"

Nikki looked around, her eyes desperate behind her dark glasses. The only word that screamed in her mind was "diversion." But who was going to create it?

"Do you see what I'm seeing?" Kathryn hissed.

"Oh, yeah," Nikki hissed in return as she stared across the Basin at Alexis, Joe Espinosa, and Maggie Spritzer. "How long do you think we have?"

"Depends on whether we have to drag these two or they can walk. We're going to need some help. I'm thinking."

"C'mon, Clyde, up and at 'em. If you aren't on your feet in two seconds, I'm going to shove this needle up your ass so far you're going to think you're at a proctologist's," Nikki said.

Clyde was on his feet, wobbly but upright. He

stumbled, and suddenly Nikki saw a tall, bronzed man was beside her, reaching down to help him to his feet.

"Follow me, ma'am."

Before Nikki could blink, the muscled giant had Clyde over his shoulder and was so far ahead of them Nikki had to double-time it to catch up. Bonnie received the same treatment from the giant's twin. Kathryn raced to keep up.

"I saw a movie once where two Navy SEAL guys carried a telephone pole on their shoulders. Kathryn, do you think . . . ?"

"Yeah, I think, but who cares? I sure as hell hope those two guys belong to Snowden," Kathryn gasped. "Can you see Alexis?"

"Yeah, they're all running this way. How long do you think we have?"

"That bus left, Nikki. We're out of time. Damn, I thought I was in shape. It's the heat, we aren't used to it. We need to split up once we get past the Sno-Cone guy."

"Right. Sun's going to go down soon. Clouds moving in. Rain, maybe." Nikki gasped again as she swiped at the sweat pooling on her neck. "This is where we split. I'll see you when I see you, Kathryn."

Nikki looked up once in her haste to get away. She loved how the Basin was surrounded by the Jefferson Memorial and the Franklin Delano Roosevelt Memorial. The 107 acres were a vision of beauty in the spring. How many times she and Jack had come here during their courtship. She had a favorite picture of the two of them surrounded by the cherry blossom branches that Jack had asked some tourist to take. It was her most treasured belonging.

Tears stung her eyes and mixed with the sweat that was rolling down her face. *Don't think, just run. Run like the Devil is on your heels. Don't look back, just run.* She was on Fifteenth Street, certain she wasn't going to make it to Raoul Wallenberg Place, where she felt she would be safe, when she heard a shout directed at her. "Hey, good lookin', you want a ride?"

Damn straight she wanted a ride, but not with some derelict on a motorbike. She looked up at the lone rider and almost fainted.

"If you slow down, I'll be happy to climb on. God, Jack, another minute, and I was going to lose it. How'd you know I . . . ?"

"Gut instinct. Hold on. Can you reach the helmet? Try, Nik. We can't risk getting pulled over now. Harry's going to report his bike stolen any minute, if he hasn't already."

"Oh, my God, you stole Harry's Ducati! This bike is his most prized possession next to Yoko, not that Yoko is a possession. You know what I mean," Nikki gasped as she settled herself on the back of the cycle.

"Yeah, but don't worry, I have a gun. Hang on!"

"Everyone knows Harry can stop a bullet in midair with two fingers. I know you can't shoot worth a damn. You're going to have to do better than that, Jack."

Within minutes, Jack weaved the Ducati into

and out of almost bumper-to-bumper traffic. Horns blared, curses following him through open car windows. He ignored it all as he barreled his way around corners and down side streets until he hit Independence Avenue.

Twenty minutes later, he slowed and cruised Virginia Avenue. "I'm going to drop you off here, Nik. You only have three blocks to go. You can hoof it, right?"

"Sure. No problem." Nikki leaned over and kissed Jack so hard he thought he was going to black out. "That's for loving me as much as I love you."

His head spinning, Jack managed to get out a garbled sentence, which was, "Call Harry and tell him I have his bike." His eyes glazed over, he managed to return the kiss Nikki blew in his direction before she sprinted down Virginia Avenue. He waited a minute to see if anyone was paying attention to her or if she had a tail. When he was sure she was in the clear, he maneuvered the Ducati back into traffic.

Nikki was heading for the main door of the Watergate when a young woman came up alongside her. She, too, had been jogging.

"I haven't seen you around here. You new to the building?" she asked Nikki.

A warning bell went off inside Nikki's head. "I'm just visiting my two aunts. Actually, I'm heading back to New Hampshire in the morning. How do you stand this awful heat?" Was the woman staring at her a little too carefully? Yes, she was, Nikki decided. She knew instinctively she had to get away from her.

"You get used to it. How do you stand those winters in New Hampshire?"

"You get used to it. No state tax in New Hampshire, that's an incentive." Nikki couldn't be sure, but she thought she saw something flicker, some sign of recognition.

Nikki was the first one in the elevator. "What floor?"

"Seventeen." The woman removed her sunglasses and stepped sideways to get a better look at Nikki. At least that was Nikki's first thought. Nikki kept her glasses on and stared ahead as she pressed the button that would let her off at the fourth floor.

"You look familiar," the woman said. Her tone was now different, not exactly suspicious but different from the casual repartee they'd been having.

Nikki's heartbeat quickened. "People say that all the time. I do soap commercials. Maybe that's where you've seen me. Ah, here's my floor. Nice talking to you."

"Hey, what apartment are you in? I'm always looking for a running partner. I'm in 1706. If you ever come back, just knock on my door."

Nikki waved airily. "Nice to know. Seventeen oh six, I'll remember that." She was out the door before the woman could ask again for her apartment number.

Nikki immediately ran down the hall to the

red EXIT sign. She galloped up the four flights of stairs to the eighth floor. She almost jumped out of her skin when she saw Kathryn sitting on the top step.

"Something's wrong with me, Nikki. I can't move."

"You need water. So do I. Just sit here, I'll be right back."

"Like I'm really going to go somewhere. If John Law shows up in the next few minutes, I'm done for."

Nikki was back within minutes, her arms full. "Drink the water first, then the Gatorade." She followed her own instructions as she sat down next to Kathryn and swigged until both bottles were empty.

"What's going on?" Kathryn asked.

"Myra and Annie are holding the fort. Annie said Charles called and said his people will be delivering a package once it gets dark. I take that to mean Bonnie and Clyde. No one else is here yet." She went on to explain how Jack had found her and brought her home. "I was ready to cave, Kathryn. How did you make it here on your own?"

"Honest to God, Nikki, I don't know. I just kept pushing. My blisters have blisters. I'm afraid to take off my sneakers and socks. Fear is my only answer."

"Some woman got a little too close to me when I hit the front door of our building. I had to ride the elevator with her. I got off on the fourth floor and walked up the other four. We need to get out of here. Listen, we both made it, that's the good thing. Come on, I'll help you. A shower and a few more bottles of water, and you'll be good as new."

"I feel like such a . . . wuss. I really thought I was in good shape, Nikki."

"Like you said, it's the heat. We trained on a mountain where the air is cool. You are in good shape, so don't go berating yourself."

"I feel like a bag of wet noodles."

"I feel the same way you do. Myra and Annie have news. Wait till you see it."

"I don't want to see anything but the shower," Kathryn said as she hobbled behind Nikki to Apartment 809, where Myra and Annie were waiting in the open doorway. "What?" she asked, curiosity getting the best of her.

Nikki pointed to the television. "Seems someone said they saw the vigilantes at the Crystal City Underground. They have it staked out— FBI, the locals, and media. That anchor, Joyce Hart, is saying the vigilantes are vain and have egos bigger than the Washington Monument, and she's staying till we show ourselves."

Kathryn started to laugh and couldn't stop as she stumbled toward the bathroom.

Annie hurried after her as she voiced motherly concerns. "What's that noise? I hope the air-conditioning isn't going to go out on us. I'll die if that happens." Annie laughed.

"Will she be okay, Nikki?" Myra asked.

"Yes, some more water and Gatorade, some food, she'll be fine. The shower is going to help. When Yoko gets here, she might give her a massage of sorts. She'll be the old Kathryn by morning. What's that noise? Oh, who cares?"

Myra smiled. "What about you, dear?"

"I got my second wind, Mummie. I'll be okay. I'm going to take a shower now. Do you think you could make us a BLT? Lots of tomatoes, the bacon nice and crisp, soft, spongy bread, light on the mayo and lettuce but load on the bacon. Two glasses full of ice with orange Gatorade, and I'll be in heaven."

Myra practically swooned. She loved it when Nikki called her Mummie. Growing up, Barbara and Nikki had both called her Mummie. Tears blurred her vision as she made her way to the kitchen.

"Don't cry, Mummie. Nik will be okay. Remember she likes her bacon to the point where you can snap it in two."

"Darling girl, I wish I was making a BLT for you, too. God in Heaven, I miss you so. Do you know if . . . ?"

"Everyone is fine. Charles is busy. Actually, he is having the time of his life right now. He pulled it off. It was really a little dicey there for a while, but it all worked out. I know you are all upset with him, but you have to get over it. And, Mummie, he wants that tulip comforter back on the bed so badly he can taste it. It's time, Mummie."

Myra managed a weary smile as she laid strips of bacon into the fry pan. "Yes, I guess it is. I can't believe the time has come when the wheel has turned, and you're giving me advice. I feel like crying, darling girl."

"No tears, Mummie. I have to go now. Nik needs me. Love you."

"And I love you more than you can ever know, darling girl. If Nikki needs you, go to her."

Myra swiped at her tears. If only she could turn the clock back to the days when Barbara and Nikki were little girls. Innocent little girls with little-girl secrets. Sisters, but not blood sisters, who shared everything.

It all seemed like a lifetime ago. The bacon sizzled, bringing Myra back to the present. She wiped her eyes as she vowed to make these the biggest and the best BLTs Nikki and Kathryn ever had in their entire lives. She needed to pay attention to her blessings.

Charles Martin let his mind race. Why did Murphy's Law have to invade his territory just when things were running smoothly? First it was Snowden telling him about the unexpected young hoodlum invasion at the Tidal Basin. Then it was Isabelle calling to say she and Yoko had chased the boys and retrieved the bags that were now safe in Apartment 809 at the Watergate. Another call saying Bonnie and Clyde would be delivered under cover of darkness.

On top of that, a vigilante sighting at the Crystal City Underground to confuse things even more. And then Nikki calling to say she thought she had been spotted by another runner residing at the Watergate, and to check out

Apartment 1706, and don't let her get away. Seven phone calls later, four agents in place on the seventeenth floor and stairwell, and he was reasonably confident the woman was no threat to his girls. The worst-case scenario for the woman runner would be that her cell phone, her landline, and her computer would be inoperable for a while until his girls were on their way to safety. If necessary, he had an agent standing by who would make the elevator just as inoperable.

Charles looked up at the large-screen monitor. He moved Lady Justice and brought up a map of Washington. With his index finger he tapped area after area, each of which lit up with bright red dots. The red dots represented agents in place, the blue dots for agents on the move. For the Sisters, along with Jack and Harry, yellow dots. Now all the dots were blinking to show that everything was more or less under control. Four green dots, bigger than the others, indicated that the special merchandise the girls had ordered was in place.

Charles took a deep breath and let it out slowly before he moved back to his workstation. He looked down at his checklist.

Lizzie Fox. No problem there.

Maggie. No problem there either.

Ted and Espinosa. No problem and no need for their help at the present.

Jack and Harry. Always a problem. But problems that worked out, for some strange reason. He'd learned along the way to let them have

their heads and somehow work around what followed.

Charles moved on to the massiveness of the
identity theft ring. Until just a few hours ago,
he had been convinced that Bonnie and Clyde
were the second tier, with someone else heading
up their ring. He'd changed his mind when absolutely no other intel came his way. The intri-
cacies, the details boggled his mind. He thought
about how many people he'd had to use to keep
the vigilantes safe from harm. How Bonnie and
Clyde kept it together without making a mistake
was something he was never going to understand.

And they'd still be out there scamming people, stealing fortunes, and ruining lives if not
for Harry Wong and his aversion to opening his
mail. Harry was going to turn out to be a hero,
and he didn't even know it.

Maybe a surprise was in order for everyone.
He needed to make some brownie points with
the girls, and cooking a gourmet dinner on
their return wasn't going to do it.

Charles jerked around when the dogs at his
feet barked. He looked to see what had warranted
the alert. Then he smiled. It was the silence.
The fax machine was quiet. There were no *pings*
alerting him to incoming e-mails. The phones,
all nine of them, were quiet—even the two spe-
cially encrypted phones in his pockets, the ones
he was never without, were silent.

Silence to the dogs meant special time. A
run, a walk, some treats. Charles obliged as he

led the way out into the early evening. He inhaled deeply as he threw two sticks. The dogs raced after them. While he waited for their return, he sat down on the bench under the old hemlock tree. He fired up his pipe, puffed, then let his body relax. The dogs returned, panting but wanting more. He threw the sticks again.

In a truly relaxed state, Charles let his mind wander. What could he plan for his chicks? A surprise! A really wonderful surprise for them. And for himself as well. All he needed to do was work out the details.

The dogs returned. They'd had enough. They stood politely, waiting for the treats Charles carried in his pocket. Bacon-flavored chews that took a whole hour to gnaw down to nothing.

Charles puffed contentedly. Right then the world looked pretty darn good.

Chapter 20

It was four o'clock on the dot when Vinny Paloma was almost finished loading up the *Post*'s delivery truck with the morning edition of the paper. He'd been doing the same job for the past twenty-three years. Most times he liked what he did because he got to read the headlines before anyone else. Even though it was four o'clock, he had his route timed so well that he could take a good seven and a half minutes to scan the front page and sip the hot coffee he bought at the 7-Eleven around the corner. He loved routine, thrived on it.

Vinny settled himself in the cab of the truck the moment he loaded the last bundle of papers into the back. The first sip of the strong brew was always the best; almost like an aphrodisiac. He looked down at the paper in his hands, then reared back at what he was seeing in front of his very eyes. He didn't need to read the article, the headline was enough for him. Today he was going to be three minutes late on his route.

He hauled out the laptop he always carried with him and kept on the passenger seat of his truck, powered it up, and sent an e-mail to Dominic Russo, his wife's brother, who had been a victim of identity theft ten months ago. He knew his brother-in-law would send his e-mail to all 120 people in his address book, and those 120 people would send it to another 120 people, possibly more, possibly a little less, and on and on it would go around the country. Then he hit his own address book and knew for a fact he had close to 250 people listed—his bowling team, softball team, neighbors, relatives, the kids' friends' parents, the whole congregation at the church, and friends he'd met online.

Then, just for the pure hell of it, he went to eBay and sent an e-mail to a few sites where he'd bought items, asking the sellers to pass the word along that the *Post* was this close to bringing in the heads of the largest identity theft ring in the country.

He was about to close the laptop and get on with his workday when he thought about how he was forever sending e-mails to television shows. He checked a particular file and fired off e-mails to Joyce Hart, Joe Scarborough, Chris Matthews, Bill O'Reilly, and Nancy Grace. His wife, Ginny, loved Nancy Grace. Ginny always said if government had a dozen Nancy Graces in office, there would be no problems in the country. Come hell or high water, at eight o'clock every single night, his house went silent, and if a ball game was on, he had to go into the bedroom to watch it on their little twelve-inch screen while Ginny rooted for Nancy Grace and whatever cause she was pursuing.

Vinny looked down at his watch. He knew without a doubt that by six AM, maybe even five-thirty, his e-mails would be circling the country and being delivered at cyberspeed. The news would be carrying the story live. He wished he had someone he could make a bet with. If the vigilantes were in town, according to the dual headline, the scum would be behind bars within hours. Guaranteed.

Vinny started up his truck and backed away from the loading dock. He had a job to do, and he'd just gone beyond the call of duty. Maybe he'd treat himself to some waffles with fresh fruit after he dropped off his last load of papers.

Nikki walked into the kitchen to see the Sisters all gathered around the table drinking coffee. She stifled a yawn as she looked down at the plate of warm sticky buns in the center of the table. She sniffed: cinnamon. She loved the smell of cinnamon. "I ache all over," she said as she poured herself a cup of coffee.

Kathryn groaned as she massaged her neck. "Tell me about it. I cannot believe I slept straight through for twelve hours."

Nikki looked at the clock on the stove and

winced. She, too, had slept twelve hours. Panic gripped her. "Where . . . ?"

"Our . . . uh . . . guests are . . . resting," Myra said. "Mr. Snowden's people helped that along. They're in the alcove, all trussed up like Christmas turkeys. Since time wasn't an issue, we decided to allow you and Kathryn the sleep you needed. We have plenty of time, so enjoy your coffee. Then we'll get down to work."

Nikki felt herself relax as she brought the coffee cup to her lips. "When are they going to wake up?"

"Any minute now," Annie said cheerfully. "I think we have a generous window of time to do what we came here to do."

Myra's cell phone rang. The Sisters froze in place as they watched and listened.

"I'll tell them, Charles," Myra said and then hung up.

"Our 'generous window of time' just disappeared," she told them briskly. "We need our guests awake right now." She looked over at the clock Nikki had just looked at. "It's seven o'clock. Every news channel is running with a tale of the vigilantes, and they're saying they have their quarry cornered at the Watergate."

The Sisters were on their feet and running to the alcove.

"Where are those backpacks? Did anyone check the contents?" Isabelle shouted.

"I did, dear," Annie answered. "Some getaway cash, ten thousand, to be precise. Papers, memory sticks, and two passports. We couldn't access the memory sticks, they're password protected. Charles is checking the names on the passports. How much time do we have, Myra?" she asked.

Myra just shook her head, her gaze going to the two huge boxes sitting in the foyer, the kind of boxes that washing machines come in.

The Sisters looked toward the guest bedroom as they dragged the protesting bound couple toward the living room. There was a strange noise filtering out into the apartment from the guest room.

Yoko's head jerked upright. She placed her index finger next to her lips for silence. Next, running feet could be heard in the hallway. Then shouts and curses.

Kathryn looked down at the bound couple. "Hey, you two, listen up. You hear what's going on out there in the hall? This is just a guess on my part, but I think it's the FBI, and they're looking for you."

Annie held up a copy of the morning edition of the *Post* so that the trussed couple could read the headlines and see the pictures.

The man started to laugh. "What makes you so sure they're here for us? I think they're here for YOU!"

"That's true," Nikki said. "but we're going to get away, and you aren't. Now, we have your backpack, and that means we have the memory sticks, which will give us access to all the funds you've stolen over the years. I want your real birth names, and I won't ask twice."

"I want a lot of things, too. Make it worth our while," the man said.

"I wouldn't give you the time if you were in a dark room," Kathryn said. "We don't have time for games."

"I think it's time to get dressed, girls!" Myra announced.

The Sisters ran to the foyer and opened the boxes. Within minutes they were dressed in white Hazmat suits. They moved slowly in a tight line back to the living room.

"In one minute we're going to open the door to that room over there," Annie told the couple, pointing to the door of the guest room. "That noise you probably thought was coming from a faulty air-conditioning unit is really coming from there. Inside are nine hives of killer bees. Either you talk, or we release the bees. Decide now," she said, her hand on the crystal knob of the guest room door.

"Oh, God, I'm allergic to bee stings. I was hospitalized once for just one sting," the woman said. "I could die if I'm stung again."

"We know, that's where we got the idea. Back when you worked at East Coast Savings Bank and were calling yourself Sara Brickman. Who are you?" Yoko asked.

"Margaret Pearson. His name is William Bell."

"Shut the hell up, Margie."

"Don't tell me to shut up. I told you we needed to stop at five years. Did you listen? No, you were too greedy. We wouldn't be in this position if you had listened to me. Maybe you want to die, but I don't. I told you we would get caught, but you wouldn't listen. God, I hate you, Bill."

"I know someone who hates him more than you do," Yoko said grimly.

The Sisters whirled around when they heard loud banging on the door. The doorbell shrilled at the same time.

"Quick!" Annie shouted. "Drag these two into the bathroom and close the door. Stuff a towel at the bottom of the door. Alexis, take the tops off the beehives."

The Sisters moved to the front door as millions of bees invaded the apartment. Kathryn opened the door, and the bees swirled ahead of her, a monstrous black swarm. The crowd of police, reporters, and Watergate security ran for cover.

"Killer bees, cover your faces," Isabelle barked as she headed for the EXIT sign. She held open the door until the others were through and on the steps. She propped open the stairwell door. On the third floor, Annie propped open that door, and Myra did the same thing on the second floor. When they reached the first floor, the swarm of bees was buzzing so loudly that people were covering their ears and trying to seek shelter.

"Killer bees! Run! Cover your faces! If you get bitten, go to the hospital immediately," Kathryn shouted over and over.

The Sisters kept up Kathryn's chant as they

made their way to the door leading to the street outside.

Directly in their line of vision was a large white van that said HAZMAT on the panel in bold black letters. As far as the eye could see, people were running down the street, away from the Watergate—except for Joe Espinosa, who had his camera at the ready. Ted Robinson was texting so fast that time seemed to stop. From time to time they swatted at any pesky bees that got too close.

The Sisters lined up, removed their headgear, and gave a slow, sweeping bow as Espinosa clicked and clicked. The pictures were on their way to the *Post* even as Alexis winked at him, then blew him an air kiss.

Their work done, the Sisters ran for the van and climbed inside. "Whoever you are, burn rubber," Annie bellowed.

"My pleasure, ladies."

"Charles!" the Sisters shouted in unison.

"They weren't really killer bees, were they, Charles?" Myra asked anxiously.

Charles laughed. "No, they were honeybees."

The questions came fast and furious. "Why are you here? What happened? Where are we going? Tell us!"

"All in good time, ladies. I have to keep my eyes on the road to make sure we arrive at our destination safely."

Kathryn looked out of one of the dark-tinted windows. "I might be wrong, but I think we have an escort, front and back. Oh, and on the left side, too."

Charles laughed. "Never leave anything to chance."

Back at the Watergate, police, FBI agents, and a lone woman were standing near the doorway to the front entrance.

"I'm not saying you were wrong, Miss Augustine, but I'm not saying you were right either," Bert Navarro said.

"Then how do you explain that photographer taking those pictures? The vigilantes took off those crazy-looking head covers and posed. I SAW it with my own eyes," Sharon Augustine cried indignantly.

"Well, when I see it with my own eyes, I will make sure the FBI acknowledges your tip." Bert moved off toward a quasifriend he knew in the police department, who was standing next to the curb looking glum.

"Those crazy-ass women did it again! Killer bees! This whole damn town is going to go to red alert. Who the hell would have thought of bumblebees? The vigilantes made jackasses out of us. Again! I'm thinking my pension is suddenly looking not so good. What's your excuse, Navarro?" Leroy Jackson demanded.

"Honeybees, not killer bees. Not even bumblebees. There's a difference! Nine hives were in that apartment! That translates into millions of bees. The queen was among them! Don't even ask me what that means because I don't know. Some beekeeper from Bethesda is on his way to take charge of the hives."

"How'd those guys from the *Post* know to be here just when the vigilantes were leaving? Seems to me if you're paying attention, and I'm paying attention, they always manage to show up to get their damn pictures. Something's fishy there. I'm going to haul their asses in and go a few rounds with them. Don't give me any of that shit that it's just good reporting, that seventh sense that newshounds have. What do the brains in the Hoover Building think?" Detective Jackson asked.

Bert forced a laugh he didn't feel. "They're saying those women are smarter than we are. I'm not so sure they aren't right."

"You know what I think, Navarro? I think they have people here in the District helping them. Powerful people, influential people. That's what I think."

"All you have to do is prove it, Jackson. That's not to say I disagree with you. On the contrary, I think like you do, but those influential, important people can bite you on the ass if you start something you can't prove. You want to haul Robinson and Espinosa in, go for it. Been there, done that. You'll have Lizzie Fox so far up your ass, you won't be able to sit for a week. She'll be at the station before you can get those two through the door. Like I said, been there, done that. By the way, you didn't hear this from me, but the rumor is she's going to be chief White

House counsel. They offered her the job. What's-his-name has some kind of medical condition and he's moving on and the job was offered to Fox. Now, that's what I call being high-powered and influential. You want to take a shot at it, go for it."

"Did those two suspects give up anything when your guys hauled them off?" Jackson asked.

"Singing like canaries! Especially the woman! She just kept howling that she's allergic to bees. The guy kept telling her to shut up. He'll break, too."

"So what happens now?" Jackson asked.

"Depends on the vigilantes. The woman said the vigilantes have all their records. Will they do the right thing and turn those records over? I think so. I'm sure the *Post* will report on it with a special edition. Stay tuned. Nice talking to you, Jackson. Call me if you want to go out for a beer sometime."

Detective Leroy Jackson watched Director Bert Navarro walk away. Yeah, like he was really going to call him to go out for a beer. His years on the force along with his cop's instinct told him Navarro knew more than he let on, but Jackson knew better than to tangle with the FBI. Those guys from the *Post,* now, that was something else entirely. That damn paper always came out on top, and he didn't think it was due to diligent reporting. He'd bet his pension they had an inside track to those damn vigilantes. He sighed, knowing when he got back to the

precinct there would be a message that the police commissioner and the mayor wanted an audience with him, and not at his convenience.

Seven more years and he could file for his
pension. *Screw influential people who perch in high
places.* Navarro was right, let some other dick-
weed go after those damn women. Seven more
years and he was home free.

"These pictures are absolutely delicious, Espinosa. I'm thinking this time, as a show of good
faith, we share them with MSNBC. We don't
want to be accused of being biased, now, do
we?" Maggie chortled. "Damn, you guys are the
best!"

Ted and Espinosa beamed with pleasure.

"Absolutely, we do not want to be accused of
being biased! How come you aren't going with a
special edition?" Ted asked.

"Because, gentlemen, we have someplace to
go in exactly ten minutes. This paper is going to
be running itself for a little while. I worked it all
out. Go home, pack a bag, and meet me out at
Dulles. Don't ask questions. Go!"

Dressed in military camouflage, the Sisters
stepped out of the white van, the two dogs in
tow. They walked in military precision to the
waiting plane. Charles and Myra were the last to
get out of the van.

"Hold on, Myra. I brought something for

you." Charles reached into his pocket and brought out Myra's heirloom pearls. He handed them to her. "I hate those chains you've been wearing. It's time to put these back on."

Myra's eyes filled with tears. She smiled as she stuffed her beloved pearls into her own pocket. "What's in the bag, Charles?" she asked when she finally got her tongue to work.

Charles laughed, a great, booming sound. "The yellow comforter."

Chapter 21

It was an island with no name. Nor was it on any map. Rumor had it that at one time the nine-mile-long island belonged to a Colombian drug lord. No one knew who the true owner was, nor did the vigilantes care. All they knew was that they were in a tropical paradise with every luxury their hearts desired.

They were enjoying an Olympic-size pool, tennis court, putting green, and a stable with six magnificent horses for the guests. There was also a guesthouse with eight bedrooms along with a dormitory-style room with a triple bath for unexpected visitors. The Sisters and guests had arrived on three Gulfstream jets, and the pilots were currently occupying the large dorm room. The staff consisted of two groomsmen, a five-star chef, three maids, two groundskeepers, and a majordomo of sorts.

The main house, or, as the girls called it, the mansion, itself held seventeen rooms, nine bathrooms, three powder rooms, a gourmet kitchen, and a dining room that seated twenty at its massive table.

The most important features of the island with no name that wasn't on any map were the impressive landing strip—just off of which the three Gulfstreams nested inside a hangar that any international airport would have envied—the sleek white yacht at anchor whose crew stayed onboard, and the paved roads leading to the mansion from the landing strip. Then there were the six all-terrain vehicles in a seven-car garage that also held massive generators and Deepfreezes.

A sea of beautiful flowers, some wild, most cultivated, were profuse and every color of the rainbow. Yoko wandered around the formal flowerbeds and through the English garden in the back of the mansion, her eyes alight as she named flower after flower. The Sisters all agreed this very private place had to be one of the most beautiful spots in the world.

An island unto itself.

The guests of the island with no name were sitting poolside.

"This is beyond anything I've ever seen, even in the movies. Who owns it, Charles? Are we safe here? How did you find it? Can we trust the people working here?" Annie babbled as she sniffed the fragrant air that permeated the island.

The others looked up, wanting to know the answers as much as Annie did.

Charles smiled. "You own it, Annie. You are definitely safe here. This island has no name and is not on any map. Everything has been camouflaged. It cannot be seen from the air. There are mines out there in the water, all compliments of the previous owner, who was indeed a drug lord. The captain of the yacht knows exactly how to maneuver through them. I am not at liberty at this time to tell you how I found this little island paradise. The staff is as trustworthy as the people who guard the president of the United States."

The Sisters stared at Annie, who was staring at Charles in disbelief. "When did I buy this . . . this little place?"

Charles laughed. "Two years ago when I asked you if you would be interested in buying an—"

"Island resort," Annie said. "This is a little more than an island resort, Charles."

"That's true, but it's how it was listed in the *Times*'s real estate section: 'Island resort for sale.' I sent an inquiry, and a very prestigious white-shoe law firm responded to my inquiry. The drug lord's funds were confiscated, and he needed money to pay for his legal defense. Fifty million was what you paid for it. I haggled. The asking price was $120,000,000. I offered cash, and the firm snapped it up. This island is almost as big as Guam, which is eleven miles in length. Of course, unlike Guam, the major portion of this island is uninhabited. A sterling investment, if I do say so. Anytime you want to develop it, you could in the end make billions of dollars. I was thinking into the future.

"I thought we might need a safe haven at some point in time. Just in case Pappy gets tired of living on your mountain in Spain and wants to return to Big Pine Mountain. It's called thinking ahead and anticipating things before they happen."

Annie looked around. "And worth every penny," she said spiritedly.

The others clapped their hands in approval.

"It should have a name even if it's just among ourselves," Isabelle grumbled.

The Sisters kicked that around for a while but were unable to come up with a suitable name for the luxurious paradise. They shelved the project, vowing to come up with just the right one before it was time to leave to return to Big Pine Mountain.

Charles excused himself to go back inside. He headed straight for the massive library. He looked around at the shiny teakwood book-shelves that covered the walls on three sides of the room. He wasn't sure, but he thought the floor-to-ceiling shelves could hold every work of notable English language fiction published in the past fifty years. He reached for a book and wasn't surprised to see that the spine hadn't been broken. He couldn't help but wonder if the drug lord was a reader. The law firm had told him very little other than that the house had been built by Guatemalan craftsmen—every board, nail, and pane of glass imported and top-grade. The law firm had attested to the fact that the drug lord hadn't had a chance to inspect or visit the finished project before he'd been arrested in Venezuela just as he was about to board his private jet.

Charles replaced the book and walked over to the strange-looking desk across the room. A monstrous slab of concrete sat on two ornate pedestals. The slab had been lacquered to a high shine and held everything he would need to stay in contact with the outside world. All wireless and secure, of course. Before he sat down in the custom-made leather chair, he looked around approvingly. Either the drug lord had exquisite taste, or his Guatemalan decorator did.

What puzzled him more than anything, though, was the fireplace. A fireplace on an island whose yearly temperature held steady at seventy-five degrees seemed bizarre. Maybe they'd fashioned the room from a picture in a magazine. Or, perhaps when storms came in off the ocean, the temperature dropped, and a fire could be built. He really needed to find out the answer because sooner or later one of the girls was going to ask him the question. He made a mental note to find out, then got down to work.

An hour later, Charles returned poolside and sat down just as one of the maids arrived with a frosty pitcher of tart lemonade and a plate of freshly baked something that looked like scones.

The moment she returned to the house, Charles whistled sharply, and everyone got out of the pool. "I have an update."

"I hope you're going to tell us why this place has three fireplaces," Kathryn said.

"Actually, Kathryn, I do know. The previous owner saw a picture in *Architectural Digest* and liked what he saw. He particularly liked the idea of having a mantel. I am assuming he had treasures he was going to place there at some point in time. And when storms come through in September and October, the temperature will drop to the fifty-degree mark. There are bundles of birch logs in the garage in case you get the crazy urge to light a fire.

"Moving right along here. I spoke to the office manager of Nikki's old law firm and to Lizzie, who is on the first leg of her delayed honeymoon. The three memory sticks we passed on to the firm held the name and Social Security number of every person whose identity was stolen. Strangely enough, one of the sticks contained only the names of the kids in foster care, which apparently was a separate operation from the others. Restitution will be made as soon as possible. In some cases, like Harry's, for instance, a substantial bonus will be paid for pain and suffering. The firm will be working directly with the three major credit reporting agencies to delete all the negatives and help the victims get their lives back on track."

"And Bonnie and Clyde?" Alexis asked.

"You'll never have to worry about them

again. They're in custody, and the FBI can truthfully say they captured them since Bert's agents freed them from the bathroom, where they were tethered to the toilet.

"Furthermore, the memory sticks had a record of the names and addresses of all their accomplices: the people who used the credit cards to buy merchandise and those who picked up the illegally obtained items and put them up for sale on the black market. The FBI will be having a field day going after those slimeballs."

"What about the banks that allowed all this to happen?" Kathryn asked.

"Well, Chase recognized that they were at significant risk of being taken to the cleaners by lawyers for the former foster-child victims whose identities were stolen by one of Chase's own employees. They will be treating each of those cases as deserving of a large payment for pain and suffering, even if the child is still in foster care and has not yet suffered any known loss."

Charles smiled. And then he laughed out loud. "Finally, I think you might really enjoy what I'm about to tell you. It seems the bank presidents recently held a minisummit of some sort, and, remarkably, they all agreed to hire a professional to handle their Internet banking security to make sure this doesn't happen again. The professional's name is Abner Tookus."

Maggie's fist shot in the air as the others whooped and hollered. "How much are they paying him?" she finally managed to ask.

"High seven figures," Charles said with a

straight face. "I'm told they had to coax him to come back from his honeymoon in Hawaii."

The Sisters and their guests laughed so hard they didn't hear Charles say, "Well done, girls, well done indeed."

They were the vigilantes, and they were women. Of course the job was well done.

Epilogue

Charles stood in the middle of the compound and rang the bell; the sound was pure and clear as it ricocheted over Big Pine Mountain. The Sisters scurried from all directions into the main building.

All were breathless as they took their seats in the command center at the round table. Murphy and Grady were panting from their long run up and down the paths with Alexis and Kathryn, something they did every afternoon.

The simple explanation was that the bell meant there was business going on in the main building, and Charles was waiting to discuss it.

"I can't believe tomorrow is Thanksgiving," Kathryn said. "I've never seen three and a half months go by so fast since we returned from the island."

The others agreed, their thoughts on the guests who would be arriving shortly to celebrate the holiday. Only Lizzie would be absent, as she was on the return leg of her honeymoon. But she'd called, and arrangements were set up to have a webcam visit after Thanksgiving dinner.

Nikki stared out the window at the last of the autumn leaves blowing in the late afternoon wind. Her thoughts were on Jack's arrival. Her heart ached with loneliness. Three and a half months of not seeing the person you loved was three and a half months too long. She brought her thoughts back to the present when Charles called the meeting to order. Suddenly she was on her feet. "I have something to say!"

Startled, the others stared at her. Myra's hands flew to the pearls at her neck. She was certain she'd never heard that tone in Nikki's voice before. She risked a glance at Annie, who was suddenly alert.

"Can it wait until we get our business done with?" Charles asked.

"No! No, Charles, it can't wait. I want to speak now. I need to speak now."

"You have the floor, dear," Myra said.

Nikki cleared her throat. "I'm sick of waiting for Martine Connor to grant our pardon. I think it's time we did something about it. She promised to pardon us. We made sure she got into the White House, and she hasn't taken one single step to keep her promise. To me, a person is only as good as her word. I want to make

another point. It's been three and a half
months since I've seen Jack. Yes, he and the others are coming up the mountain in a few hours,
and, yes, they will be here for a four-day weekend, but then they'll be gone, and we're back to
being alone again. My clock is ticking. I want to
get married, I would dearly love to have children if it's in the cards for me. That is not going
to happen unless Martine Connor gets off her
duff and keeps her promise. I'm sick of the
stalling, sick of the promises that don't material-
ize."

"Dear, Lizzie has been working on our case,
you know that," Myra said, her grip fierce on the
pearls around her neck.

"Well, Myra, Lizzie isn't here, now, is she?
She's been working on our case for so long my
hair grew three inches. What that means is Connor is bullshitting her, and excuse my language.
I thought Lizzie was smarter than that, I'm sorry
to say. Connor has been in office almost two
years. She said she needed time, we gave her
time. Then she said the time wasn't quite right,
so we waited again. Then there was that business
with the vice president. We pulled her out of
that one, and she still didn't honor her promise.
I for one am sick and tired of waiting, and I also
think we need to take a vote here as to what our
next project is." Nikki, her face red from frus-
tration, flopped down on her chair and glared
at Charles.

"Are you finished?" Charles asked calmly.

"I said what I had to say," Nikki snarled. She

looked around at the other Sisters, who appeared stunned at her outburst.

"She speaks for me, too," Kathryn said coolly.

One by one, the others all agreed.

"I think this means you have the floor, Charles." From the pocket of her Windbreaker, Myra withdrew a strand of the clanking metal circles. She was about to loop them around her neck when Charles held up his hand, panic in his eyes.

"I was going to address this particular problem at the end of our discussion, but since you are all in such a wicked mood at the moment, I will address it now.

"Lizzie informed me a week ago that she is going to be taking the job as chief White House counsel on January 2. There were many details to iron out before she would commit, and she wanted Cosmo's assurances that he was all right with what she was planning. Mr. Cricket okayed her taking the job.

"Now, the reason Lizzie is taking the job is because of all of you. She put so many restrictions on the table, she knew that if Connor agreed to them, she had the inside . . . 'skinny,' as she put it, to expedite your pardon. She said she felt she could make it happen within six months. What we're talking about here is another six months of waiting for it to happen. Six months is not a lifetime. Seven months, if you insist on counting December, but in December we will have guests for two full weeks. So, essentially six months, ladies."

"Why didn't you tell us sooner?" Alexis demanded.

"Because Lizzie wanted her new husband's approval first. She's putting her new married life on hold for all of you. That says to me she thinks she can make it happen. For all she's done for you, don't you think you owe her that vote of confidence?"

Myra moved the metal necklace from one hand to the other. The clanking noise was the only sound in the room.

"Let's table that vote until we're finished with our other business," Annie said.

Nikki was so relieved at the reprieve that she felt light-headed. She looked at the others, who were smiling at her the way sisters smiled. She had their vote, she could see it in their eyes.

"All right," Nikki said.

"There's not much." Charles picked up a square box that looked heavy. "Inside this box is a record of the resolution of all Bonnie and Clyde's identity theft victims' cases. The last checks were mailed to the recipients five days ago, just in time for Thanksgiving. They were substantial and should make for a very merry Christmas. The other banks involved, recognizing their liability for their own employees' misconduct, did essentially what Chase did for the foster-kid victims. You ladies made thousands of people very thankful this year. Your firm, Nikki, worked around-the-clock to make this happen. There is a surplus of money, mostly interest the monies earned while it was offshore. Where do you want those monies to go? Anonymously, of course."

"We talked about it earlier, Charles. We want half of it to go to St. Jude Children's Research Hospital, and the other half to the center that helps find missing children," Annie said.

"Commendable, ladies. Consider it done. Now, what name did you all come up with for the island?"

Yoko stood up. "We unanimously agreed to call that slice of paradise Flower Island."

"Flower Island it is. One last thing. I have a request for your help. The time frame will be so tight if you agree to take it on that I don't know if you want to step in or not."

"Tell us what it is, and we'll let you know," Kathryn said.

Charles squared his shoulders. "It's bleak, and it's terribly sad. A client showed up about ten days ago at Nikki's old law firm. She and her husband, with the aid of a lawyer, hired a surrogate to give them a child. They paid $50,000 to the surrogate plus legal fees. They also paid all medical expenses for the surrogate. The couple borrowed the money from relatives and friends. They had a beautiful baby daughter whom they loved dearly. Nine months later the surrogate decided she wanted her baby back. She sued. The couple lost the baby because they didn't have the funds to fight the lawsuit.

"The young mother was devastated. The father got angry and decided to do what he could to make things right, which pretty much turned out to be nothing. He went on the Net and threw things out there, hoping something would stick. Basically what he was asking was if anyone out there had gone through the same thing, or knew of someone else who had gone through it, to get in touch with him. He came up with three other couples whose babies had been reclaimed by the surrogates. The couples all used the same lawyer but different surrogates. All the couples are in the same financial situation as the first couple.

"What they want to know is this: is there a way for you to get their babies back before Christmas? I called Pearl Barnes, and she's got her people working on it as we speak. The decision, of course, is entirely up to you, but your firm would like an answer as soon as possible. The sooner you give me your answer, the sooner I can get to work."

Annie looked around the table. "How could we not take this on? Just raise your hands, and let's get on with it."

Everyone in the room, including Charles, raised a hand.

Myra slipped the noisy necklace back into her pocket.

"Are we adjourned?"

The Sisters all looked at Nikki.

"We're adjourned," Nikki said quietly.

"We didn't vote on Martine Connor," Kathryn whispered as they walked through the door.

Nikki looked up at Kathryn and smiled. "I know."

If you enjoyed *Vanishing Act*,
don't miss the next exciting novel in
Fern Michaels's
Sisterhood series!

Turn the page for a special preview of

DEADLY DEALS,

a Zebra paperback on sale in April 2010.

Prologue

It looked like a cozy building, and it was . . . in the spring and summer. Ivy covered the brick walls, and flower beds abounded, all tended by the new manager of the Quinn Law Firm, a twelve-member, all-female firm, as everyone was quick to point out. In whispered tones, of course. Previously owned by one Nikki Quinn, one of the infamous Vigilantes.

In the fall and winter, the three-story brick building in Georgetown took on another appearance. Usually smoke could be seen wafting up through the chimney from the fireplace in the spacious lobby. A wreath of colorful leaves adorned the stark white door.

The Monday after Thanksgiving, the building underwent another transformation. A fragrant evergreen wreath with a huge red satin bow almost as wide as the door arrived from a grateful client in Oregon. Inside, the fire blazed; the birch logs, from another grateful client somewhere in the state of Washington, arrived like clockwork the day before Thanksgiving.

It was a low-key firm. All the lawyers were friends, each of them helping the others. There was no shortage of clients, but that hadn't always been the case. At one point the firm had struggled to keep its head above water, but that all changed when the Vigilantes were captured and then escaped. The media had a field day as they splashed the news that the Quinn Law Firm's owner was one of the notorious women. Within twenty-four hours, there were waiting lines of women—some men, too—forming up outside to be represented by the now-prestigious, outrageous, famous law firm.

Nancy Barnes, the firm's business manager, was new to the firm but not that new. She'd replaced her aunt Maddy, who had retired to stop and smell the roses a year after the Vigilantes had gone on the run. She knew the firm inside and out, having worked there summers and holidays for as long as she could remember. She herself was a paralegal but had found out that management was more to her liking. She had a wonderful rapport with the lawyers and clients. At Christmas time alone she had to have a friend come by with a pickup truck to take all her presents home: gifts from the lawyers, gifts from all the grateful clients.

Nancy Barnes loved her job.

On the first day of October, Nancy was huff-

ing and puffing as she struggled with an oversize
pumpkin that she somehow managed to get into
the lobby after she opened the door and turned
off the alarm without dropping the pumpkin.
She knew by the end of the week there would be
about twenty more pumpkins around her scare-
crow-and-hay arrangement, all brought in by the
lawyers themselves, along with the paralegals
and the secretaries.

Cozy. A feel-good place to come to when in
trouble.

Nancy looked up to see a young woman coming through the door. Her first thought was that
she looked like a deer caught in the headlights.
Fragile. Scared. But there was a spark of something she couldn't quite define. Yet.

Nancy Barnes was a chunky young woman
who wore sensible shoes. She had curly hair, *un-
ruly* curly hair, and a bridge of freckles danced
across her nose and rosy cheeks. She wore
granny glasses and always had two or three pen-
cils stuck behind her ears or in her hair. It was
her smile that put new clients at ease, or maybe
it was her first words of greeting, no one was
ever quite sure. "Good morning. What can I do
to help you?"

"I'm Rachel Dawson, and I need to talk to a
lawyer as soon as possible. I don't have an appointment. I'm sorry. I just . . . What I did was . . .
My husband doesn't know I'm here. I can't afford to be here." The woman flapped her arms
and then said, "But here I am."

"I'll tell you what, walk around here to where

I am, and then I'll get us both some coffee, and you and I can talk. What that means is after you tell me your problem, I'll decide who it is that would work best with you. We have donuts, too."

Rachel Dawson tried her best to smile but couldn't bring it off. Nancy could see she was fighting back her tears.

Settled at her desk with coffee Rachel Dawson wasn't going to drink, she said gently, "Tell me what you're comfortable telling me so all of us here can help you. I want you to think of this firm as your extended family. Everyone here works for the client, and it doesn't matter which attorney is assigned to you. Do you understand that?"

"I can't afford to be here. My husband is going to be upset when he finds out I . . ."

"Let's not talk about payment right now. But for the record, we do quite a bit of pro bono work. I'm usually the one who makes that particular decision, so we aren't going to worry about whether you qualify or not right now. Tell me how we can help you."

Rachel Dawson fooled Nancy. Before she spoke she gulped at her coffee and drained the cup. "I can't have children. It's me, not my husband. I had every test in the book. I'm thirty-seven. My husband is thirty-eight. We both have very good jobs, but right now I'm on a leave of absence. We were so desperate to have a child, but the wait was so long, and going outside the country didn't work for us. A friend of a friend told us about a lawyer who arranged adoptions.

We went to see him a year or so ago, and in the end what we did . . . what my husband did was donate his sperm to a surrogate. It was all legal. We paid the lawyer one hundred thousand dollars. I don't know how much of that went to the surrogate. We paid all of her medical expenses. I even drove her to the doctors when she had to go. She was a student at George Washington University. We bought her clothes, food, paid her rent. She gave birth to twins, a boy and a girl. We were overjoyed. I can't tell you how giddy we were. We went into panic mode the day we found out. We had to redo the house—you know, make room for two babies instead of one.

"I guess I should tell you we had to borrow forty thousand dollars from our parents. Call us foolish, but we've been saving for a college fund even though we had no children. We hoped that we would eventually be blessed. We're savers, Miss Barnes."

Nancy watched Rachel peer into her cup. She seemed surprised that it was empty. Without thinking, Nancy reached for the cup and went to the kitchen for a refill.

"We were so happy. It was like suddenly our life was now complete. We didn't sleep. We sat up and watched the twins sleep. I guess all new parents do that. My husband took leave, too, for a month, so I could get things working. We couldn't afford a nanny, and our parents helped out. We literally thought we'd died and gone to heaven."

Rachel reached for the coffee and again

drained the full cup. She set it down precisely in the spot it had been in. Nancy waited, knowing the worst was about to be revealed. She wasn't wrong.

"Then our world turned upside down. A letter came in the mail from a lawyer saying his client, the surrogate mother, wanted the twins back. We thought about fighting it, but we had seen cases like this played out in the media, and the birth mother always got the children. Our parents offered to mortgage their houses. We were going to cash in our retirement funds and the college fund but were advised not to do that. My husband talked to several lawyers, and they basically told us to move on and put it behind us. I went to the lawyer we used to arrange the adoption. I called and called, and he didn't call back. I went to his office, and they wouldn't let me see him. I thought about going to the newspaper, but the truth was, I wasn't strong enough mentally or physically for that kind of onslaught. You'll find out sooner or later that I had a minibreakdown. That's what they called it, anyway."

Nancy looked down at the small recording machine she'd decided to use at the last second. As usual, she'd forgotten to mention it to this frail woman sitting in front of her. "Mrs. Dawson, I'm recording this conversation. I hope that's okay. I should have told you that before I turned it on."

"That's okay. Is there anything you can do for me and Tom?"

Nancy's mind raced. Was there? "I'm going to turn this off for a few moments. Then I'm going to get you some more coffee. I have to make a few phone calls. Will that be okay? I think I know just the person to help you."

"Truly? You do? Oh my God, I'll do anything. Anything at all if you help me."

"Which lawyer did you go to to arrange the adoption?"

"Baron Bell."

"Baron Bell?" The name shot out of Nancy's mouth like a bullet. "Baron Bell refused to see and talk to you after . . . . after . . . ?"

"Yes, Baron Bell. He seemed like such a nice man. He's always in the papers, and he's an advocate of everything. Everyone Tom talked to backed away when he told them it was Mr. Bell who arranged the adoption."

"Who was the surrogate mother?"

"Her name was Donna Davis."

Nancy ran to the kitchen, refilled Rachel's coffee cup, and then walked down the hall to an empty office and called her aunt Maddy. "I don't know what to do with her, Maddy. Nothing like this has ever come up before. I'll be honest, I don't think any of our lawyers here at the firm will agree to go up against someone like Baron Bell on what could become a high-profile case like this one. Talk to me, Maddy."

Nancy listened. She reached for a pad and pencil and scribbled furiously. "Maddy, are you going to do what I think you're going to do?"

"Can you think of anyone better?"

Nancy smiled. "Actually, I can't. Wouldn't it be wonderful if . . . Rachel could get her babies back for Christmas?"

"It's the time for miracles. I'll do what I can. Keep me in the loop, honey."

"Will do, Maddy."

Back in the office, Nancy sat down and reached for a small pad. As she wrote down Lizzie Fox's name, address, and phone number on a slip of paper, Rachel Dawson kept on talking. "I think this is some kind of baby ring. Tom says I'm out of my mind, but on my really bad days I would go to the park and just sit. I talked to a lot of nannies and young mothers. One of the mothers looked at me when I told her what had happened and told me about someone else the same thing happened to. I have her name right here in my purse. I even went to talk to the adoptive parents, and they're in the same position Tom and I are in. They used Baron Bell, too. Their surrogate is a student at Georgetown. Is there any way, any way at all, that we could get our babies back for Christmas? We had such plans. Our first family Christmas." Rachel burst into tears.

"Rachel, I can't answer that, but the person I want you to go see is just the right lawyer for you. Trust me when I tell you she could take on Baron Bell with her hands tied behind her back and blindfolded. If anyone can help you, it's Lizzie Fox."

Rachel Dawson bolted upright. Her tears

stopped in midflow. "She's the lawyer that . . . She was . . . the Vigilantes' attorney."

Nancy stared across the table, her gaze steady and direct. "Yes," she said softly.

"Oh! Oh! When should I go to see her?"

Nancy's phone rang. She picked it up and listened. All she said was, "Thanks, Maddy."

Nancy looked at Rachel. "Right now. You can walk to Lizzie's office from here." Nancy was out of her chair and around the desk. She put her arms around the woman's thin shoulders. "Just tell Lizzie everything you told me. Be sure to give her the other surrogate's name. By the way, is your surrogate still living wherever she was living before the birth of the twins?"

"She is. I . . . I would park down the street hoping to get a glimpse of the twins. They never seem to leave the apartment. I guess she has a babysitter while she goes to class. I was so obsessed. I don't know how to thank you. Will Ms. Fox work on a payment plan for us? Do you know?"

"You'll work something out. I wouldn't worry about that right now. Just go and talk to her, and I wish you all the luck in the world."

Nancy waited until Rachel Dawson was through the door and out of sight before she walked back to her office. She called her aunt, and they talked for ten long minutes. Nancy was smiling when she hung up the phone. Then she laughed out loud. "Rachel, honey, you are in such good hands," she murmured under her breath.

Chapter 1

1600 Pennyslvania Avenue. The most famous address in the world.

Lizzie tried her best not to gawk like a starstruck tourist at the magnificent Christmas decorations as she trailed behind the Secret Service agent escorting her to President Connor's private quarters. She was here for lunch and so much more.

President Connor herself opened the door and literally dragged Lizzie inside with a whispered, "I'll take it from here, Agent Goodwin."

As soon as the door was closed, she turned to her friend and burst out, "God, Lizzie, I am so glad to see you! I mean I'm *really* glad!"

"Me, too, Madam President." And she *was* glad; she and President Connor had a history. Then they wrapped their arms around each other in a bone-crushing hug, strange for two such elegant women.

President Connor laughed. "Stop with that president stuff. In here we're Lizzie and Marti. I *need* you to call me by name, Lizzie. I don't want to forget who I really am. Can we do that?" She sounded so anxious, Lizzie nodded.

Lizzie looked around. "Pretty fancy digs, Marti. This is my first time in the White House. I'm impressed. The Christmas decorations are beautiful."

"If you have the time, I'll give you the tour after lunch. Right now I want you all to myself. I can't thank you enough for accepting my invitation. You look so happy, Lizzie."

Lizzie smiled as she was shown to a deep off-white chair that would have held her and Cosmo. She watched as the president sat down across from her and then kicked off her shoes. Lizzie did the same thing, and then they giggled like two schoolgirls. "There are no words to tell you how happy I am, Marti. I wish I could say the same for you. You look like you have the weight of the world on your shoulders."

Martine Connor forced a smile she was far from feeling. "I *do* have the weight of the world on my shoulders. See how bowed they are? And before you can ask, the world slowed down for some reason this week to allow me time for this luncheon."

"You want to talk about it, or is it all NTK? Your approval ratings are in the 70 percent area, so you must be doing something right."

Martine shrugged. "I had a hard time getting used to every second of my time being budgeted. Sometimes bathroom breaks are a luxury. There's always a crisis brewing somewhere that has to be dealt with. You know me, I'm cool under fire. It's when I get up here that I lose it."

Lizzie blinked. "This was what you wanted, Marti."

Martine brushed at the soft bangs falling over her forehead. "Yes, and if it wasn't for you . . . and . . . your friends, I wouldn't be here. I know that, Lizzie. It's with me every second of every day. That's why you're here, isn't it? That's why you accepted my job offer, right? You're here to spell it out to me. Again."

Lizzie stared at her old friend. She gave a slight nod. "Six months. Pro bono. I walk away unless the job proves to be something beyond my expectations. I have to admit I was surprised you agreed to my terms."

Martine burst out laughing. "Oh, Lizzie, I wish you could have seen the expressions on all *their* faces when I listed your demands. I thought the lot of them would choke to death. Nine to five! Every weekend off. Pro bono. I realize one hundred sixty-eight thousand dollars is a lot of money, and yet it isn't much money to live on here in the District, what with rent, travel back to one's home state, taxes, everyday expenses, and the maintenance of two residences. It's hard to raise a family and keep up two residences all for the sake of doing one's duty. When I told them you weren't interested in adding the White House to your resume, because yours was impressive enough without it, several of them had to be resuscitated. It's safe to say your fame has preceded you. Actually, Lizzie, you're a legend in your own time, and I for one am honored to be called your friend. How does your new husband feel about you taking on the job?"

Lizzie leaned forward. "You know what, Marti? My husband is that rare breed of man who only wants to see me happy. If all it takes is his approval, he's all for it. We take turns traveling on the weekends. You need to give him a huge slice of credit for helping get you to where you're sitting right now." Lizzie looked around and then lowered her voice. "Is this place bugged? Are you recording me?"

"Lizzie!"

The president's outrage was so total, Lizzie relaxed. "What I was going to say was my husband numbers among his friends some of the most powerful, some of the most respected, some of the richest people in the world, and those he doesn't know personally, he has access to via those same friends that are in his Rolodex. You should see his Rolodex, Marti. I think it's safe to say your own cannot compare."

"What are you trying to tell me, Lizzie?" There was an edge to the president's voice that did not go unnoticed by Lizzie.

"Nothing, Marti. I was simply commenting on your question about my husband."

"Point taken. Oh, look, our lunch is ready. It's

one of the perks here. I hope you enjoy it." The president nodded to the waiter to show he could leave. "I know you don't like to eat heavy at lunch, and most days I don't have time for lunch. We're having sesame-crusted salmon, grilled asparagus, and a garden salad."

It looked delicious, but Lizzie wasn't hungry. She lifted her glass of ice tea and clinked it against Martine's. "Here's to a thankful Thanksgiving and a Merry Christmas, Madam President."

"And the same to you, Lizzie." The bite was still in Martine's voice, Lizzie noticed. Well, she hadn't invited herself here. She was the invitee. She smiled as she mashed the salmon on her plate. Martine was cutting her asparagus into tiny pieces. Lizzie couldn't help but wonder if the president was going to eat it or was just playing with her food the same way she was.

"Does my office have a window, Marti?"

Marti offered up a genuine smile this time. "It was one of your requirements, so, yes, your office has a window. You did say you would be willing to negotiate the second half of the year. Is that still on the table?"

Lizzie mashed the salmon some more. "Yes, but no promises. So, tell me now, who do I have to watch out for?"

"Everyone, would be my guess. You've been Googled so much since we made the announcement I'm surprised the site didn't shut down. You're the next thing to Public Enemy Number One at 1600 Pennsylvania Avenue. My chief of staff understands that you are to have direct access to me 24/7. Of course he went ballistic, but we're on the same page now. Everyone is replaceable. He understands that, too."

"Guess you aren't going to eat that asparagus. You must have a hundred little pieces on your plate."

"You always were perceptive, Lizzie. I'm listening when you're ready to talk."

"My friends are very unhappy, Marti. I thought you would have gotten the message when your Secret Service agents were thrown into a Dumpster, and then their weapons and badges were sent back to you."

Martine started to mash at her salmon the way Lizzie had. "We're going to have to put all this food in the disposal so the kitchen doesn't get their knickers in a knot. I did get the message. I wasn't amused. We had to do some fancy dancing to explain all of that."

"I bet you did. My friends weren't amused, either. You have six months to keep your promise."

"I can't believe you're giving the president of this country an ultimatum! And if for some reason I can't deliver on the promise in the allotted time, then what?" the president asked in the same frosty tone.

Lizzie smiled. "Marti, I might be many things, but I'm not clairvoyant."

"What? Are you seriously warning me that the Vigilantes can penetrate the White House? Is that what you're telling me? Are you telling me they're smart enough to outwit the best of the best? It's simply not possible. What are they going to do, hold a gun to my head and make me sign a pardon, and then we're all going to disappear in a puff of smoke?" Lizzie was pleased at the look of pure horror on the president's face.

Lizzie continued to smile. "I said no such thing. That's your interpretation. Although the ladies did take on the Secret Service and came out on top. And if I remember correctly, that little neighborhood White House luncheon you sponsored didn't go over so well, either. Your guests were more impressed with their ride home compliments of the Vigilantes than they were with your luncheon, the photo op, and their souvenirs."

Martine Connor got up and carried the two luncheon plates to the sink. She scraped the plates and turned on the garbage disposal. Lizzie listened to the loud clunking noise and then a shrieking, grinding sound. "The plumbing leaves a lot to be desired," Martine said.

"You could call a plumber," Lizzie volunteered.

"It doesn't work that way here. In the real world, yes. I can't even describe to you what it's like living here. I can't step out and go to the drugstore to get shampoo. If I want to do that I have to notify the Service a month in advance. Then they have to empty out the store so I can shop. I can't go to a bookstore. I can't drive a car. I can't use my credit cards or carry money. If they ever found out or find out I have that phone, they'll probably pack me off to Outer Mongolia.

"You know what I miss, Lizzie? I miss going out to the mailbox for my mail. I miss all those catalogs I used to get by the pound. I always looked forward to Sunday afternoon, when I'd browse through them and order something. You know what else? I made potato pancakes one day. They came up here on the run and said I was stinking up the White House and not to do it again. They fucking told me I can't make potato pancakes! It was the onion I put into it. I'm not excusing my language, either."

For all of a minute, Lizzie almost felt sorry for her old friend. Almost. Then she burst out laughing. "Remember that old saying, be careful what you wish for, because you just might get it. You wished for this, we made it happen for you at the eleventh hour, and now you have to live with it. And you have to honor your debt. That's the bottom line."

"God, Lizzie, how cold you sound. That's the real reason you agreed to sign on, isn't it? You're here to protect your friends, and if it means taking me down, you'll help them do it, right?" Lizzie just smiled.

"Goddamnit, Lizzie, say something."

"Where I come from, Marti, and where you've been, a person is only as good as their word. I really should be going. I've taken up enough of your time today."

Martine Connor turned to stop her furious pacing. Lizzie thought she looked great in a honey-colored suit with a copper-colored blouse underneath her suit jacket, which was open. Her haircut was stylish, and the feathery bangs falling over her forehead were new, too, since the last time she'd seen her. She looked presidential.

"But we haven't had dessert, and I was going to give you the tour. Lizzie, I'm sorry. I'll find a way, I promise you. Please, I need you to believe me."

"It's not me you have to convince, Marti. I'll pass on your message. Six months. Not one day, not one hour, not one second longer. I'll report in on January second. I hope you have a wonderful holiday. Are you staying here or going somewhere?"

"Camp David. I plan to sleep through the holidays. Do you want to hear something really sad? I don't have a single soul I can invite to spend the holidays with me. Well, that's not quite true. I had several people I was going to invite, but the Service said when they vetted them they were unsuitable. *Unsuitable!* That's what they said. I'm whining, and I didn't want to do that. I apologize."

Lizzie stepped forward and wrapped her arms around the president. She squeezed hard. "Six months, Marti," she whispered. "Now, how do I get out of here? Is that guy with the 'football' still outside the door? Oh, one last thing— watch out for Baron Bell."

Martine grimaced. "You mean the marine with the nuclear codes? Yes, he's out there. You just walk past him, it's that simple. One of my agents will take you home."

Lizzie stared at her old friend. She could feel her eyes start to burn at what she was seeing on her old friend's face. She lowered her voice to a bare whisper and said, "I wouldn't want to be you for all the gold in Fort Knox."

Martine Connor shed her personal persona, and in the blink of an eye she was the President of the United States the moment the door opened. "Thank you for that observation, and thank you for coming, Lizzie. I enjoyed our luncheon. I hope we can do it again soon. Happy Holidays to you and *yours.*"

"Don't eat too much turkey, Madam President." Lizzie flinched at the sound of the door closing behind her. She straightened her shoulders and walked alongside the agent escorting her to a black limousine, where another agent waited to drive her back to her home.

Lizzie kept her eyes closed all the way home, her mind racing as she sifted, collated, and made mental notes.

The moment Lizzie was inside her cozy little home, she shed her lavender suit and donned a pair of jeans and a fleecy, warm shirt. She had the crazy urge all of a sudden to make potato pancakes. But first she had to check things at her office, call her husband, and then call the mountain. Maybe she should call the mountain first. Or maybe she should wait, think about her visit some more, and make the potato pancakes first. Multitasking, so to speak.

Before she did anything, though, she was going to make herself a pot of strong black coffee to get her adrenaline going at full speed. While the coffee was dripping, Lizzie fiddled with her CD player and then slipped in one of Cosmo's favorite CD's. Frank Sinatra's mellow voice filled her kitchen. She immediately felt the tenseness leave her shoulders. Then she made herself a sandwich, the kind of sandwich Cosmo raised his eyebrows over but later admitted was tasty. Swiss cheese, lettuce, fire-roasted peppers, and one slice of salami. That mess she'd mangled back at the White House couldn't come close to the sandwich she was devouring. There wasn't a crumb to be seen when she finished.

Lizzie moved then at lightning speed. She called the mountain; then she called Jack Emery and then her office. She had two calls left to make when she poured her coffee. The first call was to Nikki's old law office, where she asked more questions than she answered. She had one call to go before she could call her husband. With business taken care of she could talk for hours if he had the time. At the crack of dawn she'd be winging her way to Vegas to spend Thanksgiving and the rest of the holidays with her husband. A radiant smile lit her features.

Lizzie was huffing and puffing when she opened the doors of the fireplace, placed the logs just so, and then threw in a pile of birch kindling. The fire blazed instantly. She then moved a pile of silky red cushions near the hearth so she could curl up and be comfortable.

One more trip to the kitchen to replenish her coffee. She was walking through the dining room when retired judge Nellie Easter picked up the phone. "Lizzie, Judge. Several things. I want to wish you and Elias a wonderful Thanksgiving and a Merry Christmas. I'm leaving in the morning for Las Vegas." They made small talk for a few minutes, with Lizzie asking about Elias's new grandbaby and his other children before she got down to the real reason for her phone call.

"Nellie, tell me everything you know about Baron Bell. And ask Elias if he knows anything. Better yet, use the speaker phone if he's agreeable."

"Baron was always a gentleman in court. He fights to win for his clients. He and I belong to five or six of the same organizations. He's been Man of the Year for so many years I've lost count. He used to do a lot of pro bono work. Lovely wife, kind of timid, stays in his shadow. Two grown children. One is a doctor at Georgetown, and one is a public defender in Georgia. Several grandchildren that he dotes on. No matter the cause, you can count on him for a donation, and he gives his time willingly to any worthy cause. He plays Santa every year for some children's group—it always makes the paper. He always arrives in a sleigh with his helpers, be it on wheels or with horses pulling the sleigh, and he does it at his own expense. It's usually quite an event.

As far as I know, I never heard a hint of any kind of scandal. He's quite wealthy, and, as you know, there are always a few who will take a swipe at you for that. Elias said there's a file on him at the Bureau, but nothing bad is in it. There are those who are the recipients of his generosity who think he's the Messiah. Why are you asking, Lizzie?"

"No one is *that* perfect, Nellie. What's his flaw?"

"If you believe his court record and his PR, then he is *that* perfect. Why? What happened to make you ask these questions? Did I also mention he has a pass to the White House? That means he's invited to *everything*. So he's on your radar, eh?"

"A little under it, but he's there. Do me a favor, Nellie—ask around, see if there's anything of interest there. Then call the mountain and share it with them. Are you going to spend Christmas on the mountain or just Thanksgiving?"

"We are. We're coming back Sunday night but will return the following weekend. Elias said his family is heading for a warmer climate. We both like the cold, and both of us are looking forward to spending the holidays with old friends. I'm sorry you won't be joining us."

Lizzie laughed. "Thanks, Nellie, and one more time, Happy Holidays!" She sighed happily. Now she could curl up and talk till she fell asleep. Business was taken care of. She'd packed before she left for the White House and was ready to go as soon as she rolled out of bed in the morning. Damn, she forgot to call Maggie at the *Post*. A minute later she had Maggie on the phone. She spoke quick and fast as she explained about her meeting with Rachel Dawson. "There's something there, Maggie, I could feel it. It isn't good, either. I'll be working on her case while I'm in Vegas." Her final words were, "The window of time is going to be short, Maggie. Make it work if you can. See you when I see you."

Life was good, Lizzie thought as she settled into her nest of colorful cushions.

Across town, Maggie flipped open her Rolodex and then looked at the clock. Four o'clock. She punched in the numbers and waited for Abner Tookus to pick up. He did on the fourth ring. "I thought you said you were taking my name out of your Rolodex" was all the computer hacker said by way of a greeting.

"I lied. Just the way you lied to me about working for Big Blue, and even then you lied some more, saying you were going on a honeymoon. You snookered me, Abby. I want my pound of flesh."

"Call someone who's fat and can afford to lose a pound or two. I don't have any to spare. I'm working. That means I have no time to do anything for you."

"You better find the time, and this one is for free. F-r-e-e! That job you have, the one that is paying you in eight figures? That's all compli-

ments of me. I can take it away just like . . . that,"
Maggie said, snapping her fingers.

"Go ahead, take it away," Tookus blustered. "I
hate nine to five. I hate wearing a suit and tie.
You want to fall back and regroup and call me
again like in twenty years?"

"Nah! I'm going to come over to those plushy
digs where you work and rip the skin right off
your face. What I can't decide is should I do it
before or after I sic the Vigilantes on you. Now,
if you're really nice to me I'm going to forget
you challenged me. Truce?"

"Truce. What do you want?"

Maggie's voice turned syrupy sweet. "Not all
that much. I want everything there is to get on
one Baron Bell. I want it from the moment he
came into being in his mother's womb until this
very minute, and then I want hourly updates."

"You gotta be kidding me, Maggie. Mr. Squeaky
Clean himself! Mr. Man of the Year! Mr. Personal
Buddy of every power broker in Washington!
That guy is the Easter Bunny, the Tooth Fairy,
and Santa Claus all rolled into one. He is beloved
and cherished beyond belief. What'd the son of
a bitch do to put him on your radar screen?"

"Just never you mind, Abner. At the moment
Baron Bell is *under* my radar but rising to the
top. That's all you need to know. I want this by
nine o'clock tomorrow morning. I do not care if
you sleep or eat, is that clear? If you're one
minute late, you will find yourself skinless. Nice
talking to you, sweetie."

Maggie let loose with a deep sigh. She had no

doubts at all that Abner would come through for her. But would he have anything worthwhile her friends on the mountain could use? Well, she was the master of spin, if she did say so herself.

Time to get ready to close up shop and head for the mountain with the others. She could hardly wait to sit down to a Thanksgiving dinner with all the trimmings prepared by Charles. She smacked her lips in anticipation.

At least she wouldn't be going empty-handed. Abby's file would be her gift to the host. She laughed as she envisioned Charles's expression when she handed it over.

Chapter 2

It was Thanksgiving eve, and the compound on Big Pine Mountain was quiet. The reason for the quietness was the late hour and the fact that snow had been falling for the past nine hours. A giant white blanket covered the mountaintop, making it picture-postcard perfect.

Charles Martin prowled the confines of his command center, his thoughts all over the map as he stared down at the paperwork Maggie Spritzer had brought with her earlier in the day. With the investigation his own people had done, he felt like he had a solid basis to move forward when the guests left on Sunday and they got down to the mission at hand. He walked out of the command center, slipped on a heavy mackinaw, and opened the front door. A blast of early winter air rushed through the room. He smiled at the high drifts of snow on the porch. He stood under the overhang and fired up his pipe. The smoke from the cherry tobacco in his pipe and the heady scent from the evergreens was an intoxicating mixture. He loved it. Loved seeing the steady snowfall, knowing all his chicks inside were safe and sound. For now.

Tomorrow they would all sit down to a huge dinner he would begin preparing in just a few short hours. They would all pray and give thanks for so many things. He hoped his voice didn't falter when he offered up his own thanks. He thought about his son he'd never gotten a chance to know as he puffed on his pipe. He knew if he let the tears flow they'd freeze on his lashes. He shook his head to clear his thoughts. It wasn't that he was banishing all thoughts of Geoffrey, more that it was unbearable to think about his son the traitor.

Charles listened to the silence around him. He wondered what it would be like to live in a world as silent as the one he was standing in. To never hear the sounds of laughter, never hear the wind rustling in the trees, never hear the birds chirping early in the morning. *That* was a bearable thought. He shifted his mental gears to the work at hand. Not that dinner was work; he could prepare a Thanksgiving feast with his eyes closed. What he couldn't do with his eyes closed was figure out what was going on with Baron Bell. Or with his eyes open, for that matter. He whirled around when he sensed a presence. "Myra! What are you doing up at this hour?"

"I'm up because the bed got cold. Why are you standing out here, Charles?"

"The world looks so clean and pure right now. It's so perfect I just want it to be like this forever, but that's a foolish wish on my part."

Myra reached out and nestled her hand within his. "It is beautiful. The snow came early this year. I'm ready to get married now, Charles. I thought maybe on New Year's Day. I'd like Nellie to marry us. Say something *now*, Charles, because I don't think I will get the nerve again to make this commitment."

"But you didn't ask me. You made an announcement. I'm supposed to get down on my knee and *ask you*."

"Well, what are you waiting for?" Myra asked.

Charles dropped to one knee and reached for Myra's hand. "Myra, will you marry me on New Year's Day? If you say yes, I promise to love and honor you into eternity."

"My answer is yes, Charles. Will you make the announcement at dinner?"

"If that's what you want, then, yes, it will give me great pleasure to announce our betrothal. You just made me the happiest man in the world." Charles moved his arm and wrapped it around his beloved's shoulders. "What made you pick this moment in time, if you don't mind my asking?"

"Well, Charles, we aren't getting any younger. In fact, we're getting older by the day. If that isn't enough of an answer, I realized I don't like cold beds. And you're right—this moment, right now, this instant, is so perfect it just seemed like the right time.

"I'm going to have Annie stand up for me. Who will you choose, Charles, to be your best man?"

"Elias. You don't think the boys will be upset, do you?"

"No more than the girls will be upset with me choosing Annie."

"I don't have a ring for you, Myra."

Myra laughed. "The ring isn't important. Just ask Elias for one of his cigar bands. That will do nicely."

Charles held his bride to be. "My life is now complete, Myra. I think we should go inside before we both freeze to death out here, and then there won't be a wedding at all."

"I think you might be right. Come along, my darling, I'll help you get started with your Thanksgiving dinner."

Charles pretended horror. "My dear, you are worthless in the kitchen. But you can watch me. Let's have an early breakfast. You can brown the buns and make the coffee and squeeze the juice. We received a box of Baby Bell oranges with our food order yesterday. Wait till you see them. Each one is more perfect than the last, and to think you can only get them at this particular time of year. Amazing."

Myra linked arms with Charles. "I'm going to learn to cook, Charles. I've been watching the

Food Network." Charles laughed all the way across the compound as he half dragged Myra through the deep snow.

Thanksgiving dinner was everything everyone hoped it would be. Good friends breaking bread together and giving thanks together. Chef Charles accepted the accolades heaped on him with a gracious smile. Conversation was light, at times bantering, but always in good taste. Even Murphy and Grady whooped their thanks at the heaping plates Charles set out for them, but instead of turkey they had roast chicken.

Jack passed on the pumpkin pie by saying he was allergic and went with the pecan pie. The others hooted with laughter at the remembrance of the truckload of pumpkins back in Utah. One and all agreed that it seemed like a lifetime ago.

Coffee and brandy was served in the living room in front of a blazing fire that Elias and Bert maintained. Outside the snow continued to fall. Soft music, golden oldies that no one objected to, played softly.

Even though there were football games on the big screen via satellite, no one opted to watch them. All were content to sit and revel in the peaceful atmosphere with good friends.

When Charles walked into the living room carrying a huge silver tray with two bottles of champagne, they all knew something interesting was about to happen. Myra, at his side, held an identical silver tray with exquisite cut-glass wine flutes.

Nikki looked over at Jack and winked. The heirloom crystal flutes had appeared months ago, brought to the mountain by Nellie from Myra's farmhouse. This, whatever this was, must really be important. Feeling a nudge to her shoulder, Nikki turned and wasn't surprised when she heard a whisper in her ear.

"This is Mummie's big day, Nik. She's finally going to do it."

"About time," Nikki said under her breath. She risked a glance around the room, but no one seemed to be paying attention to the fact that Barbara's spirit was in attendance.

Charles uncorked the first bottle of champagne. They all watched the cork sail upward and then spiral down to land at Myra's feet. The second cork went upward, spiraled down, and settled at Charles's feet. The little group clapped their hands.

"Nice going, Barb," Nikki mumbled.

"You should see what I can do when I put my mind to it," the spirit giggled. *"Shh, here it comes."*

Charles cleared his throat. "I have an announcement to make. I've asked Myra to marry me, and she finally said yes. I asked her on bended knee in the snow at four-thirty this morning on the front porch. I hope you're all as happy for us as we are for ourselves. So, let's drink a toast to this happy couple."

Nikki wasn't sure, but she thought she saw her spirit sister settle herself between her mother and father. Then again, maybe it was the smoke that suddenly billowed out of the fireplace before it was sucked back in and then straight up the chimney. "Nice going, Barb."

"Thanks, Nik. Give them both an earthly hug for me, okay?"

"You got it!" Nikki untangled herself and got to her feet to accept her flute of champagne. To Charles and Myra, she whispered, "I have orders to give you both an *earthly* hug. One earthly hug coming up." She wrapped her arms around Charles and Myra without spilling a drop of champagne.

"She was here, wasn't she?" Myra whispered.

"Oh, yeah, she was here." Nikki smiled. "She approves."

"I felt her right beside me," Charles murmured.

"She was between us, wasn't she, Nikki?"

"Smack dab in the middle. I am so happy for you both."

The little group started to sing "For He's a Jolly Good Fellow," and then they switched to "She's a Jolly Good Lady." All off-key, but no one cared.

Cushions and blankets appeared out of nowhere as the happy guests sprawled wherever there was room. No one noticed until later that Annie and Isabelle had left the living room and returned to the building where they lived.

"I saw how unhappy you were, Isabelle. I know how you feel. I pretty much felt like a

third wheel myself. Suddenly everyone became
a couple. Don't get me wrong, that's a good
thing. I don't think anyone will miss us, at least
not for a little while, and even then they'll think
we ate too much and are taking a nap. Everyone
has a partner but you and me. I think we should
do something about that, and I think we should
do it *right now!*"

"And that would be . . . what?" Isabelle asked
tentatively.

What indeed. "Well, you did tell me and the
others on one or more occasions that you
thought that guy in the Vegas casino was pretty
hot. For a while after we got back to the mountain, I thought you were pining for him. You said
you looked right into his eyes and liked what you
saw. You know the guy I'm talking about, the
one you socked in the eye! You even remembered his name. Stu Franklin. He said if you ever
take a vacation you'd be able to find him on the
beach in the Caymans. You said if we were ever
pardoned, that was the first place you were
going. You even asked Charles to have his people run a profile on him, and if I'm not mis-
taken, you have it in your possession."

Isabelle sighed. "All true, but that was then
and this is now. How do you suppose one would
go about finding someone on the beach in the
Caymans, someone who is hiding out from the
law?"

Annie could feel herself getting into it. "*I
know people*, Isabelle," she said vaguely as her

mind raced. "Listen, you're an architect. Draw me a picture of him from memory. Do it *now.*"

Isabelle ran to her room and returned with a sketch pad. Her drawing pencil moved swiftly, with sure, deft strokes. Ten minutes later she held up Stu Franklin's likeness.

Annie stared at the picture. "Damn, girl, the man looks *hot!*"

"He was so hot, Annie, I felt like my eyebrows were on fire. How else do you think I was able to draw such a likeness? I wonder if he remembers me or his invitation. He probably has hundreds of beach bunnies running after him."

"Trust me, honey, he remembers you. He singled you out." Annie wondered if what she was saying was true. "You're beautiful, and he was helping *you.* He didn't have to do what he did that day. I think it's safe to say he meant every word he said."

Isabelle threw her hands in the air. "What good is this going to do for me except make me more sad that I'm alone?"

"Not for long. Come on, put your jacket and boots on, and let's go to the command center. I told you I know people."

Outside the snow was still falling. "Do you think it will ever stop, Annie?"

"Oh, who cares? You need to be thinking of crashing waves, white sand, sultry breezes, and that . . . that guy on the beach. I wonder if anyone told him he's safe from prosecution. See, that's your . . . your reason for calling when we finally locate him. Even a lame reason is better

than no reason, because he probably already
knows, but there's no way for you to know that
he knows. Did that make sense?"

"Well, yes, in a cockamamie way."

They were in the command center, and
Annie was standing at Charles's workstation.
She took a deep breath, picked up one of
Charles's special encrypted phones. She dialed
a number from memory and waited. Isabelle
watched her and knew in her gut that whatever
Annie was up to, she was going to pull it off. She
walked off, sensing that Annie didn't want her
eavesdropping on her secret private conversation.

"So, do you know who this is?" Annie said to
the person who answered the phone.

"Ah, Miss No Name. Just for the record, I'm
wearing my magic decoder ring. That means
our conversation is safe. Are you calling to wish
me a Happy Thanksgiving?"

"Among other things. Are you keeping your
eyes on my half of our business, *partner?*"

"24/7. Did you have your dinner yet?"

"I did, and it was wonderful. I need a favor,
and I need it *now.*"

The voice on the other end of the line grumbled, "What is it with you women? You always
want everything *now*. Since I'm three hours behind you, that means I have not had my dinner
yet, and my now is not the same as your now
with the time difference."

"Don't worry about it," Annie snapped.
"You'll be eating turkey for a week anyway. I

want you to find someone for me right away. You did say you were . . . well, what you said was you . . ."

"The term you're looking for is . . . connected. Which I am. All right, all right. What am I going to get out of this deal? *If* I decide your request is worthy of my expertise."

Annie swallowed hard. What would the girls say? What would Myra say? "Well, Mr. Fish, partner, you get *me*." Oh God, did she really say that? Obviously she did, because Fish was sputtering on the other end of the phone. Annie listened. "Oh, get over yourself, Mr. Fish. Admit it, you don't have a clue as to what to do with me. Not to worry—I'll show you." Oh God, did she say that, too? She blinked when she heard laughter on the other end. Annie listened again. "What do you mean when? It's not like I'm free to come and go as I please. When you least expect it, I'll be there." Annie groaned inwardly. She rather thought there was a song with lyrics like that. She felt her face flame.

"So, give me your fax number, and I'm going to send you a picture of the man I want you to find. Think in terms of *rewards* for a job well-done. The kind you never dreamed of, that's what kind." Annie squeezed her eyes shut, knowing she was going to have to powwow with the girls to come up with *rewards*. Her whole body felt so hot she wanted to run out naked in the snow. Fish was still sputtering on the other end of the line.

Annie slid the drawing into the fax machine

and punched in the number Fish had managed to give her during his sputtering.

"How long is this going to take?" Annie asked. "Did I also mention that I . . . we need the man's cell-phone number, and we want a guarantee that he will answer it when we call? You can do that, can't you, Fish?"

More garbled words.

"What? What? Are you saying you lied to me? You said you worked for some secret branch of the government no one ever heard of. You said you were a terrorist and a mercenary. I believed you, otherwise I wouldn't have called you. Oh, I cannot believe I tumbled to your silver tongue. You can just forget those rewards." She listened, her eyebrows shooting upward. "Well, that's more like it. The rewards are back on the table. Of course I'll wait for your call, where do you think I'm going to go? No, I'm not sending you a list of the rewards. Well, maybe I could send the first three." Annie made kissing sounds into the phone before she broke the connection.

"Isabelle!" Annie screeched at the top of her lungs.

"Oh, no, your source said he couldn't help. It's all right, Annie. You tried, and I appreciate it. I guess it just isn't meant to be."

"Shut up, Isabelle. It's in the bag. In a few hours you will be talking to Mr. Franklin. It's what I promised—to get the information for you."

"Oh, Annie, what did you promise? Are you saying you can't deliver on your promise?"

Annie told her. Isabelle blinked. Then she blinked again before she doubled over laughing. When she finally stopped laughing, she managed to gasp, "I think we can come up with a suitable list of rewards. We might even be able to come up with *instructions*. You do realize what the problem is, right?"

"Oh God, what could be worse?" Annie groaned.

Isabelle started to giggle and couldn't stop. "Following through," she finally managed to gasp.

Annie sat down with a thump. "What should I wear?"

"You aren't getting it, Annie. Zip."

"But . . ."

"A promise is a promise, Annie."

Annie rose to the occasion. "My dear, if you can make contact with Mr. Franklin, I can certainly honor my promise. *YIPPEEEEE!*"

Four hours later, eastern standard time, Annie's cell phone rang. She bolted upright from where she'd been dozing on the sofa. She gave Isabelle a shout to wake up where she, too, was dozing by the fire. "My phone is ringing. I think this call might be for you, honey."

Isabelle reached for the phone and said, "Hello, this is Isabelle."

"Well, Isabelle, this is Stu Franklin. There's this guy standing here with a gun to my head, and he's telling me to talk pretty to you. Not that anyone needs to tell me something like that. I'd appreciate it if you'd tell him he can leave us now so we can have a private conversation. I'm going to put him on the phone right now before he blows my head off."

Isabelle managed to squeak out, "Thank you for your help, sir. I appreciate you doing this for me on Thanksgiving. I hope I didn't take you away from your dinner." The voice on the other end of the phone mumbled something that sounded like he was glad he didn't have to kill anyone on Thanksgiving. Isabelle was so light-headed she had to sit down.

The voice was soft, cultured, intimate-sounding. "Somehow or other, Isabelle, I thought you would have gotten in touch with me in a more conventional way. But I admire your aggressiveness. I'm glad you called. Are you having a nice Thanksgiving?"

"I did . . . I am . . . I was until . . . Oh, never mind. I didn't spoil yours, did I?"

"No. I just had a hot dog with all the trimmings on the beach. Did you have the whole enchilada, meaning a turkey with all the trimmings?"

"I did. I love hot dogs with all the trimmings, too."

"I saw that picture you did of me. Pretty good. Are you an artist?"

"No, I'm an architect. I feel . . . I feel kind of foolish and pushy right now. Maybe someday I can explain what made me . . . What I mean is . . ."

"Just for the record, I would have gotten in

touch, but I didn't know how. I was hoping you might take me up on my offer one of these days."

"That's kind of hard, but I'm working on it. We have two feet of snow where I am right now."

"It's sunny and eighty degrees where I am. There's not a ripple in the ocean, and it's sapphire blue. There aren't many people here right now, which is unusual. I guess the economy is as bad as they say it is."

"Has anyone told you that you're free from prosecution? If not, you can come and go as you please. We . . . we took care of that for you."

The silence on the other end of the phone lasted so long Isabelle had to say, "Are you still there?"

"I'm still here. No, I didn't know that. Well, this is a wonderful Thanksgiving, after all. But how do I know it's true?"

"Because I tracked you down to tell you. I don't lie. I think we might, I say might, be going to Washington soon."

"Is that an invitation? If it is, I accept."

"It is. If you give me your phone number, I can call you if it happens. You can call me anytime, but not on this number." She rattled off a number that Stu Franklin said he memorized.

"Let's talk, Isabelle. I want to know what happened that day at the casino. I want to know all about you."

And so Isabelle told him while Annie pretended to snore lightly on the couch.

If you love the Sisterhood series,
but are wanting a non-Sisterhood "fix" from
Fern Michaels,
you are in luck!

Her next stand-alone novel will be
coming from Kensington in May 2010.

Turn the page for a special preview of

RETURN TO SENDER,

the wonderful new bestseller by Fern Michaels.

Prologue

January 13, 1989
Dalton, Georgia

Rosalind Townsend, whom everyone called Lin, held her newborn son tightly in her arms as the orderly wheeled her to the hospital's administration office. A nurse tried to take him from her so she could tend to the business of her release, but she refused to give him up.

After eighteen hours of agonizing labor without any medication, she'd delivered a healthy six-pound eight-ounce baby boy. She wasn't about to let him out of her sight.

She'd named him William Michael Townsend. A good, solid name. She would call him Will.

Like his father's, Will's hair was a deep black, so dark it appeared to be blue. Lin wasn't sure about his eyes at this point. She'd read in her baby book that a newborn's eye color wasn't true at birth. Nothing about him resembled her, as she was fair-haired with unusual silver-colored eyes and milk white skin.

She gazed down at the securely wrapped bundle in her arms and ran her thumb across his delicate cheek. Soft as silk. He yawned, revealing tender, pink gums. Lin smiled down at her son. No matter what her circumstances, she made a vow to herself: she would devote her life to caring for this precious little child.

Lin had spent the past seven months preparing for this day. During the day she worked at J & G Carpet Mills as a secretary. Five evenings a week and weekend mornings, she waited tables at Jack's Diner. Other than what it cost for rent, food, and utilities, Lin saved every cent she made. She had to be conservative, because it was just her and Will. She'd allowed herself a week off from both jobs so she could bond with her son, adjust to her new life as a mother. While she would've loved spending more time with her son, being the sole caregiver and provider made that impossible. She'd lucked out when Sally, a coworker at Jack's and a single mother to boot, had asked her if she would sit for her two-year-old daughter, Lizzie. In return, Sally would look after the baby on the days that she wasn't working. Lin had agreed because she had to. There were still the days to cover, but Sally gave her a list of reliable sitters she'd used in the past. Dear Sally. Only five years older than

Lin but so much wiser to the ways of the world. They were fast becoming good friends. Sally was the complete opposite of Lin—tall, olive-skinned, with beautiful brown eyes that had a slight upward slant, giving her an Asian look. Lin had called three of the sitters: two high-school girls and one elderly woman. She would meet with them later in the week. Lin was sure that if Sally approved, she would as well.

Sadly, there would be no help from Will's father or her parents. Lin recalled her father's cruel words when he learned she was pregnant.

"May you burn in hell, you little harlot! You've disgraced my good name. Get out of my house. I don't ever want to lay eyes on you again or your bastard child!"

Lin had appealed to her mother in the hope she would intervene, but, as usual, her mother had cowered behind her father, accepting his word as law. Lin would never allow a man to intimidate her the way her father did her mother.

Never.

"Miss?"

Lin directed her attention back to the woman behind the administration desk. "Yes?"

"If you'll sign here and initial here." The woman slid a single sheet of paper across the desk.

Lin signed the paper, releasing the hospital from any liability. Since she had no health insurance and refused public assistance, she could only afford to stay in the hospital for twenty-four hours. She'd spend the next two years paying a hundred dollars a month until her debt was paid in full.

The woman behind the desk reached into a drawer and pulled out a thick envelope. "Here, take these. You might find them useful."

Lin took the envelope, peered inside. Coupons for diapers, formula, baby lotion, and anything else one might need. She gave the woman a wan smile. "Thank you."

"You're welcome."

Throughout her pregnancy, she had visited the local dollar store once a month. She'd purchased generic brands of baby items that were on the list of layette necessities she'd read about in the baby book given to her by her obstetrician. Lin didn't have extra money to spend on a homecoming outfit for the baby, so she'd gone to Goodwill and found a secondhand pale blue sweater set. She'd carefully hand washed it in Dreft detergent. Subsequently it had looked good as new. Someday, she swore to herself, her son wouldn't have to wear secondhand clothes.

The orderly wheeled her back to her room, where she dressed in the maternity clothes she'd worn when admitted to the hospital the day before. She ran her hand across her flat stomach. Now she would be able to wear the uniform Jack required, thus saving wear and tear on her few meager outfits. She gazed around the room to make sure she wasn't leaving anything behind. Had it only been twenty-four hours since the taxi had dropped her off at the emergency room? It seemed like a week.

Lin carefully removed the sweater set she'd placed in her overnight bag. With ease, she dressed her son, smiling at the results. Will looked like a little prince in his blue outfit from Goodwill. Briefly, she thought of his father and their weeklong affair. What would his reaction be when he saw his son for the first time? After months of indecision, she'd finally written him another letter two months ago, the first one since she had been on her own, and mailed it to his parents' address in New York, the only way she knew to contact him. She'd begged Nancy Johnson, a girl Will's father had introduced her to, for his phone number as well, but the woman had been adamant about not revealing more of her friend's personal life. She'd told Lin that if Nicholas wanted her to have his phone number, he would have given it to her. The harsh words had stung, but there was more at stake than her raw feelings. She had a child to consider. She'd written a lengthy letter, revealing her pregnancy, telling Nicholas he would be a father shortly after the new year. Weeks passed without a response. Then just last week she'd trudged to the mailbox only to find the letter she'd sent unopened and marked RETURN TO SENDER.

What's one more rejection? she'd asked herself.

Her father hadn't accepted her, either. Her mother had once told her that he'd always dreamed of having a son. At the time, Lin had been terribly hurt, but as the years passed, she learned to set those feelings aside. She'd been the best daughter she knew how to be in hopes of gaining some kind of approval, and maybe even a bit of love and affection from both parents, but that was not to be. When she told her parents about the decision to keep her baby, they were mortified and humiliated. She'd been tossed out of the only home she'd ever known with nothing more than the clothes on her back.

A soft, mewling sound jerked her out of the past. "It's okay, little one. I'm right here."

With the quilt that Irma, Jack's wife, had made for him, Lin gently wrapped Will in a snug bundle. It was below freezing outside. Lin had halfheartedly listened to the local weather report as it blared from the television mounted above her bed. An ice storm was predicted. Meteorologists said it could be the worst in north Georgia history. With only two small electric space heaters, her garage apartment would be freezing. How she wished she could take Will to her childhood home. While it wasn't filled with love, at least it would be warm.

But Lin recalled the torturous evenings of her childhood. She would rather die than subject her son to such a strict and oftentimes cruel upbringing. Every evening, as far back as she could remember, she'd had to pray while kneeling on the hardwood floor in the living room as her father read from the Bible.

A die-hard Southern Baptist who considered himself a man of God, her father had constructed a pulpit for himself in the center of the living room from which he would gaze down at

her with disdain, as though she weren't good
enough. Then, as if that weren't bad enough,
he'd make her recite the names of all the books
of the Bible in order. If she missed one, he
would make her start from the beginning until
she named them correctly. Once, when she was
about seven or eight, she remembered spending an entire night on her knees praying. She'd
prayed hard, her father watching her the entire
time. Little did he know she'd been praying for his
immediate death. Many times she'd wet herself
while on her knees in prayer. Her father wouldn't
allow her to change her clothes or bathe after-
ward.

"The devil lives inside you, girly! Taking a
shower ain't gonna cleanse your dirty soul!"

She'd winced the first time she'd heard those
words. After a while, she became immune to his
cruel words. She'd even gotten used to smelling
like urine. The kids at school were relentless,
calling her Miss Stinkypants. And she would do
what she always did when she was hurting.

She prayed.

Every night that she knelt on that cold, hard
floor, she prayed for her father's death. Not
once in the seventeen years that she had lived in
her father's house had he ever relented on this
evening ritual. She had thick, ugly calluses on
her knees to prove it.

When she left home, or rather when she was
thrown out, she made a promise to herself: she
would *never, ever* kneel again.

Freezing definitely held more appeal.

She checked the room one last time. One of the nurses waited to wheel her downstairs, where the hospital's courtesy van would take her and Will home.

In the lobby, the automatic doors opened, and a gush of icy air greeted her, smacking her in the face. She held Will close to her with one arm and carried her small suitcase with the other. The driver, an older black man, opened the door and reached for her bag. "You best hop inside, miss. This here cold ain't good for the young'un." He nodded at the bundle in her arms.

Shivering, Lin stepped carefully up into the van. Thankful for the warm air blowing from the heater's vents, she sat on the hard vinyl seat and realized she was still very sore from the delivery. Her breasts felt as though they would explode. She couldn't wait to get home to nurse Will. She'd only be able to do so for the week she was home. Then she'd have to resort to formula. She'd calculated the expense, and while it was very costly, she would manage. Unfortunately, she had no choice.

"Thank you," she said to the driver as she placed Will in the car seat beside her. When Lin had discovered she was pregnant, she'd been frightened, fearful of having inherited her parents' harsh and unloving manner. However, when Will was placed in her arms, the love she felt for him was the most natural thing in the world. Her worries had been for naught.

When mother and son were secure in their

seats, the driver made his way through the parking lot. Waiting at the traffic light, he perused a stack of papers attached to a clipboard. "Tunnel Hill, ma'am?"

"Yes, just make a left on Lafayette, then take the second right." Lin hated having to take Will home to a one-room garage apartment. Someday they would have a home with a big yard with flowers, a white picket fence, and lots of trees for him to climb. Will would have a swing set, and she'd watch him play. Yes, she would see to it that Will had a good home, and, whatever it took, she would make sure he had an education.

Lin remembered her father telling her years before that it was foolish for women to go to college, a waste of money. He'd assured her then that he would not contribute to her education, so after she'd preenrolled at Dalton Junior College during her senior year of high school, she'd saved enough money for the first year.

Having spent three terrifying nights alone in a cheap motel after her father threw her out, she'd made her first adult decision. Instead of using the money for college, she'd paid three months' rent on an apartment. In retrospect, her father's attitude had worked out well since it forced her to save for her education. If not, there wouldn't even be a place for her to bring Will.

The driver parked in her landlady's driveway. She hurriedly removed Will from the car seat and took her bag from the driver. "Thank you. I appreciate the ride."

"Jus' doin' my job, miss. Now scoot on outta here. That ice storm's gonna hit real soon."

"Yes, I know. Thanks again for the ride."

Lin felt rather than saw the driver watching her as he slowly reversed down the long driveway. She didn't feel creepy at all, because she knew he was good and decent and just wanted to make sure she made it inside safely. A stranger cared more about her well-being than her own flesh and blood. Sad. But she smiled at her thoughts. She had the greatest gift ever, right here in her very own arms.

Holding Will tightly against her chest, she plodded down the long drive that led to the garage apartment. She felt for the key in her pocket, then stopped when she heard a whining noise. Putting her bag on the ground, she checked Will, but he was sound asleep. She heard the sound again.

"What the heck?" she said out loud.

On the side of the garage, at the bottom of the steep wooden steps that led to her apartment, Lin spotted a small dog and walked behind the steps where he hovered. Holding Will tightly, she held out her hand. Its brownish red fur matted with clumps of dirt, the ribs clearly visible, the poor dog looked scruffy and cold. He or she—she wasn't sure of the animal's gender—whined before standing on all fours, limping over to Lin, and licking her outstretched hand.

She laughed. "You sure know the way to a girl's heart."

"Woof, woof."

With the ice storm ready to hit, there was no way Lin could leave the poor dog outside. She fluffed the matted fur between its ears and decided that the dog was going inside with her.

"Scruffy, that's what I'm going to call you for now. Come on, puppy. Follow me." The dog obeyed, staying a foot behind Lin as she made her way up the rickety steps while holding Will against her chest.

Unlocking the door, Lin stepped inside and dropped her bag on the floor. Timidly, Scruffy waited to be invited in. "Come on, Scruffy. You're staying here tonight. Something tells me we're going to get along just fine."

Two unwanted strays, Lin thought.

Scruffy scurried inside and sat patiently on the kitchen floor. With Will still clutched to her chest, Lin grabbed a plastic bowl from her single cupboard, filled it with water, and placed it on the cracked olive green linoleum. She took two hot dogs out of her minirefrigerator, broke them into small pieces, and placed them on a saucer next to the bowl of water. "This should tide you over for a bit. I've got to feed the little guy now."

Scruffy looked at her with big, round eyes. Lin swore she saw thankfulness in the dog's brown-eyed gaze.

With her son still clutched in her arms, Lin managed to remove her jacket before loosening the blanket surrounding him. Making the necessary adjustments to her clothing, Lin began to nurse her son. Reclining on the floral-patterned sofa, she relaxed for the first time in a long time. Her son was fed and content. She'd inherited an adorable dog, however temporarily, and she was warm.

For a while, that would do. Someday their lives would be different.

Lin stared at the sleeping infant in her arms. "I promise you, little guy, you'll have the best life ever." Then, as an afterthought, she added, "No matter what I have to do."

Part One

Chapter 1

Friday, August 31, 2007
New York University

Will's deep brown eyes sparkled with excitement, his enthusiasm contagious, as he and Lin left University Hall, a crowded dormitory for freshmen located at Union Square. If all went as planned, Will would reside in New York City for the next four years before moving on to graduate school to study at North Carolina State University College of Veterinary Medicine, one of the most prestigious veterinary institutions in the country.

"I just hate that you're so far away from home. And in New York City, no less," Lin said for the umpteenth time. "With all the remodeling and holiday parties going on at the restaurant, I doubt I'll be able to make the trip north for Thanksgiving. I don't want you to spend your holiday alone."

"Mom, I said I'd come home if I could. And I will. I promise," Will said. "Besides, I'm a big boy now. I just might like spending some time alone in this big city full of hot chicks."

Laughing, Lin replied, "I'm sure you would." She watched her son as they rode the elevator downstairs. Over six feet tall, with thick, raven black hair, Will was the spitting image of his father, or at least her memory of him.

Lin recalled all those years ago when she'd first met his father. She'd fallen head over heels in love while he'd been visiting a friend in Georgia. Briefly, Lin wondered if Will would follow in her footsteps or his father's. She prayed it wasn't the latter, though she had to admit she really didn't know how he'd turned out. But she didn't want her son to take after a man who denied his son's existence. Lin knew he was very wealthy, but that didn't mean he was a good man. Good men took care of their children, acknowledged them.

Three weeks after she'd brought Will home from the hospital, she'd sent his father a copy of their son's birth announcement along with a copy of the birth certificate. She'd shamelessly added a picture of herself just in case he'd forgotten their brief affair. Throughout the years, she had continued to send items marking Will's accomplishments, the milestones reached as he grew up. Photos of the first day of school; first lost tooth; then, as he aged, driver's license; first date; anything she thought a father would have been proud of. Again, all had come back, unopened and marked RETURN TO SENDER. After so many years of this, she should have learned, should have known that Will's father had no desire to acknowledge him. To this very day, she'd never told Will for fear it would affect him in a way that she wouldn't be able to handle. Recalling the hurt, then the anger each time she and her son were rejected, Lin tucked away the memories of the man she'd given herself to so many years ago, the man she'd loved, the man who had so callously discarded all traces of their romance and in so doing failed to acknowledge their son's existence. When Will had turned twelve, she'd told him his father had died in an accident. It had seemed enough at the time.

But as Jack, her former employer and substitute father, always said, "The past is prologue, kiddo." And he was right. She'd put that part of her life behind her and moved forward.

The elevator doors swished open. The main floor was empty but for a few couples gathered in the corner speaking in hushed tones. Most of the parents were either visiting other dorms or preparing for the evening banquet. Will hadn't wanted to attend, but Lin insisted, telling him several of the college's alumni would be speaking. She'd teased him, saying he might be among them one day. He'd reluctantly agreed, but Lin knew that if he truly hadn't wanted to attend, he would have been more persistent.

She glanced at the exquisite diamond watch on her slender wrist, a gift from Jack and Irma the day she'd made her last payment on the diner she'd purchased from them eight years ago. "I'll meet you in the banquet hall at seven. Are you sure you don't want to come back to the hotel?"

Will cupped her elbow, guiding her toward the exit. "No. Actually, I think I might take a nap. Aaron doesn't arrive until tomorrow. It might be the last chance I have for some time alone. I want to take advantage of it."

Will and his dorm mate, Aaron Levy, had met through the Internet during the summer. Though they hadn't met in person, Will assured her they'd get along just fine. They were studying to become veterinarians and both shared an avid love of baseball.

"Better set your alarm," Lin suggested. Will slept like the dead.

"Good idea." He gave her a hug, then stepped back, his gaze suddenly full of concern. "You'll be okay on your own for a while?"

Lin patted her son's arm. "Of course I will. This is my first trip to the city. There are dozens of things to do. I doubt I'll have a minute to spare. Though I don't think I'll do any sightseeing today, since I made an appointment to have my hair and nails done at the hotel spa."

Will laughed. "That's a first. You never do that kind of stuff. What gives?"

"It's not every day a mother sends her son off to college." She gently pushed him away. "Now go on with you, or there'll be no time to relax. I'll see you at seven."

Will waved. "Seven, then."

Lin gave him a thumbs-up sign, her signal to him that all was a go. She pushed the glass door open and stepped outside. The late-afternoon sun shone brightly through the oak trees, casting all sorts of irregular shapes and shadows on the sidewalk. The autumn air was cool and crisp. Lin walked down the sidewalk and breathed deeply, suddenly deliriously happy with the life she'd made for herself. She stopped for a moment, remembering all the struggles, the ups and downs, and how hard she'd worked to get to where she was. Abundant, fulfilled, completely comfortable with her life, she picked up her pace, feeling somewhat foolish and silly for her thoughts. She laughed, the sound seemingly odd since she was walking alone, no one to hear her. That was okay, too. Life was good. She was happy, Will's future appeared bright and exciting. The only dark spot in her life was her father. Her mother had died shortly after Lin had moved into Mrs. Turner's garage apartment. She'd had to read about it in the obituaries. Lin had called her father, asking how her mother had died. He told her she'd fallen down the basement steps. She suspected otherwise but knew it would be useless, possibly even dangerous to her and her unborn child, if she were to pry into the circumstances surrounding her mother's death. She'd tried to establish a relationship with her father on more than one occasion through the years, and each time he'd rebuffed her, telling her she was the devil's spawn. Her father now resided in Atlanta, in a very upscale nursing home, at her expense. Lin was sure his pure meanness had launched him into early onset Alzheimer's.

Lin thought it was time for her to proceed at her own leisurely pace, kick back, and totally relax for the first time in a very, very long time.

Lin continued to ponder her life as she walked down the sidewalk toward a line of waiting taxis. After ten years of working at Jack's Diner, when she'd learned that Jack and Irma were considering closing the place, she'd come up with a plan. Though she'd skimped and saved most of her life, for once she was about to splurge and do something so out of character that Jack had thought she'd taken temporary leave of her senses. She'd offered him a fifty-thousand-dollar down payment, a cut of the profits, and a promissory note on the balance if they would sell her the diner. It took all of two minutes for Jack and Irma to accept her offer. Since they'd never had children and didn't think they'd have a chance in hell of selling the diner given the local economy, closing the doors had seemed their only option.

Lin laughed.

She'd worked her tail off day and night and most weekends to attract a new clientele, a younger crowd with money to burn. She'd applied for a liquor license and changed the menu to healthier fare while still remaining true to some of the comfort foods Jack's was known for, such as his famous meat loaf and mashed potatoes. Within a year, Jack's was booked every night of the week, and weekends months in advance. From there, she started catering private parties. With so much success, she'd decided it was time to add on to the diner. In addition to two large private banquet rooms that would accommodate five hundred guests when combined, she added three moderately sized private rooms for smaller groups. The remodeling was in its final stages when she'd left for New York the day before. She'd left Sally, her dearest friend and manager, in charge of last-minute details.

Lin quickened her pace as she saw that the line of taxis at the end of the block had dwindled down to three. She waved her hand in the air to alert the cabbie. Yanking the yellow-orange door open, she slid inside, where the smell of stale smoke and fried onions filled her nostrils. She wrinkled her nose in disgust. "The Helmsley Park Lane." She'd always wanted to say that to a New York cab driver. Though it wasn't the most elite or expensive hotel in the city, it was one that had captured her imagination over the years. Its infamous owner, known far and wide by the well-deserved epithet the Queen of Mean, had been quite visible in the news media when Lin was younger, especially when she'd been tried and convicted for tax evasion, extortion, and mail fraud, and had died just over a week before.

Through blasts of horns, shouts from sidewalk vendors hawking their wares, and the occasional bicyclist weaving in and out of traffic, Lin enjoyed the scenery during the quick cab ride back to the hotel. New York was unlike any city in the world. Of course, she hadn't traveled outside the state of Georgia, so where this sudden knowledge came from, she hadn't a clue, but still she knew there was no other place like New York. It had its own unique *everything*, right down to the smell of the city.

The taxi stopped in front of the Helmsley. Lin handed the driver a twenty, telling him to keep the change. Hurrying, Lin practically floated through the turnstile doors as though she were on air. She felt like Cinderella, and the banquet would be her very own ball, with Will acting as her handsome prince. He would croak if he knew her thoughts. Nonetheless, she was excited about the evening ahead.

She dashed to the elevator doors with only seconds to spare. She'd lost track of time, and her salon appointment was in five minutes. They'd asked her to wear a blouse that buttoned in the front so she wouldn't mess up her new do before the banquet. She punched the button to the forty-sixth floor, from which she had an unbelievable view of the city and Central Park. Lin cringed when she thought of the cost but remembered this was just a onetime treat, and she was doing it in style.

She slid the keycard into the slot on the door and pushed the door inward. Overcome by the sheer luxuriousness, she simply stared at her surroundings, taking them in. Lavender walls with white wainscoting, cream-colored antique tables at either end of the lavender floral sofa.

The bedroom color scheme matched, though the coverlet on her bed was a deep, royal purple. She raced over to the large walk-in closet, grabbed a white button-up blouse, and headed to the bathroom. This, too, was beyond opulent. All marble, a deep Jacuzzi tub, a shower that could hold at least eight people, thick, soft, lavender bath towels and bars of lilac soaps and bath beads placed in crystal containers gave Lin such a feeling of luxury, and it was such a novel feeling, she considered staying in the room her entire trip. She laughed, then spoke out loud. "Sally would really think I've lost my marbles." She'd discussed her New York trip with her, and they'd made a list of all the must-see places. If she returned empty-handed, Sally would wring her neck. She'd bring her back something special.

They'd practically raised the kids together, and Sally felt like the older sister she'd never had. And she'd bring Elizabeth, Sally's daughter. something smart and sexy. She'd opted to attend Emory University in Atlanta instead of leaving the state as Will had. Sally told her she was glad. Not only did she not have to pay out-of-state tuition, but Lizzie was able to come home on the weekends. She would graduate next year. Where had the time gone?

She hurried downstairs to the spa for her afternoon of pampering.

Three hours later, Lin returned to her room to dress for the banquet. The hairstylist had talked her into a pedicure and a facial. After an afternoon of being catered to, she felt like royalty. Of course, it all came at a price, one so high she didn't dare give it another thought, or she'd have such a case of the guilts that she'd ruin the evening for herself and Will. No, she reminded herself again, this was a once-in-a-lifetime trip. As she had explained to Will, it wasn't every day that he went away to college. Besides, she wanted to look her best at the banquet, knowing there would be many well-to-do parents attending with their children. No way did she want to cause Will any embarrassment just because she was a small-town hick who ran a diner. Her accomplishments might mean something in Dalton, but here in New York City she would just be seen as a country bumpkin trying to keep up with the big-city folk, even though her net worth these days could probably match that of many of New York's movers and shakers.

Discarding her self-doubts, Lin took her dress out of its garment bag. She'd ordered it from a Macy's catalogue four months ago. She slid the black, long-sleeved silk dress over her head, allowing it to swathe her slender body. Lin looked at her reflection in the full-length mirror. With all the skipped meals and extra work at the diner, she'd lost weight since purchasing the dress. The curve-hugging dress emphasized her tiny waist. She twirled around in front of the mirror. *Not bad for an old woman,* she thought.

"Shoot, I'm not *that* old." She cast another look in the mirror and slipped her feet into her ruby red slingbacks she'd been dying to wear since she'd purchased them two years ago. Lin remembered buying them on a trip to Atlanta as a prize to celebrate her first million. On paper, of course, but still it was monumental to her, since she'd clawed her way to the top. It hadn't been all rainbows and lollipops, either.

Clipping on the garnet earrings Sally and Irma had given her for her thirtieth birthday, she returned to the mirror for one last look before heading downstairs.

Five-foot-three, maybe a hundred pounds soaking wet, Lin scrutinized her image. The stylist had flat-ironed her long blond hair, assuring her that it was the current style, and, no, she was not too old to wear her hair down. Her face had a rosy glow courtesy of Lancôme and a facial. The manicurist had given her a French manicure, telling her it, too, was "in vogue." After leaving the spa, she returned to her room with a few makeup tricks under her belt. Plus, her hairstylist had sashayed back and forth, showing her the fashionable way to strut her stuff so that she'd be noticed when making an entrance. While that was the last thing on her mind, she'd had a blast with the women, more than she cared to admit. Lin had confessed that she hadn't had time for such things as a girl, but she hadn't explained why.

She glanced at her watch. Six-fifteen. It was time for Cinderella to hail her carriage.

"Get off it!" If she continued thinking along those lines, she would have to commit herself.

Lin visualized her mental checklist. Purse, lipstick, wallet, cell phone, and keycard. All of a sudden her hands began to shake, and her stomach twisted in knots. It wasn't like she would be the only parent there. Unsure why she was so jittery, she shrugged her feelings aside, telling herself she simply wanted to make a good impression on Will's professors and classmates. Plus, she wasn't on her own turf, and that in and of itself had the power to turn her insides to mush.

Instead of exiting through the turnstile doors, Lin allowed the doorman to open the door for her. Discreetly, she placed a twenty in his hand and hoped it was enough. Sally told her you had to tip everyone for everything in the city. Lin calculated she'd be broke in less than a year if she remained in New York.

"Thank you, ma'am," the elderly man said as he escorted her to a waiting taxi.

Okay, that was worth the twenty bucks. She would've hated to chase down a cab in the red heels.

The inside of the taxi was warm. Lin offered up a silent prayer of thanks that there were no strange odors permeating the closed-in space. She would hate to arrive at the banquet smelling like cigarettes and onions.

More blaring horns, shouts, and tires squealing could be heard. Lin enjoyed watching the throngs of people on the streets as the driver managed to weave through the traffic. Lord, she loved the hubbub, but she didn't think she could tolerate it on a daily basis.

Poor Will. She smiled. *Not* poor Will. After

the slow pace of Dalton, he would welcome this. It was one of the many reasons he chose to attend NYU in the first place. He'd wanted a taste of the big city. Lin thought he was about to get his wish and then some.

Twenty minutes later, the cab stopped in front of the building where the banquet was being held. She offered up two twenties, telling the driver to keep the change.

"Do you want me to pick you up later?" the driver asked as he jumped out to open her door. Lin thought the tip must have been a tad too generous.

"Uh, I'm not sure. Do you have a card?" she asked.

He laughed. "No card, lady, but if you want a return ride, you gotta ask for it."

"Of course. Midnight. Be here at midnight." Now she was starting to *sound* like Cinderella.

"Will do."

Her transportation taken care of, Lin stepped out into the cool night air.

A SPECIAL
INTERVIEW WITH
FERN MICHAELS

QUESTION: With so many novels of yours published—many of which are *New York Times* bestsellers—did you ever imagine you would have such a prolific and successful career as a writer? How did you first get started? What put you on the path to becoming an author?

FERN MICHAELS: Never in a million years did I imagine I would be where I am today. I think I knew someway, somehow, that I was going to write *something* someday in the fourth grade when I wrote a story about a tadpole and the teacher gave me a big red A. What put me on the path to writing years and years later was when my youngest son went off to kindergarten and my husband told me I had to get a job. Being a wife and mother did not qualify me to go into the outside workforce. Plus, and most important, I didn't have a car to get to and from work. So I thought I would try my hand at writing a book. It was that simple. What was even more amazing was that the storytelling came easy to me. Please note, I did not say the *writing* came easy—it was the storytelling part that worked for me.

QUESTION: *Razor Sharp* marks the fourteenth book in the Sisterhood series. When you started the series with the first seven books, did you ever think it would become so successful, and you'd still be writing about the Ladies of Pinewood so many years later?

FERN MICHAELS: I've kept the series going because so many fans wrote and asked me to continue. But even I had withdrawal from the Sisterhood when I finished what I thought was the last one with number seven [*Free Fall*] and had a long break before finally starting to write *Hide and Seek.* I lived with those characters during the first seven books for so long they were part of me. The bottom line was, those wonderful characters were not ready to ride off into the sunset, and I made the decision to continue because there were so many more stories in my head that needed to play out.

QUESTION: What is it about the characters in your Sisterhood novels that allows for you to connect so deeply with readers, and how did you first conceive of these women on your pages? Is there any thread of you in any of these characters?

FERN MICHAELS: I have a lot of friends and meet a lot of people, and as women do, we moan and groan about injustices we see and experience along the way. One would say, boy, if I could just get even in some small way, or, somehow that guy/gal shouldn't be able to get away with this or that! Then I would sit down and plot all these different revenge theories that maybe would work or maybe wouldn't, but since it is all fiction, these gals could do whatever, and I could control the outcome. The "sisters" all kept reminding me I was a storyteller. In the end, I was convinced that the woman hadn't been born yet who didn't want some sort of revenge in her life. I just ran with it. The seven women of the Sisterhood and the new characters that I developed along the way are composites of those same friends, family, and to some extent some of my neighbors. Even the guys. Is there any thread of me in those characters? Oh yeah! In every single one.

QUESTION: To the disappointment of many fans, *Final Justice* was going to be the "second end" to the Sisterhood series. But to everyone's delight, the stories keep coming. When will you decide to end this successful series, and what have the reactions of your fans been?

FERN MICHAELS: To end the series after *Final*

Justice was my original intention because twelve books is a lot in a series. But . . . remember now, I am a storyteller and I still have more stories swirling around in my head. When I sent off *Final Justice* to my publisher, I stood at the FedEx place holding the box and felt physically sick. I thought I was going to cry. It was like saying good-bye to a group of my best friends that I was never going to see again. I went home in such a funk I made a pot of coffee and drank it all . . . black. Then I was so wired up I didn't know what to do. When I don't know what to do, I write. I posted a letter to my readers on my website and let it run for ten days. I asked my readers if they wanted me to end the series. I got over three thousand replies. All but twenty-two wanted me to continue it. Of the twenty-two, eleven of them said no only because they thought I wouldn't write other books. But I assured them that I am still writing non-Sisterhood books, including *Mr. and Miss Anonymous*, the upcoming *Return to Sender*, and of course the Christmas novellas I do for Zebra's anthologies every year. You know what they say: it isn't over till the big lady sings.

QUESTION: While many people know you through your writing, not many people are aware of your charitable work, which includes buying bulletproof vests for police dogs and creating day-care centers set up for the needs of single mothers. You also created the Fern Michaels Foundation, which grants scholarships to needy children. How did you get involved in these projects, and why is philanthropy such an important part of your life?

FERN MICHAELS: When I was a kid my old Polish grandmother said something to me that I didn't understand at the time but do understand now. She said when God is good to you, you must give back. I do my best. A day doesn't go by in my life that I don't thank God for all he has done for me. How could I do less? I have a new project right now, which is our local police department in the town where I live. With the passing of my daughter due to a heart condition way before her time several years ago, I wanted to do something in her memory. So I made sure every officer in the department had a defibrillator and was trained to use it, a thermal-imaging camera, plus every officer now has a taser, along with training and hiring a new police officer every year to help safeguard the people in my little town.

QUESTION: With the publication of several books a year, along with your ongoing charity work, how do you manage to balance writing, home, family, and book events with all this going on in your career and life?

FERN MICHAELS: I don't know how to answer that other than to say I take it one day at a time, look at what the day holds when I get up in the morning, and put things in the order of importance. Somehow or other I manage to do what

has to be done, even if it takes me till bedtime.
My kids tell me I have grease on my sneakers,
otherwise I wouldn't be able to do what I do. I
love it.

QUESTION: Where do you draw your inspira-
tion from? Are there any specific people—
friends, family members, etc.—that help
provide the characters found in your novels?

FERN MICHAELS: Just everyday life. I think my
brain is on overdrive from eight in the morning
till around midnight. I hear, I see, I smell, I
think, and I write it down. Sometimes it can be
something really silly. Like the day I was baby-
sitting my grandson and he was watching car-
toons and it was Alvin and the Chipmunks and
they were shouting, "Finders keepers! Finders
keepers!" I had been struggling for a title on the
book I was writing at the time. You guessed it—
turned out to be *Finders Keepers.*

QUESTION: Throughout all of the years you've
been writing and promoting your novels, what
have been the most rewarding and memorable
experiences for you?

FERN MICHAELS: Oh my gosh, there are so
many! I'm going to give you two, but they are
sad. A lady's daughter e-mailed me and said her
mother was dying, literally dying, and had maybe
a month to live if she was lucky. She had read the
first two books in the Kentucky series and

wanted to know how the third one ended because she wouldn't be here when it came out. The third book was done and in production, but there were months to go before it would be in stores. I called my publisher, Kensington Publishing, and somehow they found a way to get the advance galleys to me to send to the daughter. The daughter e-mailed me later and said every day she read to her mother and they finished the book *in time*. The second incident was almost identical, but this lady was a friend of someone who had brain cancer and was in a hospice. She wanted the fourth Sisterhood book [*The Jury*] so her friend could read it to her. I sent it along with a roomful of flowers. You just can't forget things like that, ever. And I never will. I like to think I make people's lives a little happier with my storytelling. Now, if you want to go in the other direction, I was inducted into the New Jersey Literary Hall of Fame along with such notables as Mary Higgins Clark, Peter Benchley, Belva Plain, and many others (I lived in New Jersey at the time), and you better believe that was a thrill!

QUESTION: Now that the Sisterhood is still going strong and topping the bestseller lists with every book, what is the next thing you can tell readers that you're excited about? What will 2010 and beyond bring?

FERN MICHAELS: I'm sure not ready as of this moment to put the Sisterhood series behind me, but I do have other things I'm excited about. Especially my brand-new series called the Godmothers. Again, some feisty ladies, led by eight-times-widowed Teresa "Toots" Amelia Loudenberry, getting their way in the world and having a lot of great times while they're at it. I think these books are even more fun than the Sisterhood books, and I hope my readers find them just as entertaining. The first book is *The Scoop*, in September 2009, and then I have another non-Sisterhood novel called *Return to Sender* coming in the spring of 2010. So I'm working on all kinds of things, but in my off-hours, my brain is swirling with Sisterhood stories. I can multitask.

More by Bestselling Author
Fern Michaels

___**About Face**	0-8217-7020-9	$7.99US/$10.99CAN
___**Picture Perfect**	0-8217-7588-X	$7.99US/$10.99CAN
___**Vegas Heat**	0-8217-7668-1	$7.99US/$10.99CAN
___**Finders Keepers**	0-8217-7669-X	$7.99US/$10.99CAN
___**Dear Emily**	0-8217-7670-3	$7.99US/$10.99CAN
___**Vegas Sunrise**	0-8217-7672-X	$7.99US/$10.99CAN
___**Payback**	0-8217-7876-5	$6.99US/$9.99CAN
___**Vendetta**	0-8217-7877-3	$6.99US/$9.99CAN
___**The Jury**	0-8217-7878-1	$6.99US/$9.99CAN
___**Sweet Revenge**	0-8217-7879-X	$6.99US/$9.99CAN
___**Lethal Justice**	0-8217-7880-3	$6.99US/$9.99CAN
___**Free Fall**	0-8217-7881-1	$6.99US/$9.99CAN
___**Fool Me Once**	0-8217-8071-9	$7.99US/$10.99CAN
___**Vegas Rich**	0-8217-8112-X	$7.99US/$10.99CAN
___**Hide and Seek**	1-4201-0184-6	$6.99US/$9.99CAN
___**Hokus Pokus**	1-4201-0185-4	$6.99US/$9.99CAN
___**Fast Track**	1-4201-0186-2	$6.99US/$9.99CAN
___**Collateral Damage**	1-4201-0187-0	$6.99US/$9.99CAN
___**Final Justice**	1-4201-0188-9	$6.99US/$9.99CAN
___**Up Close and Personal**	0-8217-7956-7	$7.99US/$9.99CAN
___**Under the Radar**	1-4201-0683-X	$6.99US/$9.99CAN
___**Razor Sharp**	1-4201-0684-8	$7.99US/$10.99CAN

Available Wherever Books Are Sold!
Check out our website at **www.kensingtonbooks.com**

Romantic Suspense from
Lisa Jackson